The Hope of Shridula

The Hope of Shridula

Book 2 of the Blessings in India Series

Kay Marshall Strom

Abingdon Press fiction
a novel approach to faith

Nashville, Tennessee

The Hope of Shridula

ISBN-13: 978-1-4267-0909-8

Published by Abingdon Press, P.O. Box 801, Nashville, TN 37202

www.abingdonpress.com

Published in association with the Books & Such Literary Agency,
Janet Kobobel Grant,
5926 Sunhawk Drive, Santa Rosa, CA 95409
www.booksandsuch.biz.

Cover design by Anderson Design Group, Nashville, TN

Scripture quotations are taken from the King James or Authorized
Version of the Bible.

Library of Congress Cataloging-in-Publication Data requested

Strom, Kay Marshall, 1943-
    The hope of Shridula / Kay Marshall Strom.
        pages cm. — (Blessings in India series ; book 2)
    ISBN 978-1-4267-0909-8
    1. Caste—India--Fiction. 2. Peonage—India—Fiction. 3. Families—India—Fiction.
4. Christians—India—Fiction. 5. India—History—20th century—Fiction. I. Title.
    PS3619.T773H67 2012
    813'.6—dc23

                                                                                    2011048177

Printed in the United States of America

1 2 3 4 5 6 7 8 9 10 / 17 16 15 14 13 12

I gratefully dedicate this book to the Dalits in India,
who continue to fight for respect and equality and their con-
stitutional rights. I wish I could list all of you, but such
a listing would require volumes.
God knows each of you by name.
May His grace and peace be with you all.

Acknowledgments

To say that India has captured my heart would be wrong. My heart has been captured all right, but not by the land. It is the dear people of India who bring me such joy. Most of the ones I am privileged to know personally come from the lowest strata of the caste social system—Dalits, as they prefer to be called today. In addition, most of these are also members of the Christian minority. It is through their eyes that I am beginning to make out the India that was, the India that is today, and with God's grace, the India that is still to come.

I never could have begun this project without the encouragement and assistance of so many who have willingly shared with me their stories, their heartaches, their hopes and dreams, and their emerging opportunities.

In addition to Kolakaluri Sam Paul, who first planted the seed for this project, and others I have named before—Dr. B. E. Vijayam, Mary Vijayam, Bishop Moses Swamidas, P. T. George, and Jebaraj Devashayam—I would like to express my appreciation to the family of Ruby Irene Fletchall. I never actually met Ruby Irene, but she and her husband were missionaries with the Kanarese Biblical Seminary in India during the time period considered in this book. Her family generously shared a detailed letter she wrote home that provided me with an invaluable insider's view of many details of life prior to India's independence.

To Ramona Richards, my Abingdon editor, thank you for your expertise and your patience. To Kathy Force, thank you for your time and your sharp reader's eye. To author/writing instructor Linda Clare, thank you for being my wonderful critique partner.

And to my husband, Dan Kline, thank you for your loving support, for all your help, for being my traveling companion. You are always my best editor. I could not do this without you.

The Hope of Shridula

1

South India

May 1946

The last of the straggling laborers hefted massive bundles of grain onto their weary heads and started down the path toward the storage shed. Only twelve-year-old Shridula remained in the field. Frantically she raced up and down the rows, searching through the maze of harvested wheat stalks.

Each time a group of women left, the girl tried to go with them, her nervous fear rising. Each time Dinkar stopped her. The first time she had tried to slip in with the old women at the end of the line the overseer ordered, "Shridula! Search for any water jars left in the fields." Of course she found none. She knew she wouldn't. What water boy would be fool enough to leave a jar behind?

By the time the girl finished her search, twilight shrouded the empty field in dark shadows. Shridula hurried to grab up the last bundle of grain. Its stalk tie had been knocked undone, and wheat spilled out across the ground. Quickly tucking the tie back together, Shridula struggled to balance the bundle up on her head. It shifted . . . and sagged . . . and sank down to her shoulders.

Shridula was not used to managing so unwieldy a head load. In truth, she wasn't used to working in the field at all. Her father made certain of that. This month was an exception, though, for it was the month of the first harvest. That meant everyone spent long days in the sweltering fields—including Shridula.

The girl, slight for her twelve years, possessed a haunting loveliness. Her black hair curled around her face in a most intriguing way that accented her piercing charcoal eyes. Stepping carefully, she picked her way out of the field and onto the path. Far up ahead, she could barely make out the form of the slowest woman. If she hurried, she still might be able to catch up with her. The thought of walking the path alone sent a shudder through the girl.

Shridula tried to hurry, but she could not. With each step, her awkward burden slipped further down toward her shoulders. She could hardly see through the stalks of grain that hung over her eyes.

"Please, allow me to lend you a hand."

Shridula caught her breath. How well she knew that voice! It was Master Landlord, Boban Joseph Varghese.

Afraid to lift her head, Shridula peeked out from under the mass of grain stalks. Master Landlord, fat and puffy-faced, stood on the other side of the thorn fence, ankle-deep in the stubbly remains of the wheat field. His old-man eyes fastened on her.

Shridula reached up with both hands and grabbed at the bundle on her head.

"Do not struggle with the load," Boban Joseph said, his voice as slippery-smooth as melted butter. "The women can retie it tomorrow. Let them carry it to the storehouse on their own worn-out old heads."

A shiver of dread ran through Shridula's thin body. She must be careful. Oh, she must be so very careful!

❧

All day long, as fast as the women could carry bundles of grain from the fields, Ashish had gathered them up. He separated the bundles and propped the sheaves upright side by side in the storage shed. Everything must be done just right or the grain wouldn't dry properly. One after another after another after another, Ashish stacked the grain sheaves. By the time the last woman brought in the last bundle, by the time he stood the last of the sheaves upright, by the time he closed the shed door and squeezed the padlock shut, then kicked a rock against the door for good measure and headed back to his hut, the orange shards of sunset had already disappeared from the sky.

A welcoming glow from Zia's cooking fire beckoned to Ashish. He watched as his wife grabbed out a measure of spices and sprinkled them into the boiling rice pot. But this night something wasn't right. This night Zia worked alone.

"Where is Shridula?" Ashish asked his wife.

Zia bent low over the fire and gave the pot such a hard stir it almost tipped over.

"She has not yet returned from the fields," Zia said in a voice soft and even. But after so many years together, Ashish wasn't fooled.

The glow of firelight danced across Zia's features and cast the furrows of her brow into dark shadows. Ashish ran a gnarled hand over the deep crevices of his own aging face. He yanked up his *mundu*—his long, skirt-like garment—and pulled it high under his protruding ribs, untying the ends and retying them more tightly.

"She should not have to walk alone," he said. "I will go back." Ashish spoke with exaggerated nonchalance. He would remain calm for Zia's sake.

❧

"All night!" Ashish said to his daughter when she came in at first light. He spoke in a low voice, but it hung heavy with rebuke. "Gone from your home the entire night!"

Overhead, Ashish's giant *neem* tree reached its branches out to offer welcome shelter from the early morning sun. Twenty-eight years earlier, on the day of his wedding, Ashish had planted that tree. Back then, it was no more than a struggling sprout. Yet even as he placed it in the ground, he had talked to Zia of the refreshing breezes that would one day rustle through its dark green leaves. He promised her showers of sweetly fragrant blossoms to carpet the barren packed dirt around their hut.

But no breeze pushed its way through this morning's sweltering stillness, and the relentless sun had long since scorched away the last of the white blossoms. Still, the tree was true to its promise. Its great leaves sheltered Ashish's distraught daughter from curious eyes.

Zia stared at the disheveled girl: *sari* torn, smudged face, wheat clinging to her untidy hair. Zia stared, but said nothing.

"Master Landlord told me I must go with him." Shridula trembled and her eyes filled with tears. "I said no, but he said I had to obey him because he owns me. Because he owns all of us, so we must all do whatever he says."

"Please, Daughter, stay away from Master Landlord," Ashish pleaded.

"I did, *Appa!*" Shridula struggled to fight back tears. "I dropped the bundle of grain off my head and ran away from him, just as you told me to. He tried to catch me, but I ran into the field and sneaked into the storage shed the way you showed me and hid there. All night, I hid in the wheat shocks."

"That new landlord!" Zia clucked her tongue and shook her head. "He is worse than the old one ever was!"

Zia reached over to brush the grain from her daughter's hair, but Shridula pushed her mother's hand away. Her dark eyes flashed with defiance. "Someday I will leave here!" she announced. "I will not stay a slave to the landlord!"

Boban Joseph was indeed worse than his father. Mammen Samuel Varghese had been an arrogant man, a heartless landowner with little mercy for the hapless Untouchables unfortunate enough to be caught up in his money-lending schemes.

Yet Mammen Samuel took great pride in his family's deep Christian roots—he could trace his ancestry all the way back to the first century and the Apostle Thomas. He also clung tightly to the fringes of Hinduism. The duality served him well. It promoted his status and power, yet it also fattened his purse. Even so, Mammen Samuel Varghese had not been a happy man. He seethed continually over the sea of wrongs committed against him, some real and others conjured up in his mind.

Still, it had always been Mammen Samuel's habit to think matters out thoroughly. In every situation, he first considered the circumstances in which he found himself, then measured each potential action and carefully weighed its consequence. It's what he had done when he lent Ashish's father the handful of rupees that led to his family's enslavement. Only after such consideration would Mammen Samuel make a decision. His son Boban Joseph did no such thing.

No, Young Master Landlord was not his father.

During the years of Ashish's and Zia's childhood, Mammen Samuel Varghese maintained tight control over his house and his settlement of indebted slaves. But age did not wear well on him. And the greater Mammen Samuel's decline, the more wicked and cruel Boban Joseph became.

Soon after Ashish took Zia as his wife, the elder landlord began to release one responsibility after another to his first son. Boban Joseph eagerly snatched up each one. Soon Boban Joseph began to grasp control of matters behind his father's back—always for his own personal advantage. This greatly displeased Mammen Samuel. Even more, it worried him. Boban Joseph was his heir, but something had to be done to place controls around him.

As the season grew hotter and the harvest more demanding, Boban Joseph accepted the agreement reached between the laborers and his father requiring them to work a longer day—begin before dawn and continue until after dark. But he refused to honor his father's reciprocal agreement with the workers—to allow them to rest during the two hottest hours of the afternoon.

Only when a young man fell over and died of heatstroke while swinging his scythe, and the next day one of the best workers fell off his plow in exhaustion after begging in vain for shade and water, did Boban Joseph reluctantly agree to grant a midday break. "Only long enough for a cold meal out of the sun and not a minute more!" he instructed the overseer. (Since Boban Joseph spent his afternoons stretched out across the bed in the coolness of his own room, he never knew that Dinkar allowed the workers extra time in the shade.)

"Stay away from the fields today," Ashish told Shridula.

"But the harvest—"

"The harvest is not your worry, Daughter. Busy yourself with work here in the settlement. Make it your job to be of help to weary laborers."

"How can I do that?"

"Fill water jars for the women. Gather twigs and lay them beside the cold cooking pits."

Zia scowled at her husband. "It is not right that you stand the girl up in front of Master Landlord's revenge," she said. "He is a spiteful man. And brutal."

Ashish knew that. More than anyone, he knew it.

"Master Landlord knows Shridula is your daughter," Zia pleaded. "And he will never forget."

She was right, of course. For forty years, Boban Joseph had demonstrated a seething resentment toward Ashish's family. He clung tightly to his own family's humiliation that had been brought about when Ashish's parents, Virat and Latha, dared escape from Mammen Samuel's laborer settlement. Boban Joseph, then hardly more than a boy, greatly resented his father's timid response to their capture and return. He didn't hide his feelings; he let it be known to everyone that he considered his father's actions shameful and cowardly. Boban Joseph himself had captured the runaway slaves and dragged them back in bonds. Yet his father ignored his demands to have them killed. Mammen Samuel wouldn't even order a public flogging.

"You will stay here in the settlement today," Ashish told his daughter. "You will be a servant to the workers, not to the master."

"Yes, *Appa,*" Shridula said.

"But watch out for the landlord. Should he come around, run to the forest and hide yourself. And do not come out until I am back."

At midday, Boban Joseph pushed his way through the crowd of women unloading their head loads of grain and called out to Ashish, "Old man!" (*Old man*, he said, even though he was himself almost ten years older than Ashish!) "I do not see your daughter at work in the fields today. Where is she?"

Ashish turned his back to the landlord and untied another bundle. Paying Boban Joseph no mind, he separated the sheaves of grain. Long ago he had outlived his fear of the master.

"That girl of yours is nothing!" Boban Joseph spat at Ashish's back. "Nothing but a worthless, disgusting Untouchable."

With an expert hand, Ashish tossed three sheaves of wheat into the already-overflowing storage shed, then swung around and grabbed up the next one.

"A comely Untouchable, however," Boban Joseph added. "In a dark and dirty sort of way. Yet there are those who like such girls." Ashish's eyes flashed and his jaw clenched. The landlord laughed out loud, scornful and mocking.

Ashish stopped his work and straightened his painfully stiff back. The wheat sheaf slipped from his hands. Stepping back, he turned around to look the landowner full in the face. "The pale English lady is but one day's walk from here," Ashish said. "She has not forgotten me. Most certainly, she has not forgotten your father, or anyone in your family."

The smirk disappeared from the landlord's lips.

Always, wherever Shridula went, Boban Joseph's hungry eyes followed her. At one time, he had tried to force her to come up to the big house and work in his garden. There, from dawn to dusk, she would be always in his sight. Even more, she would be away from her father's protection. But Ashish would not allow it. And although he was but a lowly Untouchable, and although Boban Joseph was his owner, Ashish prevailed because of his well-worn threat of the pale English lady.

It infuriated Boban Joseph. What did he care about that worn-out old foreign woman? That an Untouchable slave— the son of runaways, no less—should get his way was an outrage. Ashish *belonged* to him! And so did the girl. But Boban Joseph's father had warned him not to press Ashish. "The British," Mammen Samuel had said darkly. "Stay away from anything that touches on their affairs."

Boban Joseph hissed to Ashish, "The time will come, Untouchable. The time will come."

As a child, Ashish always dreaded the hot season, not for the discomfort alone, but because the heat took away the refuge of his family's hut. He found it almost impossible to spend any time inside because the interior so quickly grew stifling. One might as well step into the cooking fire pit and sit down on simmering stones. In those days, no *neem* tree stretched out above the hut with shelter in its branches. His entire life, Ashish had longed for a place of refuge. For a safe haven. For a shady protection from the world.

The *neem* tree took root and grew quickly.

It had been early morning when Zia bore Ashish their first son. She tied the baby to her back and went to work in the fields the same as she did every other day. The child had grown big enough to run through the dirt and dribble water from a bowl onto the little tree by the time Zia bore their second son. When that one grew big enough to tag along after his brother and help water the tree's roots, Zia had their third boy. By the time he was of a size to scamper about in the dirt with his brothers, the *neem* tree reached high enough to provide a bit of shade from the sun for all of them.

At night, Ashish spread two sleeping mats outside under the spreading branches, one for him and one for Zia. The three little boys curled up around them, and the entire family slept soundly and securely.

The life-giving tree; that's what Indians called a *neem*. And that's what it was, too, because each part of the tree nurtured life and brought health to the family fortunate enough to live under the protection of its shade. The bark, the twigs, the blossoms, the leaves—every part of the tree enhanced life. Even the bitter fruit could be boiled into a healing medicine.

Most certainly it was a life-giving tree—except for the one time Ashish needed it most.

2

May 1946

"Who is Devi?" Shridula asked.

Ashish almost dropped the sleeping mats he had gathered up in his arms. He shot a quick glance at Zia. An earthenware bowl slipped from her fingers and clattered to the ground.

"Tell me about Devi," Shridula pressed. "Is she one of us?" Meaning, *Is she also an Untouchable?*

Slowly, deliberately, Ashish stacked the sleeping mats in the corner, one on top of the other. He stooped down and straightened the stack, then straightened it all over again. "Yes, she is one of us," he finally said. "She *was*."

Shridula stared at her father. It seemed as though a mask had suddenly fallen over his face. The most familiar man in her life, and she hardly recognized him. In that moment he looked so old, so terribly tired.

"Who spoke to you of Devi?" Ashish took great care to keep his question casual, as though it had no real import.

"Sometimes Master Landlord calls me by that name."

Zia caught her breath and her eyes filled with tears. She turned toward the shadows and pulled her *pallu*—the loose end of her dingy sari—over her head.

But Shridula wouldn't give up. Turning to her mother, she asked, "Who was she, *Amma?*"

Zia heaved a sigh of weary resignation. "Devi was my sister. My beautiful big sister. She was the one who set my parents free."

❧

Devi.

With a nervous jerk of her hand, Zia stroked at the worn spots on her sari and smoothed the frayed cloth out over her bony frame. She was a competent woman, hardworking and kind. Toil and sorrow and years had taken their toll on her, but even before all that, no one would have called her pretty. Pleasant looking, yes, with her melancholy oval face, dark skin, and thick black hair. But not pretty like her older sister.

While Zia's parents had not considered her worthy of any name at all, they had bestowed an especially lucky one on Devi. Her name meant *goddess.* In many ways, Devi had been fortunate . . . for an Untouchable. Like her younger sister, she was hardworking and kind, but she had also been blessed with grace and beauty and pale skin. And she was loved.

"Tell me about Devi," Shridula pleaded.

Zia wiped her face with her *pallu* and sighed deeply. "The old landlord—Master's father—he gave her to Master Boban Joseph."

Devi did not measure up to the standards old Master Landlord had intended for his eldest son, Zia explained. Everyone knew that. Village gossips had already woven together tales of the lavish wedding the landlord would have for his son, and the sumptuous feast to which the entire village would certainly be invited. A bride had been selected many years earlier, chosen from a family of wealth and prestige. However, in keeping with Indian custom, young Boban Joseph had never seen or spoken to her.

"But he did not want the rich girl," Zia said. "He did not want the great wedding party."

"How do you know all this?" Shridula asked.

"Devi worked in the garden outside the landowner's house and she heard their arguments," Zia said. "Of course, she repeated everything to us."

Of course. Shridula knew all about the gossip that ran incessantly through the settlement.

"Young Master was stubborn and angry, but the landlord refused to give up on his lavish wedding arrangements," Ashish explained. "Because I was a servant of Saji Stephen, the master's younger son, I was ordered to help prepare the elephant for the groom's march. Young Master Boban Joseph said he would not ride the elephant, but the landlord said, 'A son does not go against his father.'"

Yet Boban Joseph did go against his father. He refused to have anything to do with the marriage his father arranged.

"He wanted only the Untouchable girl who worked in the garden," Zia said. "He would have no one but my sister Devi."

Landlord Mammen Samuel held the entire village under his fist, but he could not control his own willful son. So, although it brought untold humiliation and shame to his family, and though it cost him an enormous amount of money, Mammen Samuel returned the bride's dowry. He also presented costly gifts of apology to everyone in her family. He had to, in order to persuade them to agree to cancel the wedding. To quiet the vicious gossip that was spreading so quickly and to regain his honor, he forgave Devi's parents their debt in exchange for her father's thumbprint on an agreement renouncing Devi as his daughter. Her father gave his mark without hesitation. That very night her parents left the settlement.

"My sister could not stop weeping when the landlord's servants took her away," Zia told Shridula. "She was just a child, you see, younger than you are now."

Shridula shook her head. "I do not understand, *Amma*. You are still here. Why did you not go away with your parents?"

Zia would not look her daughter in the face. "My little sister, Baby, and I were not part of their agreement," she murmured. "Though we were still very small, we were sent to work in the fields in my parents' place. I never saw my mother and father again. I never saw Devi again, either."

Shridula, her face hard, declared, "I would not have stayed behind."

"It was not our choice. We could only—"

"If I could not go with them, I would have left by myself. I would not have stayed with the landlord!"

"Do not be so quick to speak, Daughter," Ashish said. "It is easy to imagine strength and bravery when none is required of you."

✍❥

Shridula had always been a curious child. With her, Ashish never found it a simple matter to tell a tale. He couldn't get through a story without her endless interruptions of, "But why, *Appa*? Why?"

Ashish did his best to answer his daughter's questions . . . in his own way. He told her . . . some things. He explained . . . what he must. Which is why Shridula knew so little.

"So you hate the landlord because of Devi?" the girl asked. "I don't understand. He owned her. Was it not his right to do with her as he wished?"

Ashish closed his eyes. His head bobbed back and forth, in the manner peculiar to his people. "I must tell you of your brothers," he said.

"Veer, our first boy, always laughed. Although still quite young when the overseer sent him to the fields, he changed from a happy child to a joyful water boy." Ashish smiled at the memory of the tiny lad who never walked but always ran, back and forth, on his short, brown legs, eager to hurry water to thirsty laborers. "Aravind, our second boy, spent his days looking after Jeevak, the smallest. Together those two little ones collected twigs and branches to trade to neighbors for vegetables and special things to eat. Aravind proved to be an especially good trader. What amazing things he would carry home to your mother for her cook pot!"

Ashish smiled in spite of himself.

"But then the dreaded smallpox sickness struck in the next village. The old landlord was so terrified he would not allow anyone in or out of the settlement. Not until the pox hit his own house."

Shridula pushed in close to her father and looked up into his dark eyes. "Did it strike the landlord, *Appa?*"

Ashish looked helplessly to Zia, but she had already turned away.

"Well, did it?" Shridula pressed.

"Yes. It struck the old landlord, Mammen Samuel," Ashish said. "They sent for me because the smallpox goddess had already kissed me. They knew she would not reach out to me again."

Shridula reached up and ran her hand over the deep scars that pitted her father's weathered face.

"When I came to him, the old landlord lay stretched out on his bed, screaming in pain. His body burned with fever. The young one, Master Boban Joseph, asked me, 'Is this the pox?' But how was I to know? I was smaller than little Jeevak when it struck me. Even so, the young landlord locked me in the room with his father and ordered me to care for him. I did his bidding because I had no choice."

"Until he got well?"

"Three days. That's how long I stayed locked in that room. When the landlord's body was cool again, and he sat up and asked for *idli* cakes and *sambar* to eat, I laughed with happiness because I thought that surely he was well. But then I saw the rash on his face and I knew. Soon that rash would turn into blisters, and the blisters into open, running ulcers."

"What did you do?"

"I called for the young master to fetch the herbalist. I pounded on the locked door and begged him to get a healing charm for his father from the holy man. But he did not. Young Master called back through the door for me to stretch his father out straight and make him comfortable, which is what I did. Then Young Master opened the door just wide enough for me to squeeze out."

"He let you go home?"

"He told me to forget I ever saw his father. I said, 'No, no! Your father will die!' But Young Master Boban Joseph slammed the door shut behind me. 'Everyone dies,' he said. 'This is the old man's karma.' And he locked the door with his father inside."

Shridula looked from her stricken father to her weeping mother. She longed to ask, *Why do you care? What did that cruel man matter to you?* But it was not the time for such questions.

"I hurried away, but I saw Devi working in the garden," Ashish said. "She had a small child tied to her back. Young Landlord's son, she told me. I lifted the baby from her and carried him while Devi broke off sunflowers for me to bring home to your mother."

Zia shook her head, as though she still found the story hard to believe.

"When I neared our hut, young Veer came running to meet me and jumped up in my arms. Little Aravind was right behind him, so I lifted him onto my shoulders. As we got closer to our hut, tiny Jeevak toddled over and I scooped him up and carried him, too."

"You hate the young landlord because he locked his father in the room and left him to die?" Shridula asked.

Ashish raised his calloused hand to wipe his face, but his hand shook so badly he dropped it back into his lap.

"No," he said in a voice choked with tears. "Because seven days after I returned home, the pox struck Devi's baby. Devi did what she could for him, but she got the pox, too. They died together, locked in the barn where they slept."

"Oh," Shridula gasped. "Poor, poor Devi!"

But Ashish wasn't finished. "The next day, our young Veer, his body damp with fever, cried over a terrible pain in his head. Soon little Aravind lay beside him, crying with his brother. They left this life together on the sleeping mat."

"But how could that happen?" Shridula demanded. "Did the pox strike you a second time, *Appa?*"

"No. But I carried it to Devi and her baby, then I took it home to my sons. We sold everything we owned to buy special sacrifices to lay before the goddess of the pox—coconut and cashews and pineapple and guavas. We begged the goddess to have mercy and not take our tiny Jeevak, too. But she had already lifted her hand against us and we could not change her mind."

"Oh!" Shridula breathed.

"With his father gone to his next life, Boban Joseph became the new landlord. He sent Sudra servants to lock us inside our hut and burn it down. They warned us to die bravely because it was our karma."

Ashish spat out those last words like bitter fruit from the *neem* tree.

"But in the end, the Sudras took pity on us. They busied themselves behind the hut while we ran away into the forest and hid. The pox never did spread in the village. When Boban Joseph no longer feared it, he turned all his efforts to making himself the new landlord. We returned to our hut and went back to work in the fields."

In the silence that followed, Shridula looked from her father to her mother, then back to her father again. "The landlord was wrong about your karma," the girl said. "Here you are . . . both of you."

Always the positive one, Shridula. Always the one to light up the darkness with a glow of hope.

"Our sons are no more," said Zia, "but we have you. We have our Shridula—our blessing. You are our karma."

Ashish's eyes flashed. "No, not karma! I will believe in blessing, but I will not accept karma!"

3

May 1946

*A*s a simmering dawn broke over the ripened fields, Miss Abigail Davidson stood on her rooftop and spoke her morning prayers. "For the poor and downtrodden, the hopeless and the oppressed, I ask your mercy, O Lord."

To her left, a pale sun rose in a sky streaked with pink and gold. To her right, the moon hovered at the horizon. "For the children who beg by the roadside and the mothers with no rice to throw into their pot, I entreat you, Lord Jesus."

Puffs of welcome breeze caught the edge of her *sari* and fanned it out around her sparse frame. "For the boy named Blessing, and the travails he must endure, I offer my supplication, Father in Heaven."

At the jingle of temple bells, a pair of birds daring enough to have built their nest in a corner of the roof awakened and offered their own morning call. "For the land of India I pray, Almighty God, with fear and trembling for what is certain to come."

A young girl tiptoed up the steep stairs bearing a tray with a china teapot and a single cup painted with blue forget-me-nots. Carefully she placed the tray on the small table and turned to go.

"Thank you, dear," Miss Abigail said.

The girl flashed a sunny smile and skipped toward the stairs.

"Lelee, wait!" Miss Abigail called after her. "Do stay and share the tea with me this morning."

"I must not," the girl said. "*Memsahib* says I am to get right back to my chores."

Miss Abigail sighed. Alone, she breathed in the fragrance of the steamy-hot tea, spiced with cloves and ginger and cardamom and just a pinch of pepper. Silky with rich water buffalo milk and sweetened the way she liked it with raw sugar. *Chai*, the flavor and aroma of Indian mornings. How accustomed Miss Abigail had become to it over the past forty years.

The spicy tea, sunrise prayers from the rooftop, days of relentless heat—some things never changed. But so much else had. For many years, it was Miss Abigail who had run the English Mission Medical Clinic. Doctors came and went, but she remained the constant. She treated injuries. She bandaged the injured limbs of lepers. She saw the villagers through horrific epidemics. She also cared for any children who found respite in the mission compound—fed them, mended their bodies, told them stories of Jesus, and gave them their first lessons in English.

No more, though. Not since Dr. William Cooper and his wife, Susanna, moved down from Calcutta. The first thing they did was order the construction of this small cottage and move her into it, well away from the real work of the clinic. The second thing they did was make plans to send the children away.

Miss Abigail sank down into one of the two chairs and poured steaming *chai* into the single forget-me-not cup.

Dr. William Cooper, readjusting himself uneasily in the great room of the clinic compound, sipped from his own cup of tea—English, not Indian. Unsweetened, the way he always insisted it be served, without "that disgusting gray cast of wretched milk." He sneaked furtive glances at his uninvited guest—an Indian man dressed in a western shirt worn loose over his native *mundu* sarong-like garment.

"What is this pressing matter you wish to discuss with me?" Dr. Cooper asked. But before the Indian could answer, the doctor added, "Please do keep in mind that this is a British clinic. Must I remind you that it is firmly under the protection of his majesty, King George?"

"Yes, yes, I am being most aware of that," the visitor answered, summoning up his best command of the English language. "This clinic, it is being treating the poor and ill for many years now, and we are being most grateful. But you are surely understanding that change is being underway in India. Unrest is being here, spread from the north of the country down to us here in the south. Now we, too, are experiencing turmoil of our own. With this agitation against you, the British, being increasing, I must to be most eagerly expressing words of great caution for you. It is true that threatenings are made against your safety."

"Our safety! I cannot see as how the poor beggars we get out at this clinic could prove much of a threat to our well-being. We have been and shall remain firmly under the protection of the British Crown."

"Yes, *sahib*, that is so. But as things are standing, I am being—"

"I say, did you state your name to be Rajeev?"

"Yes, *sahib*."

"Well, now, that alone does not tell me much, does it? Who exactly might you be, Rajeev?"

"I am being Rajeev Nathan Varghese. I am being a member of the most respected and most important landowner Varghese family. Surely you heard of us. My uncle Boban Joseph—he is being the most important man in the whole of the area. I am coming to you on his behalf."

"I see. And exactly to what end have you come, might I ask?"

"My uncle tells me to be asking you that we can be cooperating together to be keeping peace in this part of India."

Dr. Cooper's jaw tightened. He set his teacup down and straightened his back. "Could it be, Rajeev, that you yourself are one of the agitators of whom you speak?"

"No, no, *sahib*. I am being—"

"A follower of the criminal, Mohandas Gandhi, perhaps?"

"I am to be following the Mahatma, yes. The Great Soul, most certainly. But I am being no agitator. I am to be seeking a peaceful solution for India, the same as the teacher Gandhiji is doing. And more than that, I—"

"Peaceful solution, indeed!" Scowling, Dr. Cooper jumped to his feet. "Stirring up Indian mobs so that they riot and strike against the Crown—a great empire which has benefited your people on every side, I must stress!—can hardly be called seeking a peaceful solution. Not at all. No matter what the complaint might be."

Rajeev Nathan remained in his seat. As Dr. Cooper looked on impatiently, the Indian took his time downing the last swallow of his tea. When he finally stood and spoke again, the friendly tone had disappeared from his voice. "Change is to be coming, Doctor," Rajeev Nathan stated. "You must be choosing a side. But I warn you: choose most carefully. You will not be having a second chance."

"Oh, my!" Miss Abigail exclaimed when she stepped into the compound's great room that evening. In her day, she had always used that room as a reception area for the clinic. Now here it was set up as a formal English dining room. Abigail's cottage was just across the courtyard, yet how long had it been since she was last here? One month? Two? She shook her head to knock away the cobwebs that fogged her memory. Time and events did seem to drift together in a most disconcerting way.

"What is it?" Susanna Cooper asked in her clipped manner. The young woman always sounded impatient to get the present interaction over with and to move on to something more important. That's how she looked, too—breathless and harried, the color always rising in her pale cheeks.

"Nothing, dear," Miss Abigail said. She brushed the question away with a wave of her hand. "It's just that everything has changed so. Dr. Moore's large green chair is gone, and . . . what else? Oh, my secretary desk!"

"It is about time, I should say. That dusty old furniture looked as though it had been here for a century."

A century? Of course it had not! The mission clinic opened just a few years before Miss Abigail arrived in 1905. She opened her mouth to say as much when she realized how long ago 1905 actually was. Forty-one years! She looked at Susanna's fresh face and slim figure. Surely, that would *seem* a century ago to one so young. So Miss Abigail sighed and said nothing. She eased herself down into the new straight-backed chair (such an uncomfortable contraption!), adjusted her yellow cotton *sari* (her nicest), and folded her hands in her lap.

"My dear Miss Davidson." Dr. Cooper, who had quietly entered the room, reached for her hand and touched her fingers in a most cursory manner. "How good of you to join us this evening. We shall take utmost care to get you back to your bed before too late an hour."

Miss Abigail rolled her eyes.

The doctor settled himself in a more comfortable-looking chair, picked up a book, and resumed reading. Susanna sat on the sofa across from him and extracted her needlework from the bag at her feet.

"How are the children?" Miss Abigail asked. "I never see any of them running about. I suppose they keep busy, what with their chores and studies to mind."

"Children?" Susanna looked mystified.

"The abandoned ones. The little castaways."

Susanna glanced at the old lady with pity in her eyes. The doctor never looked up from his book.

"The other Indian children such as young Lelee. I see that sweet girl when she brings me my tea each morning, though she never stays to talk. Well, I suppose that's to be expected, is it not? She must be eager to get back to the others."

"Lelee is quite adequate as a servant girl," Susanna said. "We have no need for any others."

Servant girl! Miss Abigail stared at Susanna. Lelee had come to the clinic as a tiny child, and she, Miss Abigail, had taken her in. "Lelee is not to be treated as a servant," she insisted. "Oh, my, no! She is capable of so much more. Why, she can read. In English. I taught her myself."

Dr. Cooper looked up and shot his wife a warning glance. Susanna pursed her lips and stabbed the needle into her stitchery.

When the cook announced that dinner was ready, Dr. Cooper assisted Miss Abigail to her seat at the table. It was beautifully laid with a linen cloth, English porcelain dishes, and fine English cutlery. The doctor waited patiently while

Miss Abigail arranged her *sari* and settled herself, then he moved on to seat his wife.

"I do wish we could serve you a lovely roast of beef," he said as he sat down in his own chair. "But I fear that such a meal is not to be had in this wretched country. It is indeed a tragedy, is it not?"

"I shouldn't think so," Miss Abigail replied. "We are in India, after all."

"*British* India," Dr. Cooper corrected, as though he were talking to a schoolchild. "Rule of India is still in the hands of the Crown. Long live King George."

"Long live King George," Susanna echoed.

Miss Abigail said nothing.

Roasted mutton with mint. Potatoes and onions and spinach. Baked bread with butter and jam. When all was served, Dr. Cooper recited grace, then picked up his fork and knife. Susanna did the same. Miss Abigail did not. In expert Indian style, she swiped her hand around her plate, grabbed up a generous bite of food, and lifted it expertly to her mouth.

Susanna gasped out loud.

"We are in India, are we not?" Miss Abigail said with a note of amusement.

For some time, they ate in silence. Finally, Dr. Cooper said, "I have a matter of great importance to discuss with you, Miss Davidson. I do believe the time has come for you to leave India."

"Whatever do you mean?"

"Only that your work here is done."

Miss Abigail started to protest, but Dr. Cooper held up his hand. "You have accomplished a great deal, madam. No one could expect more of you. You have earned the right to return home to England and live out your days in comfort."

"Poppycock!" Miss Abigail exclaimed. "Why, I hardly remember England. India is my home, and I shall live out my days right here."

"No need to make a hasty decision," Susanna said. "The wise course would be to think on it. If you were to go home—"

"There is nothing to think on," Miss Abigail said. "I am at home. If that is why you invited me here this evening, then I greatly fear that you have wasted your hospitality."

Miss Abigail dropped her bread onto her plate, swirled it through the leftover spinach and gravy, and popped it into her mouth. "Delicious," she said. "Though I might suggest that next time you add a hot pepper or two."

*

On the walk back across the courtyard, Miss Abigail leaned heavily on Krishna's arm. Almost fifty years old, Krishna was, but in Miss Abigail's mind he was still the stringy little child she had taken in when he showed up at the clinic so badly burned. Except for the gray in his hair and his grown-man height, he didn't seem that much different from back then. Perhaps because his severely scarred face was wrinkle-free, giving him an ageless look.

Krishna opened the door and walked Miss Abigail across the parlor to her bedchamber.

"You made my bed for me," she said when she opened the door. "Really, my dear, you needn't care for me like an old woman."

"I do not," Krishna said. "I care for you like a dear friend."

To Abigail, Krishna was more than a friend. A son—that's how she thought of him. He had been with her since he was a child of seven years—eight, perhaps. Except for the time she sent him to Madras to attend the school for orphaned boys.

He always was such an intelligent lad. And he did study hard. Still, before long he had come back to her. Life was hard for a burn-scarred Untouchable, even one who could read and write English.

"Dr. Cooper told me I should leave India," Miss Abigail said. "But why should I, Krishna? India is my home."

"The doctor worries for you." Krishna picked up the candleholder that stood on the chest beside her bed and lit the candle. "He knows that trouble is coming, and he wants you to be safe."

Miss Abigail reached out and patted Krishna's twisted hand. "If trouble truly is coming, then I thank God that you are here beside me."

4

May 1946

Except for a few Sudras scattered throughout the settlement, every person the landlord owned was Untouchable. They all lived side by side in whichever huts the overseer assigned to them, and they all worked together in the fields. But that didn't mean all Untouchables were the same. Carpenters looked down on barbers, who looked down on washer folk, who looked down on basket makers, who looked down on fisher folk. And so it went until it came to the *chamars*, the leather makers. The handlers of dead animals. Everyone looked down on them. By birth, by caste, and by *jati*, Ashish was a *chamar*.

Being a gentle man, like his father before him, Ashish had always made it his habit to ignore the personal slights and insults other bonded laborers tossed his way. People were people, he insisted. Let each one prove his value in the fields and paddies. But by the age of forty-six, Ashish had begun to grow old and to wear out. More and more, the daily struggles of life weighed heavily on him. One evening he came back to his hut, exhausted from many hours in the wheat fields, to find a most troubling change. The family of potters who had lived in the hut next to his for as long as he could remember were gone. A scraggly woman with two boys had taken up residence in their hut.

Ashish looked askance at the disheveled woman. In a tone that left no room for excuses, he demanded, "Who are you?"

"Jyoti," the woman answered without looking up. She was tall and angular, but so thin Ashish didn't see how she could possibly lift a bundle of grain onto her head. Her *sari* hung around her in tatters.

"Your boys. Who are they?"

"The big one is Hari. The small one, Falak."

Actually, at fourteen, Hari couldn't truly be called *big*. Ten-year-old Falak, however, was definitely small.

"Where is your man?" Ashish asked.

"Dead." Jyoti kept her eyes fixed on the ground. When Ashish didn't leave, she shifted uncomfortably and added, "I borrowed money from the landowner to send my husband to his next life in flames." Still Ashish didn't leave, so she said—without rancor, "He died cleaning night soil for the comfort of our betters."

Ashish gasped and jumped back in disgust. A family of *thottis*—scavengers. Cleaners of latrine pits and gutters! This woman belonged at the absolute bottom of the absolute lowest of the Untouchables. Ashish turned his back and hurried away.

Zia, busy at her cooking pit, watched the entire exchange. But she noticed something her husband never saw: an elegantly carved wooden necklace hanging around the woman's neck. Extraordinarily beautiful, she thought, and surely something of real value. What a strange adornment for a starving woman!

When Jyoti saw Zia watching her, her hand went instinctively to her throat. "A wedding gift from my grandmother," she mumbled.

"Beautiful," Zia said.

"I never take it off. It has grown to be a part of my neck."

"Yes," Zia said. "I understand." But she didn't really, because no one had ever given her anything of beauty.

❧

That night, as Ashish and Zia lay together on their sleeping mats watching the stars twinkle in the black sky, Ashish shook his head and complained, "Scavengers! They should not be allowed to live here among us!"

"Many would say the same about you," Zia reminded him.

"But scavengers are hopelessly filthy."

"Because they handle filth and pick up dead animals? So, too, did your father."

"You do not understand," Ashish protested in growing exasperation. "That woman and her sons have no dignity. They eat *rats!* It is not good for Shridula that we have them living next to us."

"I do not mind, *Appa*," Shridula called from her sleeping mat.

Ashish squinted toward his daughter, but in the dark he couldn't make out whether she was lying down or sitting up. Still, simply thinking about her filled his heart with pride. Shridula was a good girl . . . a good person . . . He would set his mind on her and forget about his frustration over the scavenger woman.

Something rustled in the branches of the *neem* tree, but Ashish made no move to investigate. Some creature, most likely. If it could find comfort and shelter in his tree, then he wished it all the best. Perhaps the gods would credit his generosity to the creature as an act of kindness.

"Poor Jyoti," Zia sighed. "She has no man to bring in extra rice."

One handful of rice each day, the allotment for a working man. Half that for a working boy. Less for a working woman. For a girl, working or not, only a pinch. Ashish tried to push the landlord's accounting system out of his mind.

"The harvest is over," he said in a carefully gentled voice. "Very soon every family will receive an extra allotment of rice. Spices, too, and a measure of wheat to grind into flour."

Zia shook her head. "One woman and two boys. Even that will not be enough."

No, it wouldn't. Which was why industrious families dug small gardens and grew vegetables to add to their rice pots. Almost everyone sent their children into the forest to search for nuts or fruit or small creatures to supplement their diet. Zia was right. With no man to bring in the full handful of rice each day, and with two hungry boys to feed, Jyoti would find her job most difficult.

A flicker of sympathy flashed through Ashish's eyes, but only for a moment. "We are Untouchables," he said, "but we are not scavengers. Scavengers have no place among us!"

⚬❧

"The gods took away your three sons and gave you a girl in their place?" the men had said to Ashish when his daughter was born. "Too bad, too bad. Surely the landlord paid the Brahmin to place a curse on your house."

"No, not a curse!" Ashish had insisted with resentment. "A blessing!"

"But here you are, robbed of sons and laden with a *girl!*"

"Not just any girl," Ashish said. "My Shridula. My blessing."

After the men drifted away, clucking their tongues and whispering to one another, Ashish had taken the baby from Zia and lifted the little one up in his arms. Holding her close, he whispered in her ear, "Perhaps the name will bring you hope, my little one. More hope than my name has brought me."

Hope, he had said. Not luck. Not karma. *Hope.*

Like his father before him, Ashish struggled to lay aside the superstitions that haunted the lives of everyone around him. The position of the planets . . . the alignment of stars . . . amulets and lucky charms from holy men . . . blind dependence on the capricious will of a million gods and goddesses . . . the eternal turn of the wheel of karma. Ashish determined to reject them all. What he clung to was hope—for himself, yes, but even more for his child and her children, and all the children of all the generations that would follow.

"Hope!" the laborers repeated to Ashish with mocking laughter as he planted rice beside them. "Hope!" they called to him as he struggled behind a stubborn water buffalo, doing his best to maneuver his plow through thick mud. "Hope!" they taunted as he mopped his face and staggered under the blazing sun.

Hope might be a rare commodity, but hatred was not. It seethed throughout the settlement and simmered in the village. In the large cities of Madras and Bombay and Calcutta, it boiled up and erupted like so much scalding lava as the people rioted and the British army poured out destruction to quash their uprisings. Still, most of that hatred was aimed at the British and their iron grip on India.

Ashish knew nothing of that. All he knew was the sea of personal resentments accumulated over a lifetime of insults and prejudice. What could such a lofty concept as a struggle for independence from Britain matter to one such as him?

"The sheds are full. There is not room for any more grain," Ashish said to Dinkar.

"Master Landlord will be pleased with the harvest," the overseer replied. "Surely he will reward us with a particularly fine feast, and with extra rice and spices to fill our own grain jars."

For a moment, Ashish's mind drifted away from the empty fields. "I wonder, what would it be like to be rich?"

"You will never know," Dinkar assured him. "Nor will I. Riches are not in our *karma*. Men like us never get what we want. Certainly not in this life. Maybe in the next, though."

"You, Dinkar? What have you done good enough to earn you a place of riches in the next life?"

"What did I do to doom me to be an Untouchable in this life?" Dinkar said with a laugh.

But Ashish wasn't laughing. "Do you really believe that? Do you think we were born untouchable because we did something so awfully bad in our past life?"

"I do not know," Dinkar said. "But I won't take any chances. I will do good in this life because I never again want to be born an Untouchable."

When Ashish got back to the hut, Zia and Shridula had his meal waiting—*sambar* made from dried lentils and seasoned with crushed chili peppers. Shridula handed him his earthenware bowl of rice with the *sambar* spooned over it.

"Mmmmm," Ashish sighed. He took the bowl and settled down under the *neem* tree.

Do good in this life, Dinkar had said. Ashish could not forget those words. *Do good in this life*. Through the tree branches, he fixed his eyes on the bright patterns of twinkling stars.

"Certainly we would never allow our Shridula to marry a scavenger," Ashish said to Zia, who sat away from her husband, waiting patiently for him to finish his meal so she could eat. "And we will never eat in a scavenger's house. But I have decided that if a scavenger should come and sit next to us, we will not turn our backs and walk away."

Zia said nothing.

"I will do good in this life," Ashish said. In his mind he added, *Perhaps then, even though I am an Untouchable, my family will know hope.*

At Boban Joseph's insistence, the women scoured the ground in search of wheat heads and dropped stalks. Zia and the others worked together in order to accomplish the job more quickly. All the others except Jyoti. Jyoti pulled off to one side and worked alone, because the other women refused to work beside her.

When evening came and Dinkar released the workers to go to their huts, Zia watched the scavenger woman. Jyoti ran to get her empty water jars, then hurried to the well. Immediately the other women ceased their chatter and gossip. Without a word, they grabbed up their jars and drew away.

"Filthy!" one called out.

"The stink of the dead is on you!" another accused. She covered her nose and mouth with her *pallu*.

An old woman with three teeth spat at the scavenger woman.

Zia wanted to speak a kind word, but while she still struggled to think of something, Jyoti finished filling her water jars. Taking care to keep her head lowered, she turned and hurried away. The women laughed and shouted out more ridicule after her.

That night, as they lay under the stars, Zia whispered to Ashish, "I watched the scavenger woman today. When she thought no one was looking, she tucked heads of wheat into her *sari*."

"She is a fool," Ashish said.

"Her family must be very hungry for her to risk such a thing."

"The harvest has been a good one," Ashish told his wife. "Soon the landowner will reward all of us with a great feast and bags of extra grain. Don't worry. Her stomach will soon be filled again."

✒

With the harvest over, the laborers had more time to sit together in the shade and complain. All their faithful work, and still no feast to celebrate the harvest. Grain supplies running low for everyone, and still no extra allotments.

"Be patient," Dinkar pleaded. "Master Landowner gave us his word. He is an important man in the village and his life is busy, but he will reward your hard work just as he promised. He will celebrate the successful harvest with you."

The men gathered in whatever shade they could find and grumbled to one another. The landlord was responsible for their misery. The British were to blame. It was the fault of the rioters in the city, or the fault of the army that shot those same rioters down in the streets.

The women also clustered together, but away from the men. As they watched the cook fires dying out, they voiced complaints of their own.

"Look over there," said the woman with three teeth. She gestured toward Jyoti, who was careful to keep her distance from the other women. Jyoti was on the ground, bent over on her knees.

"Just look at her!" said Cala, an especially tall worker. "Digging in the dirt with those filthy hands of hers!"

"She's pulling up roots!" Zia exclaimed. "The poor woman is starving!"

Zia looked over at the men. Ashish was no longer listening to the others. His eyes were on the desperate woman clawing at the ground.

5

May 1946

On the last day of her life, Parmar Ruth Varghese told her sons the truth. That is, she told them as much of the truth as they needed to know.

"Boban Joseph, you have grown into a selfish man," she said to her eldest. "You have no wife and no children, yet you hoard your father's house and everything in it for yourself. One single room you allow for me and Glory Anna to share. Two small rooms for your brother, even though he has two sons with wives of their own, and three grandchildren. It is not right."

At first, Boban Joseph stood dumbstruck. His mother had always been such a quiet woman, at all times submissive to the man who served as head of the household—which now meant him. But he quickly found his tongue.

"It is not your place to criticize me," he said. "You may be my mother, yet you are still an old woman. What do you know of such things?"

"I know what is right and what is not right," Parmar Ruth answered.

"Father spoke his wishes, and his wishes are the law," Boban Joseph said. "Saji Stephen would inherit the poorer field. That is now in his charge—for all the good it does him. The best rooms of the house would be mine—those that face east and south, including the great room and both of the kitchens. Saji Stephen would have whatever was left. I would own all the good lands, and all the animals, and all the laborers listed in father's leather book. I would control the family wealth of jewels and gold coins—had any remained from his self-indulgent ways! That entire bequest was left to me to do with as I wish."

"What choice did your father have?" Parmar Ruth asked. "He knew the person you were. He saw your eyes cling to the young girls that did not belong to you. Yet what choice did he have?"

A deep flush rose in Boban Joseph's face.

"The harvest is well past, my son, and you have yet to celebrate with the laborers. You have not yet spread the promised feast before them. No gifts of grain and spices have been offered them. Your father would have immediately rewarded each one for so great a harvest—and rewarded them richly. He would not have stopped there, but would have spread his generosity throughout the village. Even beyond, all the way to the village boundaries."

"I am a busy man." Boban Joseph's voice was bitter, his tone insultingly dismissive.

"Your father would have—"

"Father wasted the wealth of our family, not me. My father squandered the jewels and gold coins that should have been mine!"

"There is much you do not know," his mother said.

"I know I do not have his luxury to spend my days on the veranda preening for the public, bragging about my expensive Persian carpet, showing it off for all the village to see."

Parmer Ruth shook her head. "You are a selfish man, my son."

Saji Stephen, Boban Joseph's younger brother, heard his mother's harsh words and unaccustomed tone. He hurried in to see how he might take advantage of the family discord.

"Just look at my own family's quarters," Saji Stephen chimed in. "Three men, two women, and three children all squeezed into two small rooms while you, Boban Joseph, amble alone though the rest of the house!"

Boban Joseph opened his mouth, a bitter retort hanging on the edge of his tongue, but it was Parmar Ruth who spoke. "And you, Saji Stephen—always my pet, forever my baby. Tell me, what is your use on this earth? You take and you take, from one person and the next, but what do you give back?"

"I am a man of wisdom and the arts," Saji Stephen huffed. "You know that!"

"I know only one thing," Parmar Ruth said. "Your daughter was not to blame for the death of her mother. Only because I would not allow you to abandon the newborn to the hungry animals, but took her as my own, is she still alive today. You do not even acknowledge her as flesh of your flesh. But acknowledge her or not, she is still your daughter."

Saji Stephen's face flushed hot.

Boban Joseph pushed his brother aside and faced his mother. "You are an old woman and the day is hot," he said impatiently. "Go back to your bed. I will instruct the servants to bring you tea."

Parmar Ruth made no move to obey. "You believe your father wasted his wealth, my son? He did not. He would never be such a fool."

Boban Joseph started to argue, but his mother turned her attention back to Saji Stephen. "Glory Anna will marry in her fourteenth year," she said. "That will be next year after the rice harvest is complete. Your sister's Uncle Dupak has already arranged the marriage."

Smirking in spite of himself, Boban Joseph answered, "Sunita's Uncle Dupak? He won't find much of a husband for Glory Anna, I fear. Saji Stephen has no money for a dowry."

"It is not a matter for Saji Stephen to decide. Or you, either."

Boban Joseph glared at his mother. "If you think for one minute that I will be willing to pay—"

Parmar Ruth swayed. Brushing her hand across her face, she looked with glassy eyes into her son's angry face and murmured, "I warn you, Boban Joseph: stay away from Glory Anna. If you do not, you will lose everything. I warn you: this night your soul will be required of you."

☙

Early the next morning, Glory Anna's horrified shrieks shook the household awake. "Come! Hurry!" she screamed. "Someone come and help!"

The Sudra servant Udit ran in from outside. Saji Stephen's sons rushed from the veranda where they slept. They all pushed the distraught girl aside and hurried back and forth, but they could do nothing. Parmar Ruth was already cold in her bed.

The entire day, everyone scurried back and forth through the house. And the entire day, Glory Anna sobbed alone in their room. In her room.

Without her grandmother, Glory Anna was truly alone. She had never thought of Saji Stephen as her father, though she knew he was. All she knew of her mother was that she died giving life to her. Saji Stephen's married sons didn't acknowledge Glory Anna's existence, and neither did their wives . . .

although Sheeba Esther, wife of the second son, was kinder to the girl than anyone else.

So sad! Glory Anna had never been without her grandmother. So lonely! She had no one else to care about her or protect her. And suddenly, so afraid. Surely her father and her uncle would want her gone. The quickest way to accomplish that would be to arrange an immediate marriage for her and send her away. But her Uncle Boban Joseph would not be willing to pay much of a dowry, and her father would not be able to do so. So what sort of husband might she expect? A sick old man with one leg? A humpback who would beat her with a stick? Perhaps someone like her father—or, worse, like her uncle Boban Joseph.

"I will take mother's room for my own," Saji Stephen announced to his brother as they waited on the veranda for the priest to arrive.

"You will do no such thing!" Boban Joseph shot back. "That room faces south, so it is rightfully mine."

"You never step your foot into all the rooms you have now! Soon the rains will come and my sons and their wives and children will no longer be able to sleep outside. Where is the shelter for all of them, I ask you?"

"Your ever-expanding family is not my concern," Boban Joseph said with a dismissive wave of his hand. "Take that worthless field of yours and build yourself as large a house as you want on it. And when you go to live there, take Glory Anna with you."

Though Saji Stephen had lived for almost half a century, though his belly had grown flabby and much gray now sprinkled through his hair, he sprang up off the floor with amazing agility and stomped his feet the way he always had as an angry child. Boban Joseph burst out laughing. Not a laugh of mirth, but a hoot of derision and ridicule.

Blind with fury, Saji Stephen pointed at his brother and bellowed his mother's words: "This night your soul will be required of you!"

Boban Joseph, still laughing, jumped up and stamped his feet in an exaggerated mock tantrum. "Your soul, your soul!" he whined in a ridiculing, childish voice. "Cling tightly to your soul!"

Sputtering with rage, Saji Stephen struggled to find a searing retort to toss back, but he could think of none. He turned and ran from the veranda.

✒

Because she was a Christian and not a Hindu, Parmar Ruth Varghese's body was buried in the church courtyard. For the rest of the day the family stayed inside the house. Servants waved fans over them in a vain effort to stir up a cooling breeze. Children of the servants ran back and forth with trays of sweets and pots of tea.

When the sun finally set, Boban Joseph called for Udit, his most responsible servant. "Arrange a harvest feast for the laborers," he instructed. "It should be quite fine, but not costly. We have plenty of rice in the storehouse. Make good use of it."

To his brother, who had returned to the veranda and was pouting alone in the corner, Boban Joseph said, "You will be in attendance at the feast." It was an order.

Saji Stephen said nothing. That was a matter for his brother to decide. Saji could stomp and pout, but in the end he would do as his brother said. To obey was his job—his only real job.

"And you will be on your best behavior, too," Boban Joseph warned. "Unity and family loyalty."

Yes, of course. Always unity and forever family loyalty. Never mind that Boban Joseph was a selfish *thag*—a rogue who bullied and cheated the entire village. Unity and family loyalty. Never mind that whenever Boban Joseph prowled the streets, fathers from all castes hurried to hide their young girls from him. At all costs, unity and family loyalty.

✐

The first rays of morning sun glowed deep orange over the still-black fields. Shridula roused herself. She stepped out from the shelter of the *neem* tree and looked around in surprise. This was to be a day of celebration. A day of rest. No one had to go to the fields, yet the entire settlement was already awake and buzzing with excitement.

"*Amma! Appa!*" Shridula called joyfully. "What food will the landlord bring for our harvest feast?"

"Two harvest feasts every year of your life," Ashish said with a laugh, "and every one you ask us that same question!"

Shridula flopped back down onto her sleeping mat. "But it is so delicious to hear the names of the food and think about their tastes!"

"*Dal,*" Zia said. "*Dal* and rice."

Yes, yes, lentils ground and boiled into a thick soup, and spiced with curry and hot peppers. So good!

"*Sambar,*" Ashish said.

Mmmm, vegetable stew. Her father's favorite.

Zia smiled. "*Rasam,* of course."

Oh, the thought of that tangy, spicy, soupy tamarind concoction! It made Shridula's mouth water.

"And rice with *ghee?*" Shridula asked.

"I do not know," Zia answered. "Young Master is not as generous as his father was." Rice smothered in melted butter was, after all, the food of the gods. "But perhaps. Perhaps."

"Fried yams," said Ashish. "And curds. All kinds of delicious fruits, too."

"And *payasam!*" Shridula exclaimed. "Sweet milk pudding! Oh, that is my favorite!"

Who could sleep while the air brimmed thick with such delicious dreams? Who wanted to? Ashish piled away their sleeping mats as Zia and Shridula hurried off to join the women already busy washing and stacking fresh-cut banana leaves. Those large leaves would serve as plates for the day's wonderful meal.

At midday, a group of children dashed into the settlement calling, "It is here, it is here! The food of Master Landlord is here!"

Shridula couldn't help herself. As if she were a child too, she ran to watch. Sure enough, the landlord's bullock cart lumbered down the path. Huge metal pots stacked in the back rattled and clanked together on the rough road. Rice, most likely. Smaller pots had been propped in between the large ones—surely they held the delicious dishes of Shridula's imagination. In every spare opening she saw piles of mangoes and guavas, and long stalks of red bananas.

"Look!" an excited woman cried. "Even a sack of cashew nuts!"

In the courtyard, cut wide by the men and swept clean by the women, laborers feasted until their hungry stomachs were so full they could hardly move. Sometime during the feast,

Boban Joseph and Saji Stephen rode up in the horse cart and sat together—watching.

"They eat like animals," Boban Joseph said, though he was careful to keep a smile on his face and his voice low.

The two made their best effort to look pleasant. But neither had the least interest in watching the workers eat, certainly not while sitting in the hot sun. Besides, other than ridiculing the workers or criticizing one another, they had absolutely nothing to say to one another. They put up with it as long as they could. Before long, however, they could suffer no more of each other's forced pleasantness.

Boban Joseph stood up in the cart. "We are pleased to celebrate this wonderful harvest with all of you!" he called out. "Tonight, we invite you to eat your fill. Tomorrow, we give you a gift of one more day with no work!" He waited, smiling, while everyone cheered. "Dinkar will see that you get fresh allotments of rice, wheat, and spices. Enjoy the feast!"

Boban Joseph didn't wait for the cheering to die down. He sat down, turned the horse around, and immediately headed for home. One more day with no work. After that, Dinkar could do whatever he wished to get the laborers back to the fields. And the sooner the better.

✍

That evening, after the men had finished their meal and Saji Stephen's sons had drifted away toward the village, Boban Joseph said to his brother, "Generosity is a wearisome pursuit."

"Perhaps that might be because it is a pursuit so foreign to you," replied Saji Stephen. "As our mother so rightly said, you are a selfish man."

The stresses of the day had already worn Boban Joseph's nerves to a frazzle. He turned on his brother, teeth bared. "And you," he hissed. "What did she say to you? Forever a baby! No use on this earth except to take, take, take!"

Saji Stephen, shaking with fury, glared at his brother. Boban Joseph clenched his teeth and glared right back.

Aaaaaahh . . . lo!

A sudden shriek shattered the stony silence, startling the brothers. Boban Joseph jumped breathlessly to his feet while Saji Stephen sat rooted, screaming for his servant.

Aaaaaahh . . . lo! Aaaaaahh . . . lo!

"It's only that foolish peacock!" Boban Joseph said with an embarrassed laugh. "Who does he think will admire his beauty in the dark of the night?"

"While he sits on a tree branch, hidden by leaves?" Saji Stephen added.

Two servants hurried to the veranda, but Saji Stephen waved them away. For several minutes, he sat in uncomfortable silence while his brother stared out into the dark.

"We are wonderful men from a great family," Boban Joseph finally said. He hefted himself back down onto his father's Persian carpet. "Perhaps what mother meant to say was that an increased show of generosity could further stretch the good will that already exists between the village and us. It is true. That could actually extend the reaches of our business."

"I take no part in the business because no part is offered me," Saji Stephen said with a pout. "But I wish I had thought to remind Mother that I alone contributed sons to carry on the family name. Two fine Varghese men, and they have given me two Varghese grandsons. So far."

"And I provide for all of them," Boban Joseph reminded him. "Quite generously, I might add."

On the last day of her life, Parmar Ruth Varghese had told her sons the truth.

6

May 1946

*F*or three days after her grandmother's death, Glory Anna refused to come out of the room that the two had shared for as long as she could remember. She opened the cupboard and lifted out each one of her grandmother's *saris*, all thirty-nine of them. Tenderly she unfolded them one by one. The purple and white silk—so luxurious and soft. It was the one her grandmother had worn to weddings and funerals. The scarlet one, thickly embroidered with gold thread all around the edges and up the front. Oh, how beautiful her grandmother had looked in that one! Like Queen Esther in the story from the Bible. The blue and green *sari*. Sometimes Grandmother had dressed Glory Anna up in it. The orange *sari* . . . The yellow *sari* trimmed in brown . . . Glory Anna buried her face in each one and breathed in the singular scent of her grandmother. The sweet fragrance of love.

The girl restacked the *saris* on the cupboard shelves, carefully laying each one back in its place. But before long, she returned to the cupboard and lifted them out all over again. One at a time. All thirty-nine of them.

Parmar Ruth had many lovely things, and each one held memories for her granddaughter. The gold jewelry she always wore—rich and beautiful, though not so many pieces as she used to wear. A silver brush and comb and a mirror to match. A music box carved with a jungle scene and a tiny ivory elephant inside that spun around in time to the music. A shelf filled with books, all of them in English. Her leather-bound Bible.

Glory Anna moved from one thing to the next to the next, caressing each one but leaving them all in their places. All except her grandmother's Bible. That she slipped behind the cupboard where no one would find it should they come to take her grandmother's belongings away.

On the fourth day, Glory Anna dried her eyes, changed into her grandmother's blue and green *sari*, and stepped out of the room.

From the back of the Varghese house came sounds of rambunctious family life: the wife of Saji Stephen's elder son shouted her disagreements with the wife of his younger son, while Saji's three grandchildren ran in circles around the two women, yelling and laughing. Boban Joseph, seated cross-legged on the veranda, growled his displeasure.

"Will no one quiet them?" he exclaimed in disgust.

Back when his father had sat on the veranda, everyone who passed by on the road would pause to bow low and call out a respectful greeting. No more. Now, when people passed by Boban Joseph, they averted their eyes and hurried on their way.

His irritation growing, Boban Joseph turned to bellow an order at Saji Stephen's noisy family, but at that moment he caught sight of Glory Anna drifting by in the blue and green *sari*. Her black hair hung loose, and her red-rimmed eyes shined dark and sad. Heartrendingly melancholy. So, so lovely!

"Devi!" Boban Joseph gasped, his voice strange and breathless. He reached out his arms. "Come to me, Devi!"

Glory Anna stopped and stared at her uncle. What was she to do?

"Please, Devi. Come to me!"

Her whole body trembled, yet Glory Anna found it strangely pleasing that her uncle should speak to her at all. He had never done so before. *If* he had actually spoken to her now. What was that name he said?

"What did you call her?" Saji Stephen demanded.

Boban Joseph started at the sound of his brother's angry voice.

"*What* did you call Glory Anna?"

Boban Joseph shook the dreams from his head and croaked an awkward laugh. "Would you deprive an old man of his memories?" he asked.

A cold fear settled in the pit of Glory Anna's stomach.

"I would deprive a disgusting old man of yet another young girl!" Saji Stephen spat.

With a gasp, Glory Anna turned and dashed back to her room. She slammed the door behind her. Then she shoved her grandmother's heavy chest in front of it.

❧

"No, no, Ashish!" Zia insisted. "You must not take our Shridula to the house of the landowner. You must not!"

Ashish looked at the ground. "What is my choice?" he said. "If I do not take her myself, a servant will come and carry her away from us."

"But we must not allow her to be so close to Young Master Landlord!" Zia cried. Panic rose in her voice.

Ashish laid a hand on his wife's arm. "It was not Master Landlord Boban Joseph who sent for her. It was his brother, Saji Stephen."

"But Young Master Landlord is right there," Zia said. "Who will protect our Shridula from him?"

"I will," said Ashish, though he shuddered at the memory of that house.

The threat of the pale English lady. It had protected him all his life, and now he counted on it to protect his daughter, as well. Miss Abigail, at the English Mission Medical Clinic. Many years had passed since he had actually seen her, but once long ago she had stood up against Boban Joseph's landlord father, and had proven that she was stronger than he. The pale English lady—who had the power of the entire British Empire behind her—was the only person the landlord feared. And she had promised to watch over Ashish. Miss Abigail . . . and the British Empire . . . and the Christian God. Shridula would be in their care.

$\mathcal{L}$

Shridula followed her father down the path, past the far-thest field and to the back of the landlord's fine house. She gasped out loud at the sight of it.

"All this is the house of the landlord?"

"For his family, yes."

"It is wonderful," Shridula sighed.

"No." Ashish struggled to pull his mind away from the har-rowing memories of that place, and of his childhood tormen-tor who forced him back. "It is not so very wonderful," he said. "In fact, it is not wonderful at all."

Ashish and Shridula took care not to step their polluted feet onto the landlord's veranda. Her father stood still, his head bowed, but Shridula gazed around her in wonder. She couldn't help herself. Flowers and blooming vines and trees heavy with fruit. Glorious birds with magnificently colored plumes—green and red sunbirds, majestic trogons, and iridescent blue peacocks eager to show off their extravagant tails. Perfume drifting on the breeze from mango blossoms and jasmine in bloom.

"Hello, Ashish." Saji Stephen, bathed and oiled and scented with sandalwood, stood before his childhood playmate. The sun shone bright against the pure white of Saji's silk *mundu* and set the golden threads of the edging to glimmering. Ashish pulled self-consciously at his own dusty garment, just as he had as a child.

Although Saji Stephen was gray-haired and pudgy around the middle—no longer the spoiled child of so many years ago—Ashish stepped back, half expecting him to throw a rock at his stomach.

"This is your daughter?" Saji Stephen asked.

Ashish stood mute.

"She looks small. Still, I suppose she should be adequate to tend to the girl and raise her spirits." Saji Stephen clapped his hands and a servant appeared. "Take this girl to Glory Anna," he said.

Standing at the edge of the garden, among spinach and onion plants, Ashish fought his memories. He had not seen that garden since the day he held Devi's baby and watched Devi break off sunflowers to celebrate the end of his smallpox duty.

"My Shridula must never be far from me," Ashish said.

Saji Stephen stiffened and his face grew dark.

But Ashish stood tall and looked Saji Stephen full in the face. "We are laborers only. You have no other rights over us. If that is not so here in this place, the pale English lady will want to know."

"Come, come!" Saji Stephen said with a sudden laugh. He motioned around the corner of the house to a patch of dirt alongside the veranda. "Sit! You can hear her call from here."

Saji Stephen stepped on up to the veranda and settled himself in a shady spot on his father's expensive Persian carpet. Boban Joseph—seated on the other side of the veranda, his father's leather-bound book of accounts open on his lap—didn't bother to look up.

"My boyhood playmate!" Saji Stephen called to him with a smile. "Remember the mischief we made together?"

Ashish kept his eyes down and his mouth closed.

"We would run out into the pouring rain to that big mango grove on the side of the house and pull ripe fruit off the tree. We would gorge ourselves! We didn't care a bit that water streamed down and soaked us. Remember, Ashish?"

Ashish remembered. One of Saji Stephen's favorite torments was to force him out into the downpour and up into the tree. It was Saji who ate the mangoes. Ashish got the whip.

"Oh, the joys of our childhood!" Saji Stephen said with a laugh.

Boban Joseph looked over at his brother. "Do you think that poor wretch does not remember how you tormented him? Do you think any of us could forget?"

"We have a friendship, he and I," Saji Stephen said to his brother. He spoke as though Ashish were not even there. "He thinks of me as his guardian, and I look on him as my child. His kind is always in need, of course. They could not live without us. If they are good to us, we are good to them."

"But if they offend us, we make their lives impossible. Is that not so?"

"Yes, yes!" Saji Stephen agreed. "Exactly."

Ashish sat silently in the dirt, his eyes fixed on his hands folded in his lap. He could feel Boban Joseph's eyes on him.

"Ones like him do not need anything," Saji Stephen said to his brother, "because they have never had anything. They are not like us, you see."

✑❦

All day, Ashish sat in the dirt beside the veranda, listening for Shridula's voice. Saji Stephen came and went, but Ashish sat in his place. A servant brought trays of food, which Boban Joseph and Saji Stephen ate noisily. Not a morsel was offered to Ashish. He continued to wait in motionless silence.

"Uncle." Rajeev Nathan, Saji Stephen's elder son, stepped out onto the veranda and bowed first to Boban Joseph, then to Saji Stephen. "Father."

"Sit, sit!" Boban Joseph said with an air of impatience. "Eat."

As Rajeev Nathan reached his hand to the food platter, he glanced up at Ashish and raised his eyebrows. "A Harijan from the fields? Sitting at our doorstep?"

"An Untouchable," Saji Stephen corrected. "He is an Untouchable."

Rajeev Nathan splayed out his fingers and pressed his palm flat on his plate. Faster than the eye could follow, he drew his fingers together and raised his hand to his mouth. "The Mahatma calls them Harijans," he said. "Children of God."

"The Mahatma did not see the father of that one crawling down this road to beg our father for money." Boban Joseph gestured toward Ashish. "I did. He had a broom tied to his back to brush away his filthy footprints, a cup over his mouth to protect us from his polluted breath, and a drum to warn us of his disgusting presence. I saw him and I can tell you, that Untouchable was no child of any god."

Ashish sat perfectly still. Even when a fly landed on his forehead and walked down over his nose and to his mouth, he never so much as blinked his eyes.

"Those were the days when grandfather lived," Rajeev Nathan said. "Mahatma Gandhi promises a new day for a new India."

"Promises, promises, always promises." Saji Stephen scowled. "But in the end, nothing ever changes."

Rajeev Nathan lifted his head in an assumed air of superiority. "Look at my family, Father. I am from a Christian heritage, my wife is Muslim, and we live successfully in peaceful harmony in a land of Hindus. Already I am achieving the first fruits of the Mahatma's promise of change. Gandhiji. Dear teacher Gandhi."

"Do you think yourself superior to your uncle?" Boban Joseph demanded. "I am the one with wealth, and I am the one with power. And in case you did not notice, Nephew, I am the one who owns the house you live in and the land that supports you."

"And you are the one who acts a fool whenever a young girl happens by," Saji Stephen said dryly.

"Would you have me be more like you, then?" Boban Joseph shot back. "An overgrown child, too irresponsible for anyone to respect?"

Rajeev Nathan grabbed up a large bite of rice and curry in his *chapati*. With his mouth full he said, "For four years now, ever since I first heard of the Quit India call of Mohandas Gandhi—the demand that the British immediately withdraw from our country—my eyes have been fixed on the great man."

Who could this wonderful man be? Ashish wondered. *Surely he must be even more powerful than the landowner.*

"He is not unlike me," Rajeev Nathan said. "A Hindu of high caste, deeply influenced by Christian ideas, yet fully Indian."

Boban Joseph laughed out loud.

"Your Mahatma cannot even keep himself out of prison," Saji Stephen sneered.

"Through his practice of civil disobedience, Gandhiji will lead India to independence," Rajeev Nathan stated with a note of disdain. "And when he does, I shall be standing by his side."

Boban Joseph pushed the bowl aside and cleared his throat, but he did not speak.

"Live in peace, then," Saji Stephen scoffed. "Find your success. Just do not cause an uproar in my house."

Boban Joseph cast a scathing glare at his brother. "My house!" he declared. "This is *my* house! Do not forget it."

❧

All through the hottest part of the day, Ashish sat in his spot in the dirt beside the veranda.

"Go to the barn to wait for your daughter," Saji Stephen suggested. But Ashish kept his eyes on the ground and refused to move.

In the afternoon, Brahmin Rama walked up the road. But with Ashish sitting in the dirt, he stopped well away and called out, "Boban! Boban Varghese!"

Ashish looked back. At first, he saw only the white *mundu* tied high under the slight man's ribs. But then he saw the sacred thread, emblem of exalted caste status, that hung over the Brahmin's left shoulder, across his body and under his right arm. Quickly Ashish scrambled to his knees and pressed his forehead to the dirt.

The Brahmin ignored him. Once again, he called, "Boban Varghese! Come and speak with me!"

"Yes, yes," Boban Joseph called back as he made his way out to the veranda. "What do you want?"

"I wish to talk over a matter of great concern." Brahmin Rama glanced at Ashish, who still bowed with his face to the ground. The Brahmin's eyes hardened. "But a piece of trash lies at your doorway."

"You! Untouchable!" Boban Joseph ordered. "Wait in the barn."

"Please, Master," Ashish said without moving. "Your brother agreed that I should stay near my daughter."

Boban Joseph shrugged. "She has already been in my house too long. I am tired of the both of you!" With a great show of impatience, he called for his servant to bring Shridula around to the garden. "Wait for her there," he told Ashish, "then take her away from my house."

"Now I shall have to suffer the time and trouble of bathing myself in a ritually purifying bath, and all because you do not have the decency of a proper outcaste," Brahmin Rama complained. "I must say, Landlord, it appalls me that you should allow one so polluted to lie across the threshold of your house."

Yet the Brahmin's dismay didn't stop him from stepping up to the veranda—from the far side, away from where Ashish had sat.

When he had settled himself, Brahmin Rama informed the landlord, "Your nephew is stirring up trouble."

"Rajeev Nathan is young. He dreams and he talks."

"He can dream all he wants," the Brahmin said, "but his never-ending talk must stop. Children of God! Which god is that, I ask you? It matters not what Mohandas Gandhi says. Untouchables are polluted and cursed by all the gods. To tell them otherwise is folly. It is begging for trouble."

"Come, come," Boban Joseph said, a glint of mischief flashing in his eye. "Surely a man with such vast powers as yours, one who can tell the future and call down curses on his enemies, need not fear the boastings of one foolish young man."

The Brahmin, his lips pursed tight, adjusted his wire-rimmed spectacles. "This is not a matter for levity. Your nephew Rajeev stirs up trouble by claiming that change is on the horizon."

"Perhaps he is right."

"Perhaps he is," said the Brahmin. "But it will take something far deeper than foolishly spread words to change the karma that controls our lives."

"Why, then, do you fear his words?"

"I fear the ones to whom Rajeev speaks," said Brahmin Rama. "It is bad enough that your nephew talks of strikes and resistance and riots and home rule to the people. But now he goes to the English with his words. That, my dear sir, is nothing short of madness!"

"It is you who are mad!" Boban Joseph shot back. "My nephew has no contact with the English."

"Can it be that you know so little of what happens under your own roof?" the Brahmin countered. "Rajeev wants the British and their mission medical clinic gone. All of them: the new doctor and his wife, and the old woman who has reigned over the clinic for forty years. And what's more, he intends to bring it to pass."

"I do not believe any of it," Boban Joseph said.

"Believe it or not, his plans are already in motion."

7

June 1946

"Faster!" Dinkar called to a clutch of women who had fallen behind. The line filed in from the roadside, each woman balancing an enormous load of chopped grass on her head.

"Why must you command this of us?" Ashish demanded of the overseer. "We have had no rest since the end of harvest. Now is the time we should be planting rice, yet you pile more work on us!"

"It is not for me to decide," Dinkar answered. "Master Landlord insists that we have everything ready for his new dairy before the rains come. Shelters for all his valuable new cows, he says, and stronger fences around their grazing fields."

"No!" Ashish insisted. "It is too much to ask!"

"You are not the master," Dinkar said dryly. "It is not for me to say, and it is not for you, either."

But even as he said it, Dinkar was well aware that Ashish wasn't the only one complaining. Unrest had begun to spread throughout the settlement.

A young man with an old man's face grumbled as he struggled to fell a tree. "We work and work until we can hardly stand on our feet, and for what? To make the rich landlord richer still!"

"We owe the landlord a debt, but we do not owe him our lives!" seethed the young man's friend Jinraj. Despite the deep, bleeding scratches that crisscrossed his hands and arms, Jinraj pulled up another thorn bramble from the road and piled it on top of the barrier that surrounded the new dairy's field. "We do not owe him the flesh from our bodies, either!"

Finally, Dinkar, his head bowed low in humility and fear, had no choice but to carry word of the workers' anger to the landlord.

Boban Joseph listened impatiently. "Have you lost all control over the laborers?" he demanded. "Do they not understand that I own them?"

"Please, Master Landlord," Dinkar pleaded. "It is too much for them. Your father would have—"

"I am not my father! Nor do I need your advice on how to work my laborers. I know perfectly well how to deal with them."

Hunger.

"From this day forth, rice allotments will be based on productivity," Boban Joseph ordered. "Workers who work fast and hard will receive a fair share. Those who fall behind will feel the harsh pangs of hunger."

Fear.

"Make them see that the work is for their own good. Consider Bengal, up in the north of India. So many workers have starved in that horrible famine that it is impossible to count the dead. Thousands upon thousands, and all because the laborers refused to work hard and prepare for the inevitable." Boban Joseph glared at the overseer. "You go back to the workers and tell them they can do the work assigned to them, or they can prepare to wrap up the bodies of their children for the fire. After that, they will wrap up their women, too, and then they will dig their own graves."

Terrified, Dinkar ran back down the road. He didn't hear Boban Joseph's laughter. Nor did he see Saji Stephen step out from behind his brother and challenge him:

"We only just heard about that horrible famine in Bengal on the radio, and it had nothing to do with the efforts of laborers," said Saji Stephen. "But, of course, you know that."

"Of course I know that," Boban Joseph answered with another chuckle. "But a tragedy is not a complete tragedy if a wise man can use it for his benefit."

*

The next morning, Dinkar passed the landlord's words on to the laborers. "I can do no more," he said. "I am but a laborer, the same as you."

But young Hari, Jyoti's oldest son, would not let the overseer off so easily. "I am the man of my family. I should be paid the same as any other man!" he insisted.

Dinkar inspected the boy with a critical eye—skinny arms and bony legs, narrow shoulders. "When you can do the work of a man, then you can demand the pay of a man."

"Give me a man's job, and I will prove to you that I can do it."

Dinkar hesitated.

"I can help you get Master Landlord's work finished," Hari insisted. "You need more willing backs if you are to meet his demands."

The overseer glanced from the boy to his mother, who sighed in resignation. She was equally skinny and wan. "Wild elephants and boars trample the far field," Dinkar said. "The young men up ahead are heading out to drive them away. Go with Jinraj and see what you can do."

Hari leaped forward and ran after the young men.

"He didn't even take a stick with him." Dinkar scowled. "Ashish! Run and fetch that boy back before he is trampled to death." As Ashish rushed after Hari, Dinkar muttered, "That scrawny boy is no man!"

☙

Ashish had already finished his evening meal and settled himself to rest under his *neem* tree, and his wife and daughter sat beside the dying cook fire with their dishes of spiced rice when Jyoti and her boys finally dragged themselves in from the fields.

"Cook over our fire tonight," Zia called to Jyoti, her voice gentle. "It is already hot. And do not bother to go to the well. I have enough water to fill your pot."

Ashish watched, but he said nothing.

Jyoti bowed her gratitude and hurried to her hut to get her own cooking pot.

While Jyoti waited next to the cooking fire for the water to heat, she unwrapped a new packet of rice and poured a portion of it into the pot.

"Your carved wood necklace," Zia cried. "It is gone!"

Jyoti's hand jerked to her neck. Gently she caressed the place where the necklace had fit so perfectly against her skin.

"Oh." Understanding passed over Zia's face. "The landlord?"

Jyoti's dark eyes filled with tears.

"But it was your grandmother's wedding gift to you!"

"My grandmother would understand," Jyoti whispered.

The scavenger woman's two skinny boys hunkered down in the shadows, watching impatiently as their mother stirred the bubbling pot.

Ashish also watched, but in silence from his place under the *neem* tree. It made sense to him that Jyoti would trade the necklace for food. Even though it had grown to be a part of her, it made perfect sense.

"Shridula," Zia called in a voice of false lightness. "Pull off a generous handful of greens from the garden and bring them here." To Jyoti she said, "They will add color to your meal and strength to your sons' bones."

Ashish shook his head. *A few pieces of vegetables won't help those scrawny boys!* he wanted to say. But he kept his mouth closed.

❧

With the dawn, Arun, a wiry man who limped on a twisted foot, squinted toward the rising sun and announced to Ashish, "Today the sun will be hot."

Mist lay over the flooded fields where trenches from the river had been opened onto the harvested fields. Every man not building fences or cow shelters was at work with a plow pulled by a water buffalo. Either he churned up the mud or he worked mounds of manure into the ground. Hari had no plow. He worked alone on his knees, mixing up the stinking muck with his hands.

"Look at that disgusting scavenger boy," the wiry man said to Ashish. "He is exactly where he belongs, on his hands and knees in the filthy mess!"

But he's doing a man's job, Ashish thought. What he said was, "Yes, Arun, the hot season is most certainly upon us."

Teams with harrows followed the plows to flatten the soggy ground and level it for planting. After so many years working behind a water buffalo, Ashish was a master with the harrow.

⚜

On the other side of the field, Zia worked alongside her daughter, tending the rice seedlings in flat baskets, carefully covering them with straw.

"They tell us our forefathers were dirty and ate pigs and cows, and that is why we are unclean," a woman with a loud voice stated. "Maybe that is true and maybe it is not. I do not know. But we are clean now. We do not eat cows or pigs. And yet the high caste still says we are unclean."

"I do not eat cows or pigs because I don't have any cows or pigs to eat," the woman with three teeth said. "Give me some meat and just watch me eat it!"

"*Amma*," Shridula whispered. "Look at Jyoti. What is she doing? Did she lose something?"

Zia peered over in the direction of Shridula's gaze. Actually, Jyoti didn't exactly look as though she were searching for anything. She looked more like she was watching for something, out toward the fields. Expecting someone, perhaps.

"I do not know," Zia said to Shridula.

"Maybe she is going to hide some of the seedlings in her *sari*."

"Why would she do that? She cannot eat seedlings."

"Or maybe—"

"Maybe we should mind our own business," Zia said firmly. "What Jyoti does is her own affair. If we slow down in our work, it is our rice pot that will go wanting."

⚜

As the white disc of the sun turned to pale yellow and sank toward the far field, the women mopped at their perspiring faces and turned back toward the settlement, eager to gather wood and water and light their evening cooking fires. As the edges of the mountain faded to gray, the exhausted men unyoked the water buffalo and headed to the well to pour water over their mud-splattered bodies. As the setting sun flooded the valley with its amber light, young Hari rose from the stinking muck and made his way to the edge of the paddy. He sprinted across the road and forced his way through the fence to the field adjacent to the storage sheds. Like a shadow, he slipped along the far side of the darkened path. Under a sky that had already given up the last of its color, he shinnied his scrawny body up the side of the shed and eased down through the narrow opening at the top.

Hari was a good son. He did his best to be the man of the family. Hari was also a good brother. He knew what it was to be despised, and he tried hard to protect his little brother, Falak, from jeers and cruel gossip. Hari was a good worker. Though it meant spending the entire day in backbreaking labor on his hands and knees in stinking mud, he did the job assigned to him without a word of complaint.

But Hari was a terrible thief. Dinkar caught him before he even got out of the storehouse.

"I will work!" Hari pleaded. "Just give me a man's job and I will do it!"

Dinkar bound Hari's hands with coarse rope and led him back to the settlement. In the courtyard, he untied the boy and forced him to hug the trunk of a young tamarind tree so he could bind Hari's wrists together on the opposite side. Ignoring the boy's pleas, he set a guard to watch him until daylight.

"Please, please!" Jyoti begged. "My son is only a boy. Please! He did wrong, but only to get food for his mother and his brother. He did not do it for himself."

Dinkar pushed her away with his foot.

❧

Ashish lay on the sleeping mat between his wife and daughter and listened to the weeping of the woman who sat crumpled outside the hut next to his.

"What will happen to Hari?" Shridula whispered.

"That is not your business," Zia said. "Your business is to sleep so you can work hard tomorrow."

Ashish said nothing.

All night he lay awake under the shelter of his *neem* tree, listening to the muffled sobs of the scavenger woman who now had no one with her but one hungry young child.

8

June 1946

$\mathcal{T}$he sun rose over a hot and steamy day, but the laborers could not start work. Jinraj and his band of young men barred them from both the paddies and the dairy construction site.

"What is happening?" Shridula asked.

"I do not know," her father said. Whatever it was, he was certain it would not be good.

"Look!" Shridula gasped. "Master Landlord is coming!"

Laborers who had been gathering in the courtyard since dawn quickly stepped to one side or the other, splitting the crowd down the middle. Boban Joseph's Sudra servant steered the horse-drawn cart through the open passageway, all the way through to the well. He didn't so much as glance Shridula's way. Dinkar, his face drawn, fell to his knees and bowed before the landlord. "The boy is ready, master," he mumbled.

Boban Joseph stood up in the cart and looked out at the tattered throng. "I own this land!" he proclaimed. "I own the grain that grows on it, and I own every one of you!"

Young Hari, his arms still bound around the tamarind tree, started to whimper.

"I am a fair man. I give you fair return for fair labor. But I will not abide thievery!"

Jyoti ran to the cart and fell on her face before the land-lord. "Please, please, show mercy to my son!" she cried. "He is but a boy trying to be a man. For the sake of his mother and brother, show him mercy."

Boban Joseph looked at her with disdain. "Remove your-self, woman, or you shall join your son for his punishment."

Zia rushed forward and grabbed hold of Jyoti. "Come," she begged. "You will only make things worse for Hari."

As Zia pulled Jyoti away, Boban Joseph's servant climbed down from the cart. In his hand he clutched a whip.

"Do not expect mercy from me," Boban Joseph declared—not only to Jyoti, but to the entire crowd of workers. "I am not like my father!"

The Sudra servant, his eyes fixed on the trembling, sobbing boy, slowly uncoiled his whip. He cracked it in the air once, twice, then brought it down hard across Hari's bare back. The boy shrieked with pain.

"No! Please, no!" Jyoti screamed.

Another crack of the whip, another lash. Then another, and another. Hari screamed with each lash, but already his cries were growing weaker.

Jyoti's legs gave way and she fell to the ground.

Another crack, another lash. Another. Another. Tears poured from the boy's eyes. He opened his mouth, but all he could do was utter strangled, gurgling noises.

Hari crumpled and collapsed. Still tightly bound around the tree's trunk, he hung by his arms, moaning.

Ashish glanced at Shridula. She was sobbing in her moth-er's arms.

"Stop it!" Ashish cried to the Sudra. "How can you beat a starving boy?"

Another crack, another lash.

"Stop! We are not animals. We are people!"

Another crack, another lash. Now Hari moved only slightly at the blows. He was barely conscious. But by the look on Boban Joseph's face, he neither knew nor cared.

Ashish jumped forward, positioning himself between the Sudra servant and Hari.

"Move aside immediately," Boban Joseph ordered, "or my servant will whip the life out of both you and him!"

Ashish raised his head, stood tall, and held his ground. Shridula pulled away from her mother and ran to stand beside her father. Zia opened her mouth to protest, but instead she, too, stepped up beside them.

Boban Joseph shook with rage. "You think I will not beat you? I most certainly will!" he bellowed. "Raise the whip!"

But before the Sudra could follow the landlord's orders, Dinkar rushed up and stood beside Ashish. The young man with the old man's face pushed forward, too. Then Jinraj did the same, and the entire group of young men followed him.

The Sudra servant, forced to step back to make room for the growing crowd, looked about him in confusion. He turned to Boban Joseph, but all the landlord did was growl and sputter and grind his teeth in frustrated fury.

More laborers pushed forward, forcing the Sudra to step back still further.

Boban Joseph turned from the Sudra to the growing crowd, his look of rage fast deteriorating into desperation tinged with fear.

The Sudra had already raised his whip, but he hesitated, still holding it high in the air. Finally he dropped his arm and let the whip fall.

"Come!" Boban Joseph called abruptly. "We have taught the thief his lesson. We are finished here."

Ashish didn't dare to move.

The Sudra hurried into the cart and lashed wildly at the horse. The poor animal leapt forward and bolted up the pathway toward home. Boban Joseph did not look back.

Jyoti pushed forward to tend to her son. The laborers—looking blankly at each other—turned in silence toward their huts.

"What happened?" Dinkar asked Ashish when they were alone.

"Civil disobedience," Ashish said. "Like the Mahatma teaches."

Although Mohandas Gandhi had been irritating the British Empire for longer than Ashish had lived, Ashish had never heard the leader's name before he spent the day in the dirt beside Boban Joseph's veranda. Sitting perfectly still, remaining absolutely quiet, he learned much about the Mahatma's words and methods that afternoon. The high caste men had talked on that day, ignoring the Untouchable's presence. As far as they were concerned, he was not even there. Such a one as he was of no more consequence to them than a fly or a mouse.

Years before, when the Communist Party of Malabar had gone through the countryside recruiting members, they came at night to the settlement and whispered to the workers who sat around their cooking fires. Ashish's father, Virat, perked up his Untouchable ears and listened to their message: *Everyone will be treated the same. No one shall be privileged over any other. No more caste.* Strongly drawn to that message, Virat joined the party.

When Ashish's voice changed from that of a boy to that of a man, he had followed his father and received his own party membership card. It didn't take long, however, for him to see that Untouchables still fell victim to attacks by the upper castes. And, as always, most of those attacks went unreported. Their landowner and his son were the worst offenders of all.

"We must force them to stop!" Ashish had railed to his father back then.

But Virat simply said, "Be patient, my son. It will take time."

The Communists spoke long and loud, but they did not speak for the Untouchables. So Ashish tore up his membership card and turned his back on the Communist Party.

✍

Nihal Amos, Saji Stephen's second son, had no idea that anyone in the settlement had the least knowledge of the Communist Party. Not only did he himself carry a membership card, but he was active in the organization and totally dedicated to it. So quickly was he moving up the ranks that he was slated to soon be awarded a place of leadership.

"You, a Communist?" his uncle Boban Joseph mocked him. "How can that be? You are from a Christian family!"

"I am a Christian Communist," Nihal Amos huffed.

Which was not as unlikely as it sounded. The area's Marxist rulers were unusual among Communists in that they did not condemn religion. On the contrary, they emphasized the areas on which they agreed with religious leaders. Over caste issues and matters of land reform, they clashed equally with Hindus and Christians.

"Actually, Communism and Christianity have much in common," Nihal Amos told his uncle. "Both fight for justice among the poor. Surely Jesus would approve of that."

"I suppose you want me to set all our workers free," Boban Joseph said. "I suppose you are offering to plow the land yourself, and then to plant the crops and bring in the harvest with your own hand."

"Certainly not," Nihal Amos answered. "As a matter of fact, I am saying that the slave castes are a different breed of people than we high castes. They are the true sons of the soil. They are the ones who descended from the earliest inhabitants of India. Therefore, they deserve our help and compensation for all that their kind has suffered at the hands of those who invaded their land, killed their kings, and stole their homes."

Boban Joseph's eyes narrowed and he glared at his second nephew. "And who is supposed to provide this help and pay all this compensation?"

"Well . . ." Nihal Amos hesitated. "I suppose . . . uh . . . well, all of us—that is, to some extent."

"I will begin to this extent," Boban Joseph said. "By the new moon, you and your family will leave my house. Whatever expense I have previously wasted on you and your wife, I will expend on my new dairy, which will provide extra work—and therefore, extra rice—for the laborers."

"Now, Uncle, do not be hasty," Nihal Amos said. "All I meant to say was that—"

"By the new moon."

"Uncle, please. This is our home. It is our only home. We have nowhere else to go."

"Join the beggars by the side of the road, then. Become one with them."

"You do not understand my point, Uncle. It is simply that—"

"You will be gone by the new moon!"

9

June 1946

"Come! Gather around and listen to what I have to say!" Nihal Amos called as he walked through the workers' settlement. "Come, come and hear!" Nihal's lean, unpretentious appearance attracted the attention of the Untouchable laborers. This could be no well-fed, pampered high caste landowner—could it?

Still balancing her water pot on her head, Shridula stopped to gape at the thin man, his *mundu* flapping around his brown legs. Not like a Brahmin, though. For with the *mundu* he wore an Englishman's white shirt.

"Come! Come!" Nihal Amos called. "Gather around. What I have to say is important to all!"

Ashish kept his mouth shut tight. He recognized Saji Stephen's second son. And he knew perfectly well why Nihal Amos had come to the settlement.

It wasn't difficult to persuade the workers to toss their plows and hoes aside and forget about the weeds that threatened to overtake the paddies. The men clumped together in groups, staying far enough back from the stranger to feel safe, but inching close enough to hear what he had to say.

"I am Nihal, nephew of the landowner."

The workers cast anxious eyes to their idled working tools. Slowly, they began to edge back toward them. But as they whispered worried suspicions to one another, Nihal Amos quickly added, "Please do not worry. I have not come here to oppress you further. Nor do I intend to force more work from your tired backs. On the contrary, I have come to help you."

The whispering hushed. Every worker fixed his eyes on the skinny man in the white man's shirt.

Nihal Amos began by telling the laborers what they already knew: "The landlord forces you to work too hard. He rests on his bed through the searing heat of the day. Why should he deny you the right to do the same? It is through your sweat and labor that the rich landlord grows richer still. Why then should you struggle to work when you are so weak from hunger you find it difficult to stand? Why should your starving children cry themselves to sleep at night? It is not fair! It is not right!"

"Yes, yes!" the workers said to one another. "Everything the man says is true. He knows. He knows!"

Nihal Amos spoke of the workers' suffering. Of their breaking backs as they stooped over in the paddies hour after hour, planting the rice seedlings. Of their hands, blistered and raw, as they hoed the ground under the scorching sun. Of their parched mouths as they cried out for water that didn't come. Of their head-swimming weariness with no rest in sight.

"Yes, yes! That is our plight!" the laborers called back. "You know! You understand!"

"And you have no hope. That is the worst of it," Nihal Amos said sadly. "With the curse of karma hanging heavy over you, how can you hope that your lot will improve? It will not. Not for you and not for your children."

"No," the people murmured. "We have no hope. No hope at all."

❧

Ashish watched the energy with which Nihal Amos waved his twig-thin arms about and listened to the amazing passion of Nihal Amos's message. He looked around at the intensity of the crowd, too. How easily his friends and neighbors called out their agreement to this son of the landlord's brother! All the people he knew so well suddenly seemed complete strangers to him.

"It does not have to be this way!" Nihal Amos said. "You do not have to be slaves to the high castes!"

The crowd grew hushed. Ashish could tell they did not quite believe what Nihal Amos had just said, even though they badly wanted to believe it. He could see the disbelief in the slump of their shoulders and the way they turned their eyes away from Nihal Amos.

Nihal Amos saw it too, so he quickly changed his approach. "Who of you knows of Mr. B. R. Ambedkar?" he bellowed.

The gathered workers all stared back at him with curious eyes.

"No one? But every one of you should know of this man! He is one of you—an Untouchable. But he is no slave to a landowner! He does not spend his days groveling in the stinking mud of rice paddies or his nights in the shabby hut of a laborer. No, he practices law at the Bombay High Court."

A gasp of disbelief arose from the crowd.

"I tell you the truth! This important lawyer is an Untouchable, the same as you!"

Nihal Amos paused to let the enormity of this revelation sink in.

"Mr. B. R. Ambedkar is not exactly like you, however, for he insists before everyone that the caste system is a terrible evil."

The crowd stared in shocked silence. Could the landowner's nephew actually be saying such a thing?

"Mr. B. R. Ambedkar stands up in public and calls the members of the Indian Congress hypocrites. Yes, and he says the same of Mr. Gandhi, too! Mr. B. R. Ambedkar insists that every person who is a member of the upper caste must be required to pay for what they have done to you Untouchables!"

Ashish glanced around at the rapt faces. This had to be some sort of a trick. Yes, surely the landlord's nephew was attempting to fool the workers, to get something more out of them.

"So you see, to pull free from your bonds of oppression is more than just a wishful hope. It is a real possibility! Mr. B. R. Ambedkar has made a path to freedom for you. He has shown Untouchables the way to a whole new future!"

❧

As long as Nihal Amos talked, the workers listened eagerly. Men pushed up close to Nihal Amos while the women held back, but they also listened. Even the children, who couldn't begin to understand the concepts, listened to the words and grasped the excitement.

Finally, Nihal Amos stopped talking. He wiped the dripping perspiration from his face with the sleeve of his shirt, and gratefully accepted the cup of water a worker held out to him. To everyone's amazement, the son of the landlord's brother actually drank water from an Untouchable cup!

"Mr. B. R. Ambedkar may not know it, but in his heart he is a Marxist," Nihal Amos said. "For Marxists also believe all people should be treated the same. Everyone who expects to eat should toil in the fields and paddies, regardless of the caste of his birth. And every person who works, in whatever capacity, should enjoy and share equally in the fruits of his labor."

Yes, the workers agreed. What the landowner's nephew said was most certainly true. Every word of it!

"You, too, can be a part of this exciting future," Nihal Amos cried. "All this hope and possibility belongs to you as well! Every one of you! All you need to do is come up here to me, and join the Communist Party. I will add your name to my list, and you can seal your membership with your thumbprint. I will give you a membership card to prove which side you are on. Come and add your name! Come and help change India! Come and give power to Untouchables!"

As the men pushed forward, Ashish jumped up onto a stump and called out, "Wait! Do you not understand that this is the son of the landlord's brother? Who is he to speak to us of freedom and hope? He is part of the family of our oppressor, yet he dares tell us we should not be oppressed! We stamped our thumbprints on the landlord's sheets before—or our fathers did—and look where that got us. I beg you, do not be too quick to trust this upper caste man!"

"Do not think of it as joining with me!" Nihal Amos countered. "Think of it as joining with the great B. R. Ambedkar!"

"Is that so?" Ashish challenged. "Then let Mr. B. R. Ambedkar come and talk to us. Let Mr. B. R. Ambedkar invite us to join with him!"

At the head of the line, eager to stamp his thumbprint and join with the Marxists, was Dinkar. Young Hari, still hurting badly from the whipping, limped up behind him. Jinraj followed, and the young man with an old man's face came along behind him. Two more men stepped up, and another and another. The line grew, but it grew neither fast nor long.

"Can girls join too, *Appa?*" Shridula asked eagerly. "If they can, I want the landlord's nephew to add my name to the list."

"No!" Ashish said. "I forbid it. Even if you were a son and not a daughter, I would still forbid it."

"Why?" Shridula demanded to know.

"Because the Marxists do not really speak for us. Even if they want to, they cannot. The upper castes will continue to attack us, and the police will continue to defend and protect them. That is how it has always been and that is how it will continue to be."

"But the Communists are our only hope!"

"Be patient, my daughter," Ashish said. "Real change will come someday, but it will not be like this."

10

June 1946

*A*s the summer sun rose, a sizzling disk in an already scorched sky, Shridula followed her mother out to the closest rice paddy. Ankle-deep in water, she hiked up her *sari* and tied it high, then hunkered down in the mud to start the arduous task of planting the morning's first basketful of rice seedlings. One by one by one. Each six inches apart. Row after row after row.

Across the road in the field beyond, her father steadied himself on a wooden harrow and steered the black water buffalo through the uneven mud toward the east. Soon that paddy, too, would be ready for planting.

Boban Joseph, ensconced on his father's Persian carpet and shaded by fragrant jasmine blossoms, cast a haughty gaze around the veranda at his brother and two nephews. From his seat of honor Boban Joseph declared, "I agree with my friend, the Great Soul Gandhiji. Whether an Untouchable calls himself a Christian, a Muslim, a Hindu, or a Sikh, nevertheless he remains an Untouchable. He cannot change the spots he inherited from Hinduism. He may change his clothes, he may call himself a Christian Untouchable or a Muslim Untouchable or whatever he wishes, but he nevertheless remains an Untouchable."

"Mahatma Gandhi never uses the word 'Untouchable,'" Nihal Amos pointed out. "And even if he did, that statement makes absolutely no sense."

"You would say that, of course, since you are a Communist," Boban Joseph said in his most dismissive tone of voice. "Why are you standing on my veranda, anyway? This night the moon will be full. You are no longer welcome under my roof."

Nihal Amos ignored the last comment. "Mahatma Gandhi does indeed speak of all Harijans still being Harijans regardless of their religion. Yet even as he says it, he restricts his social care to Hindu Harijans alone. Do you not find this a striking contradiction, Uncle?"

"Not in the least. Gandhiji is absolutely right. Social funds *should* be used only for Hindu Harijans."

"Perhaps you have forgotten that you yourself are from a Christian family," Saji Stephen said with a smirk.

Wagging his finger in his uncle's face, Nihal Amos insisted, "Mr. Gandhi's real concern is not for the plight of the Untouchables at all. It is for his own political interest."

"If you believe that, there is much you do not understand," Rajeev Nathan proclaimed. "The Mahatma fights a battle without weapons. Nonviolence is his way. Truth, too. That is his real power. Truth so strong that the whole of the British Empire will not be able to stand against it!"

"My friend Gandhiji is no coward," Boban Joseph said. "But, as I advise him, he must also learn the persuasive power of violence. For while he sits safely in prison, we, the truly brave, are the ones left to carry on the fight."

The noonday sun beat down relentlessly on Shridula's aching back, scorching her dark skin through her mud-caked *sari*. Despite her mother's repeated warnings, she dipped her hand into the muddy paddy water and poured it over her arms. It felt so good that she dipped her hand in again and splashed the stinking water onto her sweltering face.

Over in the next paddy, her father, splattered with mud and flushed crimson under his dark skin, stopped the water buffalo and called for the water boy. He waited and waited. When the boy didn't come, Ashish bellowed for him. Still no water boy. Still no water.

"You say Gandhiji is a personal friend of yours, Uncle?" Rajeev Nathan allowed himself to smile at the ridiculous thought. "Surely, then, you know that Jesus' Sermon on the Mount was his revelation for Passive Resistance."

"Pshaw!"

Rajeev Nathan cleared his throat. "If I may say, I have made an extensive study of Mohandas Gandhi and his teachings. To him, *Ahimsa* is not so much nonviolence as action founded on a refusal to cause harm. We all know that the masses have been exhausted by endless servitude. Yet Gandhi does not teach them to avoid suffering. He teaches them to cease *fearing*. That is a big difference."

Boban Joseph waved his nephew aside and strutted across the veranda. "Yes, yes. But I could teach the Mahatma a few things. 'Quit sweeping the floor and clean up your own mess,' I would tell him. 'Hold onto the old Hindu social order,' I would say. 'That social order has served you well.'"

Rajeev Nathan opened his mouth to argue, but Saji Stephen interrupted. "Come, come!" he said. "We should not spend our evening talking politics."

"*You* should not spend *your* evening talking politics," Boban Joseph retorted, "because you have nothing of value to add to the conversation. What do you know of such things? You seldom listen to the radio reports with me, or even read what is written in the newspapers."

"Much wisdom and understanding come from listening to the ideas of others," Rajeev Nathan pointed out.

"Oh, yes, you with your Muslim wife and brood of mixed-blood children," Boban Joseph mocked. "So much I could gain from you!"

"The point is—" Nihal Amos began.

"The point is that at least Rajeev Nathan's belly makes him look like an upper caste person. But you, Nihal Amos: Your emaciated asceticism is an embarrassment to this family. And are you so foolish you cannot see the uselessness of Marxism? No, I alone am in a position to discuss politics. But to do so, I need more intelligent companions than the likes of any of you!"

☙

Glory Anna, panting in her stifling room despite the wide-open window shutters, wiped perspiration from her face and eased her door open. Seeing no one about, she crept out—but only far enough to catch a bit of a breeze from the veranda. Rajeev's children called out to each other from the back of the house, their voices drowning out the gossip of her brothers' wives. But at the sound of her uncle Boban Joseph's voice, Glory Anna jumped back into the room and pulled the door closed. The very thought of his eyes on her set her to shivering. And of his hands reaching out to her—oh, it was too terrible to imagine! Uncle Boban Joseph was the main reason Glory Anna endured the searing heat of the day closed up inside her grandmother's airless room.

"Call her what you will, Saji Stephen, but bring that Untouchable girl back here," Boban Joseph was saying. "Only this time, leave her old father where he belongs—at work in the fields."

Saji Stephen answered, but Glory Anna couldn't make out the words. Boban Joseph laughed out loud.

They were talking about Shridula! That was a puzzlement. Why had Saji Stephen sent that Untouchable girl to her in the first place? To be a servant? A companion? It made no sense. Glory Anna knew perfectly well that she could live her entire life closed up inside her room, or she could disappear tomorrow and never be seen again, and her father would never give her a second thought. So why bring Shridula to her?

Evidently, Shridula hadn't known either. While she was there, the two girls never spoke a word to each other. The entire time Shridula was in her room, Glory Anna sat on her grandmother's bed and stared at the wall. For a long time Shridula stood in silence, but she finally slipped to the floor and spent the rest of the day sitting against the wall, staring at her hands. Only once did the two have the misfortune of sneaking a glance at each other at exactly the same moment. But they quickly looked away and made certain it didn't happen again.

" 'White monkeys.' That is what mother used to call the English." It was Uncle Boban Joseph's irritated voice again. "So many taxes they pile on our backs. Tax on our land, tax for our water, tax to walk along our own road through our own town. The British government has sucked the blood out of our bodies and left us with hardly a bit of life remaining!"

"That's why we must demand self-rule for India." Rajeev Nathan said that. He was never at a loss for words.

"The rest of you do well to fear the English," Uncle Boban Joseph said. "But fear is not necessary for me. I can buy off their officials. The police may come for the rest of you, but they will not come for me." This was followed by a sharp laugh. Uncle Boban Joseph, most likely. Yes, certainly Uncle Boban.

For a while, all was quiet. Glory Anna let down her guard and risked moving a few steps closer to the veranda. Then Rajeev Nathan spoke again, and this time his voice dripped with bitterness. "If you think you are safe, Uncle, you are the biggest fool of all. The English will bring more disaster on India than this country has ever known. Why should they spare you?"

Glory Anna caught her breath. Horrible disaster? In this place? Oh, but where would that leave her? Her head spun. She felt as though all the blood had drained from her face. Glory Anna ran back to her room. She didn't dare so much as breathe until she had pulled the door shut behind her.

❦

"Overseer!" the old woman with three teeth cried out, "When is our time to rest? Do you intend to work us until we all drop dead in the fields?"

Dinkar wiped his calloused hand across his sweat-streaked face. "It is not my decision," he said. "I must follow Master Landlord's orders."

"Well, I cannot work anymore today," she said. "I quit!"

The old woman struggled to pull herself upright and stumbled away through the paddy.

"Me, too!" said the woman with the loud voice. She also stood up and walked away.

"Come, *Amma*," Shridula said. "Let us go, too."

Zia hesitated, but Shridula had already gotten to her feet and was adjusting her *sari*. "Daughter," Zia warned, "the land-lord will not allow this disobedience. He will not let it go unpunished!"

In the next paddy, Ashish halted the black water buffalo and shaded his eyes. He stared in disbelief at the women.

"What have I started?" he murmured.

☙

Boban Joseph sat alone in the gathering darkness, watching the full moon cast a ghostly glow over the mango grove. An owl called out from somewhere in the shadows. Boban Joseph shivered in spite of himself. He was not used to being alone. But after he sent Nihal Amos and his wife away from the house, the rest of Saji Stephen's family retreated to the back. The evening drew out long and lonely.

"Master!"

Boban Joseph started at his servant Udit's unexpected call. He opened his mouth to scold the fool for creeping up so silently, but the servant said, "Big trouble by the entrance to your new dairy, master. The workers caught an intruder and they say you must come."

"A thief, then. Is that what you mean to say?" Boban Joseph demanded as he leaped to his feet. "Prepare the cart!"

"Begging your pardon, master," Udit said, "I have your horse already prepared. You must make all haste!"

Boban Joseph hesitated.

"Your overseer . . . he has gathered workers. Already they prepare to fight the intruder, but they need your wisdom and guidance."

"I shall leave at once!"

Although Boban Joseph used to ride often, he seldom attempted to get up on a horse anymore. Yet it did make sense, for haste was most certainly called for in this situation. "Get me the whip!" he ordered. "And my knife, too."

Boban Joseph mounted his horse and rode awkwardly past the garden. He followed along the paths that led through the fields. He started at a face-saving trot, but as soon as he was out of sight, he slowed to an easy walk.

Even under a full moon, the narrow road was heavy with shadows and lined with dangerous thorn brambles. It made for a murderous combination. "Perhaps we should have insisted on the cart," Boban Joseph said to the horse. It gave him courage to hear a voice, even if it was only his own.

Boban Joseph passed by two fields not yet prepared for planting, then turned down the path that ran alongside the rice paddy Ashish had finished leveling that very day. The night was perfectly still. Not even an owl called out. Boban Joseph could hear nothing but the clop, clop, clop of his horse's hooves.

As the shadows shifted, Boban Joseph made out two men on horseback up ahead. They looked to be waiting at the juncture of two field paths.

"There they are. The thieves!" Boban Joseph breathed. Icy fear rose in his throat. He gasped for breath, his heart pounding.

Frantically, Boban Joseph looked about for Dinkar and the band of workers. He sighed in relief at the sound of muffled voices coming up behind him. From the tramp and clatter, it sounded to be a sizable number of men. Boban Joseph laughed out loud, his fear dissipating, replaced by a fresh bravado. He kicked at his horse's sides and plunged forward, bellowing, "Stop the thieves! Grab them!"

To Boban's surprise, the men on horseback didn't try to escape. Instead, they moved slowly toward him and stopped their horses in the middle of the path ahead. Boban Joseph glanced around in confusion. He started to call out to the group of men, but as they drew closer he saw by the light of the moon that they had pulled their *chaddars* off their heads and wrapped them so low over their faces that he couldn't make out who they were. Puzzled, Boban Joseph turned and stared from the men on foot to the two men on horseback.

Suddenly the group on foot ran toward him, yelling and swinging heavy clubs. Boban Joseph had no room to move his horse. He was trapped between the men advancing on foot and the two on horseback. On either side, bramble fences hemmed him in.

Boban Joseph's horse, panicked by the wild terror from behind and bellowed threats in front, did a quick-stepping sort of dance that nearly threw Boban from its back.

Some men in the advancing crowd thumped their clubs on the ground. Others waved them in the air. *What are you doing?* Boban Joseph wanted to ask. *Stop it! Stop it now!* he wanted to shout. But everything happened so fast that he couldn't get his wits about him. He couldn't think!

A hard blow smashed against Boban Joseph's shoulder and his arm went numb. Terror rose in his chest. He tried to jerk his frightened horse around, but the angry mob completely blocked the path. Another blow struck him squarely in the back, almost knocking the breath out of him. Fumbling for his knife, he tried again to turn his horse around, to head for home and safety. But before he could get his hand on his weapon, a long staff caught him a sharp blow in the head and knocked him off his horse. Boban Joseph tumbled directly into the needle-sharp barbs of the brambles.

Stunned, wounded, and bleeding—and helplessly entangled in the thorns—Boban Joseph screamed, "I will give you money! Let me go and you can have anything you want!"

But the men, now a vengeful mob, rained blow after vicious blow down on him. Boban's screams turns to piteous wails, his wails to whimpering pleas for mercy.

Using the last of his strength, Boban Joseph pulled himself painfully off the brambles and toppled to the ground. He curled up, his arms over his head in a vain attempt to block the beating. Even with his dying words, punctuated by the impact of the pounding clubs, he still sought to appease his unknown tormentors: "Please . . . please . . . Anything . . . I am . . . the landlord . . . and . . . I can give you . . . give you anything . . . Anything."

❧

As the sun rose in a scorched sky to start another day, Shridula once more followed her mother to the nearer rice paddy. Again she hiked up her sari and tied it high. Again she hunkered down in the muddy water to plant yet another of the endless basketfuls of rice seedlings. One by one by one. Each six inches apart. Row after row after row.

In the field beyond, her father steered the black water buffalo through the clumped mud toward the east. That's when he saw the battered body of landowner Boban Joseph.

"Thieves," Dinkar said in answer to Ashish's cries for help. He clucked his tongue and shook his head. "It's the only answer for such an assault. An attack by thieves."

Ashish pointed to the lavishly carved knife that lay by the landlord's side. "Could thieves have missed that?"

Dinkar kicked the knife into the muddy water of the paddy. "I will call the landlord's men," he said. "You take the day off and rest yourself. You deserve it after so much extra work. We all do."

11

June 1946

"*M*iss Abigail! Come quickly, Miss Abigail!" Krishna called. "Two policemen be asking questions of the doctor and *memsahib* in the great room, and now they demand to be seeing you, too!"

"Whatever for?" Miss Abigail asked. She knew better than to react too quickly to demands from Indian police. "Has something happened?"

"They be telling me nothing," Krishna said. "Only to fetch you, and bring you most quickly."

Miss Abigail Davidson slipped her shoes on—she seldom wore them in her own rooms—and adjusted her *sari*. As she and Krishna made their careful way across the mission clinic yard, Miss Abigail was struck by the silence in the compound. No one hoed in the garden. No one pumped water at the well. No children ran about, calling out or playing in the dirt. Why, she could remember when the entire place rocked with noisy activity. When every single person . . .

Miss Abigail shook her head. No! She must not recall those long-ago times. She must not torture herself. Past was past; what was gone was gone.

As soon as Miss Abigail entered the great room, she knew something was terribly wrong. Dr. Cooper sat stone-faced on the settee, his wife sagging beside him. Susanna had gone quite pale and she twisted nervously at the handkerchief clutched in her hands. Both she and her husband kept their eyes away from the two Indian policemen who had positioned themselves beside the fireplace.

The moment Miss Abigail entered, Dr. Cooper jumped to his feet and reached out to her. "Miss Davidson. Awfully good of you to come straightaway. Please, sit down. Do sit down!"

Miss Abigail slipped into the nearest chair—that uncomfortable straight-backed thing she so disliked—and gazed cautiously from doctor to policemen to anxious wife and back again. "Well?" she asked. "What is this all about?"

"The landowner, Boban Joseph Varghese," said Dr. Cooper. "He is dead."

Miss Abigail raised her eyebrows. "Oh? Well then. A death is always a sad event for a family, is it not?"

"Tell her, William!" Susanna hissed.

"Murdered, it would seem."

Miss Abigail caught her breath. "Oh? Goodness me!"

"Yes," said Dr. Cooper. "Indeed."

Never one for emotional displays, Miss Abigail turned her attention to the two policemen. One was tall and clean-shaven, the other short with a bushy beard and mustache. "You came all the way out here to bring us this news, then?"

Dr. Cooper cleared his throat. Susanna dabbed at her eyes with her handkerchief.

"What dealings have *you* had with landowner Boban Joseph Varghese?" the tall policeman demanded of Miss Abigail.

"I beg your pardon?" Miss Abigail looked questioningly from the policeman back to the doctor. "Why, absolutely none. No dealings at all."

The short, bushy-faced policeman's eyes narrowed. "His family has a different story to tell. They say Boban Joseph Varghese was a kind and generous man that Indians, both his family and the villagers, held in the highest esteem. But they say that you English harassed and threatened him."

"Especially you," the tall policeman said to Miss Abigail.

"Why, not a bit of it!" Miss Abigail protested. "I have never so much as made the man's acquaintance!"

Or could it be that he was that nice man who came to see me? Miss Abigail wondered. Fortunately, she had the presence of mind not to say out loud every thought that came to her mind.

The policemen fixed Miss Abigail fast in an accusing stare.

"My entire life I have worked among the outcastes of your society," Miss Abigail said. "I tended to the sick who came to the clinic for help, and I took in the little ones tossed aside because no one else wanted them."

"Hindu children or Muslim?" the bushy-faced policeman demanded.

"Whichever needed my help, sir."

"You will do well to determine with which side you will align yourself," the tall policeman stated. "Christians caught between Hindus and Muslims will soon be in for a sore squeezing."

"In no such manner as you suggest have I ever imposed myself," Miss Abigail huffed. "Nor have I ever interfered with the landlord or his business. No, sir, not in the least!"

Maybe there could have been some disturbance, Miss Abigail thought. *Once, long ago. When was it? I can't quite recall . . .*

"Not in the least, you say?" The bushy-faced policeman thrust his face close to Miss Abigail's and assumed a most accusatory tone. "You are certain of that?"

"Quite certain!"

Well, why not "quite certain"? It couldn't have been much of a disturbance or I would remember it, wouldn't I?

"Then why does Boban Joseph Varghese have a laborer who continually invokes your name as a threat in order to avoid undesirable work?"

Miss Abigail stared at the policeman in confusion. She looked to Dr. Cooper (he hardened his gaze unsympathetically) and to Susanna (she continued to blot at her red-rimmed eyes). Miss Abigail shook her head and tried to understand.

"Oh!" she suddenly exclaimed. "You must mean Ashish!"

✍

Long after the policemen had left, Dr. Cooper continued to grill Miss Abigail for details. ("Do not expect this to be our last visit," the tall policeman had warned on his way out.) Miss Abigail patted a handkerchief across her wrinkled brow and willed her mind to stop skipping around so. How she longed to retire to the calm of her rooftop and watch the sun sink over the mountains. But Dr. Cooper would not stop talking.

"I did my utmost to warn you, Miss Davidson! 'Do not get overly involved with the natives,' I said. Did I not warn you?"

Miss Abigail heaved a heavy sigh. "Ashish is just a child. He and Krishna play together."

"Your Krishna is an old man!" Susanna exclaimed in exasperation. "Can you not remember that?"

"Do not get involved, that was my counsel. Yet look at you! Dressed in Indian clothes. Eating with your hands like a native from the jungle. Speaking their gibberish language!"

"Yes, yes, Dr. Cooper. I am guilty on every charge. All of them! But I did not interject myself into the landlord's slave business."

"Slave business! There you are, rousing up trouble again! We can only thank God that the policemen were not around to hear you say that."

Miss Abigail looked at Dr. Cooper's flushed face and flashing eyes. She could not help but notice the pulsing at his temples. *Best not to tell him I gave Ashish my Bible,* she decided.

Age and experience had their benefits. This was a truth Miss Abigail Davidson understood in her more lucid moments. And she had both at her disposal. She was painfully acquainted with India's decades-old struggle for independence, and even more with her own country's determination to thwart those efforts. The "Quit India" movement, for instance, when the Indian Congress had demanded immediate independence. The British response was to call out fifty-seven fully armed army battalions. Horrible! They had fired on the peacefully assembled, unarmed Indians and had killed thousands. When Miss Abigail tried to tell Dr. Cooper and Susanna about it the next day, they told her to stop spreading such ridiculous tales.

"Really, we've nothing to fear from the Indian police, have we, dear?" Susanna asked her husband.

"I shouldn't think so," Dr. Cooper said. "We know those fellows to be nothing more than an irritating nip at the heels of the unshakable Empire."

"It really is quite funny, when one considers it in that light," Susanna said. "Those two Indians, standing before us, were making such a show of looking official."

"That they would actually threaten us and expect us to fall into line behind them would be a grave insult, were it not so absurd," Dr. Cooper agreed.

Miss Abigail said nothing.

The doctor turned to her. "Although you most assuredly have nothing to fear from them, Miss Davidson, it does not lessen the import of our previous warning to you. I do hope you will try to understand."

Still Miss Abigail held her peace. So Dr. Cooper turned his attention back to his wife. But while he laughed with Susanna over the policemen's visit and joked about a "silly puppy barking at the feet of a tiger," Miss Abigail trembled. Because she knew. She knew.

As Abigail stood to excuse herself, Susanna Cooper interrupted. "Pardon me for being so blunt, Miss Davidson," she said, "but at times like this, I feel that one must be honest. You are a woman of considerable years, are you not?"

Miss Abigail smiled. "Indeed. Full of age and experience, and, at times, a fair share of wisdom. Would you agree, Doctor?"

Dr. Cooper cleared his throat.

"What I mean to say is that someone of your age really should be residing in a civilized country," Susanna pressed.

"I see. A country of aggressors as opposed to a country fighting for its right to govern itself. Is that what you mean?"

"Miss Davidson," Dr. Cooper interrupted, "what my wife is trying to explain is that, for your own good, at this time of your life you should be surrounded by your own kind."

"Ahhh. I see. And what exactly would you consider to be my own kind, Dr. Cooper?"

"Englishwomen who are . . . of an advanced age where . . . what I mean to say is, elderly women who have earned the right to . . . to drift a bit now and then and to . . . to . . ."

"Who have spent their lives lifting women and children out of a human dumping ground? Who have dedicated themselves to rescuing unwanted little ones who would otherwise have no chance of escaping poverty? Who have spent the better part of half a century showing the love of Jesus Christ with their hands as well as their words? Is that what you mean?"

"Well . . . I suppose . . . That is, you see . . ." Dr. Cooper stammered.

"Do tell me, good Doctor, where exactly am I to find this gathering of my own kind with which you would have me surround myself?"

"We are only thinking of your welfare, Miss Davidson. My wife and I are exceedingly concerned about your well-being—most appropriately concerned, I might add."

"I did not come to India with the intention of digging a well only to give thirsty persons a single sip and then send them on their way."

Miss Abigail's blue eyes lost their blur and fairly flamed with passion.

"No, my dear ones. I shall remain exactly where I am."

Susanna turned to her husband with a desperate look of *whatever-shall-we-do-now?*

"You two are free to leave, of course, and to find a place where you can be surrounded by people you find more to your liking," Miss Abigail hastened to add. "But as for me, I am already with my kind."

12

June 1946

Saji Stephen, his hands and feet freshly washed and his hair damp from oil scented with sandalwood, strolled out to the veranda. Without pausing to acknowledge his elder son, he headed directly to the fragrantly shaded spot under the twisting vines of sweet jasmine and settled himself in the choice place his brother had always reserved for himself— on his father's valuable Persian carpet. No, on *his own*—Saji Stephen's—valuable Persian carpet.

"Imagine, Father. Now you are landlord," Rajeev Nathan said. "Everything belongs to you."

"Yes." Saji Stephen nodded, and a smile spread across his face. "Everything is mine."

"What will you do?"

"Do! Why, settle myself into the best rooms of the house, of course!"

"I mean about the rice that is not being planted. About the laborers who no longer go to the paddies to work."

Saji Stephen shrugged his shoulders and raised his palms to the sky. "The laborers are the overseer's responsibility. The rice planting is a job for workers. They all know this. Everyone knows this. Why should I worry myself over such things?"

Even so, Saji Stephen's smile faded. Always, it was Boban Joseph his father had called to sit beside him while he printed notes next to the names listed in his book of accounts. Always it was Boban Joseph he had invited to accompany him in his cart as he went about his business errands. Always it was Boban Joseph he had trusted to oversee the planting and the harvest. Never Saji Stephen. Never the baby.

Ah, but Boban Joseph was no more. Now everything belonged to Saji Stephen. He threw back his head and laughed out loud.

"I will take the best room in the house for myself, and I will have this Persian carpet spread out on my floor. The sitar in the great room now belongs to me, and so does every book on every shelf in this house. All of them are mine. Father's leather-bound book of accounts is mine, too. I shall call for it whenever I will, and I shall sit with it on my lap and make my marks in it in any way I wish."

Saji Stephen folded his arms across his chest and roared with laughter.

Rajeev Nathan didn't laugh. His jaw clenched and his eyes narrowed as he watched his father.

"Where is Udit? That lazy servant!" Saji Stephen bellowed, "Udit! Bring me food! Not only fruit and tea, but real food! Now!"

Saji Stephen relaxed, but only for a moment.

"My old friend, Ashish, the Untouchable! Bring him here immediately, Udit. I want him to see me sitting on this Persian carpet, eating my fill in the middle of the day. He must bow down before me. He must call me Master Landlord!"

Ashish was at work in the field when the servant came running, bellowing out his name. Because he had no choice, Ashish laid his hoe aside and followed the servant back to the landlord's house. He didn't hurry, though. Saji Stephen, who paced impatiently in front of the garden, was not at all pleased with the delay.

"Go to your place by the veranda!" Saji Stephen ordered.

Ashish stood obediently in the dirt and gazed impassively at the new landowner who pranced and crowed before him like a ridiculous peacock.

"Look around you, Ashish. Everything you see is mine— and much more than that besides. Every tree, every field, and every worker—all are mine. You, too! You belong to me. I can make you overseer if I wish, or I can send you to clean the latrine pit."

Ashish didn't move and the expression on his face never changed.

"I am not going to do things the way my brother did. I do not yet know all the changes I will make, but I will be a different landlord than he was," Saji Stephen said. "I will be a better one. Much better!"

Ashish stood so still he hardly seemed to breathe.

"You and all my other laborers must work especially hard, because I want my harvest to be the best one ever. I can put you in charge, but if I do, you must bring in the best harvest ever recorded on this land. If you succeed, I will reward you. But if you fail, I will have you sorely punished."

"I am an old man," Ashish said. "Overseer is a job for a young man."

Saji Stephen's eyes flashed. "It is a job for whichever man I choose!" But then, stepping closer, he lowered his voice and confided, "The truth is, you are smart for an Untouchable. Not smart like me, of course, but smart for your kind. I think most likely it is because of the time you spent with me when we were boys."

Ashish's face remained impassive.

Suddenly Saji Stephen's mood darkened. "That is it, then? Not a word of gratitude from you?"

Ashish would not look at Saji Stephen. He couldn't trust himself to hide the disgust he felt for the oppressor who dared call himself a friend. He half expected the landowner to stamp his feet and heave a rock at him. But instead Saji Stephen pointed his finger and declared, "You make certain the rice harvest is a good one. I will hold you personally responsible!"

✐

The day was half gone, yet no laborers worked the paddies. They didn't exactly refuse, they simply discovered reasons to be elsewhere. And since they had neither seen nor heard anything from Saji Stephen, they didn't fear him. But Ashish knew. He shaded his eyes against the sunny glare and gazed above. Already traces of clouds had begun to show in the sky. The rains could well come early.

"We must get the laborers back to work," Ashish pleaded to Dinkar. "The plowing is not yet completed in even the first paddy, and in the next, the planting is hardly begun!"

"Yes," Dinkar said, "but not today. Today everyone is celebrating the cows' birthday."

Of course! According to Hindu legends, this was the birthday of Blaram, the older brother of Lord Krishna. How could Ashish have failed to notice?

"See? Already women and children file out to the animals' field with jars of water and baskets of flowers on their heads."

Yes, yes. The women would wash the cows and children would decorate the poor beasts with blossoms. Then the men would come along behind with special food for the cows.

With a disgusted sigh, Ashish headed back to his own hut.

"Look, *Appa!*" Shridula called out. She stepped back so he could see the picture of the cows on the front of their hut. She had painted it with blue rice paste.

"Birthday of the cows!" Ashish grunted. All the cows would be treated with great love and care, never mind the unplanted rice. Never mind the landlord's demands on him. Never mind what would happen tomorrow.

The cows' birthday celebration lasted only one day. Unfortunately, it wasn't the only problem. Without the imposing Master Landlord Boban Joseph's iron fist hovering over them, the laborers were of no mind to break their backs in the rice paddies. Why should they bend over in the hot sun hour after hour only to return at night to their own meagerly filled cooking pots? "At least we can tend our gardens and climb the trees in search of fruit," they said. No one spoke aloud of stealing rice from the fields.

"I do not want to be overseer," Ashish said to Dinkar.

"That is a good thing," Dinkar said, "because you are not. I am overseer."

"Yes. But if the rice harvest is not good, the new landlord will hold me responsible. All of us will suffer his wrath. The workers have to get back to work in the paddies."

"Why do you care? The sun still shines and the rice we helped ourselves to is not yet gone from our rice bags. Rest yourself under the trees with the other men and enjoy the gossip. Time to work will come soon enough, you can be certain of that. Enjoy your rest while you can."

Ever since he was a small boy, Saji Stephen had been intrigued by the silky smooth rosewood sitar that stood propped up in the corner of the great room. His sister Sunita Lois used to play it for him before she married and moved away. His mother played it, too. But Saji Stephen was never allowed to touch it. When their father died and everything in the house passed to Boban Joseph, Saji Stephen tried to get the sitar for himself. Although Boban Joseph never much cared for the instrument, and though he never once so much as plucked at the strings, he refused to allow his brother to try to play it. Well, now everyone else was gone and the sitar was his. He could pluck it or strum it or break it into firewood if he so desired. It belonged to him!

Seated on the veranda with his legs crossed, Saji Stephen clamped the bowl of the instrument between his feet and propped the long neck up against his shoulder. Closing his eyes, he imagined his fingers plucking the strings as mournfully beautiful music poured forth. Alas, it was not to be. All he produced from the sitar was a squawking racket so jarring it stunned the birds in the trees into shocked silence.

Fury overtook Saji Stephen. He clamped his teeth tight and jabbed at the strings with a vengeance. That only made the racket worse.

So intent was Saji Stephen on forcing a decent sound from the instrument that he failed to notice two policemen approaching the veranda. For some time they stood off to the side and waited patiently for the landowner to acknowledge their presence. The taller policeman wore his black hair greased back slick in a way that accentuated the droop of his lower lip. It gave him a decidedly menacing look. When he finally grew tired of waiting, the taller policeman puffed out his lip and uttered a loud "Ahem!"

Saji Stephen looked up with a start.

"We are from the next village over," the taller policeman informed him. "We received a complaint about your treatment of cows that have strayed from our village to yours."

"I know nothing of that," Saji Stephen said. He turned back to his struggle with the sitar strings.

"In that case, we must speak to the one who does."

Saji Stephen plucked out another dreadful screech.

"Sir! Must you torture us all day?" the policeman's dark-skinned companion demanded. "We must see the landowner immediately. I insist!"

Anger flashed across Saji Stephen's face. He motioned for Udit to take the sitar from his lap. "I am the only landowner here," he said. "You would do well to remember that!"

The dark-skinned policeman pushed forward. "In that case, we must settle this dispute with you, sir." He waved out to the road where a crowd of twenty or so men stood clumped together, all murmuring angrily. Saji Stephen didn't recognize any of them.

"Come," Saji Stephen said to the policemen. "Sit with me."

As the two settled themselves on the veranda, a hefty man shouted from the crowd, "Three times you sent your men to my field to beat my son, Landlord!"

"I did no such thing!" Saji Stephen shouted back.

"And all my son ever did was search for our straying cows. Nothing more!"

Saji Stephen looked at the policemen but said in a voice loud enough for the men on the road to hear, "It would be a better world if everyone lived in his own house and minded his own business. Do you not agree?"

But the tall policeman with the droopy lip warned, "You, sir, would be most unwise to mock so angry a crowd."

"I know nothing about that man or his son," Saji Stephen insisted. "I only became landowner upon the recent death of my brother. What happened in my fields or his before that is not of my doing. Nor is it my affair."

"Please, sir," the dark-skinned policeman warned. "These villagers are not in a charitable mood."

"Neither am I!" Saji Stephen snapped. He folded his arms across his chest and sat, sullen and simmering.

"Please reconsider, sir. These villagers are angry. They have been wronged," the droopy-lipped policeman said. "If you are to be a successful landlord, if you hope to sit on this veranda for many years to come, heed this advice: do not provoke the villagers. Do not give them reason to riot against you."

Saji Stephen glowered at the policemen in petulant silence.

"Well, then . . ." the taller policeman said as he stood to his feet. When he got no response from Saji Stephen, he shrugged and strode toward the crowd, shouting for them to disperse.

But the dark-skinned policeman didn't follow him. Alone on the veranda with Saji Stephen, he bowed and said, "Sir Landlord, may I speak freely?"

"Yes," Saji Stephen said—but warily, as he suspected a trick.

"I live in the next village with my wife and two daughters. The eldest is of an age to marry, but I have no money for her dowry. You do see the problem I face, do you not?"

Saji Stephen said nothing.

"Please, sir, I wish to talk with you about securing a loan." When Saji Stephen didn't answer, the policeman added, "It is, of course, in my power to strike a favorable settlement with the villagers . . ."

The sweltering afternoon faded into a steamy evening. The crowd had long since drifted away. Even the dark-skinned policeman had left once he secured the promise of a loan, accompanied by a signed agreement from the landlord. Still, Saji Stephen sat cross-legged on the veranda, on the Persian carpet under the jasmine vines. He had decided he would not move the carpet to his private room after all. Back there, no one could see it. What was the value of such a treasure if no one saw it? What did it matter if he couldn't use it to stir up envy and jealousy?

"Bring me my sitar!" Saji Stephen called to Udit.

No sooner had the instrument been brought to him and propped up in his lap than Saji Stephen pushed it aside. "Take it away!" he ordered.

Saji Stephen wanted to make beautiful music, but when his fingers plucked the strings, the notes came out shrill and unpleasant. He wanted to bring in the greatest harvest ever, but the fields lay barren and weedy because he had no idea how to get the laborers to work. He wanted to be loved and admired and, most of all, respected by all, but the best he could elicit from those around him was grudging compliance in exchange for his favors.

"What am I to do?" Saji Stephen demanded. Since no one was around, he spoke to the shadows that drifted through the trees. "I am the spoiled child of my parents. I was never even allowed to go out in the rain. I never had a chance to supervise laborers in the fields the way my brother did. Now I am grown, and I cannot go back. But neither can I go forward. What am I to do? I ask, what am I to do?"

13

June 1946

Cool air had not yet touched his face, nor had the first whiff of damp earth reached his nostrils, yet Saji Stephen knew for certain that rain was on the way. For the first time since he was a child at his mother's knee, he considered the wisdom of bowing down to mumble a prayer for help.

But instead of praying, Saji Stephen stepped out to the road to get a better view of the mountains. Thoughts of those first billows of dark clouds quickly left him, however, for down on the road he saw Brahmin Rama hurrying toward him.

"What do you want?" Saji Stephen called out. He made no attempt to disguise his irritation.

"I came to offer prayers for you and your household," the Brahmin said.

Saji Stephen waved him away, but the Brahmin chose to ignore the rebuff.

"The rain clouds grow heavy," Brahmin Rama said.

"And why should they not? The monsoons come to us every year at this time."

"Ah, but this year is different, is it not? This year—were it not for the sturdy weeds—your rice paddies would sit empty."

Saji Stephen's face flushed hot. "My rice paddies are no concern of yours."

"Oh, but they are. They most certainly are. Your paddies are the concern of the entire village. Do we not all depend on the success of your rice harvest to ensure grain for our kitchens?"

Saji Stephen scowled. "And I suppose the entire village is gossiping about the state of my paddies?"

"Most certainly. Gossip is the way of the village."

"Well, you can tell the villagers to tend to their own concerns," Saji Stephen snapped. "God will send me my harvest." Turning his back to the Brahmin, he hurried back to the veranda and slumped down in his corner under the jasmine vines. Already the blossoms had begun to fade and wither. Saji Stephen scowled at them, too.

Brahmin Rama followed the landlord. Without waiting for an invitation, he settled himself on the other side of the veranda.

For a long while, the two sat in silence—Saji Stephen staring out at the road, and Rama's eyes fixed on Saji Stephen's sullen face. Finally Brahmin Rama spoke. "The whole of the *Bhagavad Gita* is summed up in this maxim: *Your business is with the deed, and not with the result.*"

Saji Stephen clenched his jaw and glared at the Brahmin.

Rama calmly adjusted his wire spectacles and cleared his throat. "Which is to say, each individual has a special part to play in the drama of life. Everyone must choose the right course according to the circumstances given him, without any consideration for his personal interest. Everyone must act for the good of all."

Fury burned inside Saji Stephen. Through gritted teeth he asked, "That is the practice of Brahmins, then? Even as you refuse the low castes and outcastes spiritual equality? Even as you keep the most powerful positions of temple priests for yourselves alone? Even as you deny the people the right to communicate with Hindu gods in any language but Sanskrit, which only you Brahmins are allowed to learn?"

"You may be an Indian by birth, Saji Varghese, but you have no understanding of the Indian way," Brahmin Rama said. "Every class has its particular function. And every man has the responsibility to fulfill his particular task to the best of his ability, but always with devotion to the gods and at all times without personal ambition."

Saji Stephen's lips curled in a mocking grin. "Good," he said. "Fine. Shall we begin by taking up Mr. Ambedkar's suggestion that in the newly independent India we oppose both Brahmanism and caste oppression? We can accomplish this goal by publicly burning the *Manusmriti*."

Brahmin Rama jerked back, as though he had been hit in the face. With a shaky hand, he pushed his slipping spectacles back up on his nose. "The virtue of the Brahmin class is wisdom, which is what I came here today to offer you. You have repaid my kindness with an attack on our sacred writings. You are indeed a foolish man."

Rama stood up, turned his back to Saji, and walked away.

Saji Stephen wanted to laugh at him. He wanted to mock him and call out ridicule that would ring in the Brahmin's ears all the way back to his house. But the sky had suddenly grown quite dark. As Brahmin Rama retreated down the road, the first drops of rain splashed onto the dry earth.

At the first patter of rain, Glory Anna gingerly pushed open the door of her room. Seeing no one about and eager to feel the fresh drops on her face, she eased out and headed toward the veranda. *Tears of God.* That's what her grandmother used to tell her of the rain. Well, Glory Anna was badly in need of God's touch, even it was nothing but his tears.

But Glory Anna never made it outside. For at the very moment the rain called to her, it also drove Saji Stephen into the house. Glory Anna rounded the corner and, for the first time in her life, found herself alone, face to face with her father.

"Oh!" Saji Stephen exclaimed. "Are you still here?"

Still here? What possible answer could Glory Anna give to such a question? She eased back toward her own door.

"You cannot stay in that room," Saji Stephen informed her. "It is the one I intend to take for myself. Tomorrow you will move in with the wife of my youngest son."

Glory Anna shrank back, her eyes searching for a way out.

"Sheeba Esther will serve as your guardian," Saji Stephen told the girl. "See that you cause her no trouble."

Glory Anna wanted to cry out that she would not leave her grandmother's room. She wanted to beg Saji Stephen to have mercy on her and let her be. To plead with him to forget all over again that she was still there. But when she opened her mouth, all that came out was a soft, mewing cry.

⌇

Rain beat down on the roof, but it could not drown out the angry voices that echoed through from the back of the house. Saji Stephen groaned. His two daughters-in-law were at it again. Their families were simply too crowded, especially when rain drove them all inside.

Saji's elder son, Rajeev Nathan, allowed—no, he *encouraged*—his wife, Amina, to rule over the women of the household. And Amina did so eagerly and with a heavy hand, for she was by nature a bossy woman. Nihal Amos's wife, Sheeba

Esther, was of a more agreeable temperament—though her husband constantly pushed her to stand up for herself. But Sheeba Esther was still young. She had been raised to hold her tongue in the presence of her elders, a trait Saji Stephen greatly appreciated.

I shall give each family a room of its own, Saji Stephen decided. Glory Anna will be under Sheeba Esther's care, but the girl can bear the responsibility for Amina's children. Maybe then, I will finally have some peace in my house.

Saji Stephen pushed his way through Rajeev Nathan's whining little ones, intent on delivering his message to the two daughters-in-law. But Amina met him with a message of her own.

"Do you see how I must work?" she said to Saji Stephen. "It is too much to expect of me. Now that you are landowner, you can get us the servants we need. And not only servants. Now that you are landlord, you can . . ."

Saji Stephen turned and hurried back out to the safety of the veranda. Tomorrow he would tell his daughters-in-law. Yes, tomorrow would be soon enough to deliver his message.

Sons who consider themselves so wise they should offer advice to their father! A daughter-in-law who dares issue demands to her father-in-law! Villagers who shout out accusations to the landowner! Lectures from that skinny Brahmin! It was all too much for Saji Stephen. He was the new landlord. He was the most important man in the village. He was the one with all the power.

I will show them I am in charge! Saji vowed.

Yes, but how?

They will see me display my power in an unforgettable way!

But in what way?

I will force every one of them to respect me!

But how to accomplish such an end?

Saji Stephen made it a point to stay away from the back of the house and let his sons and his sons' wives battle their way through their days on their own. He didn't go to the village either for fear of being confronted by angry villagers. Day after day he sought refuge in his private rooms. He sucked on the bones of roasted lamb and went over and over the offenses committed against him. As his fury grew hard and sour, he laid his plan.

In the dusk that followed the first full day of the rainy season, without speaking a word to anyone, Saji Stephen crept out of the house through the rain-soaked veranda door. He edged his way along the muddy garden far enough to allow him a good look at the road. It was deserted. Saji Stephen hurried down, taking care to stay tucked away in the shadows. Keeping a watchful eye in all directions, he made his way to the beginning of the Brahmin settlement. The entire way, he didn't pass another person.

Once in the Brahmin section of the village, Saji Stephen hunkered down low and eased into a stand of tamarind trees. He knew the area, though not well. Certainly he knew of the enormous anthill that stood between the trees and the back of Brahmin Rama's house. Everyone knew that. Because a great snake with especially dramatic markings had taken up residence in that anthill, the Hindus looked upon it as a particularly holy place.

Squinting into the rain, Saji Stephen could make out the knobby edges of the anthill. It was not yet the month of *Naga Panchami*, which meant it was too soon for the dedicated worship of the revered snake goddess. Pity that. Even so, the anthill flowed red with rain-streaked vermillion powder. The gift of worshippers. Spiced turmeric offerings floated in the muddy puddle at its foot.

A glance behind him—one to the right side and another to the left—then a quick step back. Saji Stephen's foot slipped, sending him sprawling. As he pulled himself from the mud, a knot of fear rose up in his throat. Not that he believed Brahmin Rama's boasts about possessing magical skills and an ability to see into the future. Still, the rains had started early. And they were falling exceptionally hard. And one could never be too careful around the house of a Brahmin, especially one with such an anthill beside it.

Swiping a hand over his rain- and mud-streaked face, Saji Stephen stared at the anthill. It stood waist-high and was as big around as a tree stump. Home of the revered cobra. Saji Stephen edged closer until the anthill was close enough to reach out and touch. Only then did his resolve began to quake.

The sun had long since set in a moonless sky. Soon the earth would be black. But in the lingering twilight, Saji Stephen caught sight of a rise beyond the anthill. On top of the rise someone had constructed a crude fire pit.

Quickly Saji Stephen clawed his way up the slippery hillside. He grabbed one of the large stones out of the pit and tossed it at the anthill. The rock struck the side with a thud, knocking away a good-sized chunk. Congratulating himself, Saji Stephen grabbed up another rock. He eased his way closer to the edge of the rise and took more careful aim, then he threw again. This time he managed to smash away the entire red-streaked top.

Trembling with fearful excitement, Saji Stephen grabbed up the last rock—the biggest one of all. He grasped it in both hands, eased his way to the edge of the rise, and took careful aim. Then, with all his might, he heaved the rock at the anthill. The rock pounded into the ground, and the muddy anthill collapsed.

Hardly able to contain his glee, Saji Stephen hurried through the river of mud, back to the safety of his house, before the Brahmin—or the snake—could catch him.

14

July 1946

*P*salm 39," Shridula began to read. "*I said, I will take heed to my ways, that I sin not with my t . . . t . . . my t . . .*"

"My *tongue*," Ashish said.

" *. . . my tongue: I will keep my mouth with a b . . . a br . . .*"

"A *bridle*. It is a metal brace that fits in the mouth of a horse so that the rider can guide where the horse goes."

" *. . . a bridle, while the w . . . the wicked is before me.*"

Shridula hunkered down next to her father, Miss Abigail Davidson's Bible open in front of them. By the flickering candle stub, she carefully pointed to each word as she read it.

"*Be . . . hold, thou hast made my days as an hand . . . b . . . br . . .*"

" *. . . handbreadth*, I think. I don't know what it means."

" *. . . as an handbreadth; and mine age is as nothing before thee: v . . . verily every man at his best state is altogether v . . . van . . .*"

"*Vanity. Altogether vanity.* That means 'too proud.'"

Zia looked at the two hunched together over the Holy Book and frowned. They took no notice, so she uttered a sigh. When they still didn't look up, she sighed again—more loudly this time. Shridula went right on reading:

"*Surely every man walketh in a vain shew: surely they are dis . . . dis . . .*"

"I don't know that word. Read what comes after it."

". . . *he heapeth up riches, and knoweth not who shall gather them. And now, Lord, what wait I for? my hope is in thee.*"

"There! Do you see what it says, Daughter?" Ashish said triumphantly. "The son of landowner son is wrong. Our hope in not in him, and it is not in the Marxist Communists. All those people will do what is best for them, just as the landlord does what is best for him. If we have any hope at all, it has to be in the God that is hidden away inside this Holy Book."

"But can we find that God?" Shridula asked.

"Enough. Close the book and put it back in its hiding place," Ashish said, because he didn't know the answer to her question.

When Shridula was very young, Ashish would draw English letters in the dirt with a stick and read them to her. "This letter is A," he would say. "It makes this sound . . . *aaaa.*" By the time she was old enough to gather twigs for the fire, she could pick out words in his Bible and read them.

"You must stop, Husband," Zia warned him. "What you are doing is too dangerous. Someone might hear you!"

But Ashish shrugged off her warnings. "Which one of the workers has ears so good he could hear us over the pounding rain?"

"Perhaps someone curious enough to stand close by the door," Zia said.

"Pshaw! No one cares that much about what I do inside my hut. Everyone is too busy following their own karma to worry about ours."

In truth, had anyone in the settlement happened to overhear the English words, they wouldn't have understood them. And if by some miracle they did understand, no one would have suspected Shridula and Ashish of reading the words. For not one other person in the settlement had ever even seen a book.

But Zia was not satisfied. "What if a nosy neighbor mistakes that English book for the holy Veda? You know the punishment that would bring down on you."

Ashish did indeed. According to the Hindu scriptures, hot molten lead should be poured into the ears of any unworthy person who heard the words of the holy script recited. Of course, all Untouchables were unworthy. Should an unworthy person actually dare to read the holy Veda, that person was to be pulled to pieces.

"But this is not the Veda," Ashish explained yet again. "It is the Holy Bible. And it is not written in the forbidden holy language of India. It is written in English."

Zia glowered at him. "If nothing else, it is most certainly a waste of our precious candle nubs."

✍

"*Psalm 37. Fret not thyself because of evildoers, neither be thou en . . . envi . . . envious against the workers of in . . . in . . .* "

" . . . *workers of iniquity*," Ashish said. "That means, do not look at wicked people and wish you were like them."

"*For they shall soon be cut down like the grass, and wither as the green herb.*" Shridula paused in her reading. "Is this talking about the landowner, *Appa?*"

"I do not know," her father said. "Maybe. But there are many other wicked people besides him."

"Yes," said Shridula. "The British."

Ashish frowned. "Not all of them."

"The landowner's son said so. That is why we needed to join the Communist party and get our membership cards."

"The pale English lady is British," Ashish said softly. "She saved my life. She believed I was a blessing, and she gave me this Holy Book." He ran his hand over the page before him. "Wherever there are wicked people, there are also good ones. Remember that, Daughter."

Z

"Trust in the LORD, *and do good; so shalt thou dwell in the land, and verily thou shalt be fed. Delight thyself also in the* LORD; *and he shall give thee the desires of thine heart."*

Shridula stopped reading. "What does that mean, *Appa?*"

"I do not know," Ashish said.

"Be fed means that I will have enough rice for the pot," Zia said. "And vegetables to add every day. It means our stomachs will not ache from hunger."

Ashish nodded his agreement. "But I do not understand the part about *delight in the* LORD. I cannot understand the meaning of the word *delight.*"

"I wish you did," Shridula said. "If we could do it, the Lord would give us the desires of our hearts."

Ashish smiled. "What is the desire of your heart, my daughter?"

Shridula leaned in close and lowered her voice to a whisper. "To walk away from this place. Like your parents did, Amma, and yours, too, *Appa.* To walk away and never come back. But all of us together. So we would all be free."

"Close that book!" Zia ordered. "What good is it to make an Untouchable girl displeased with the life she has been born to?"

"But *Amma* . . . "

"The English lady was wrong to teach you to read, Ashish. She was wrong to give you that book. It does not belong with our kind." Zia turned to face her husband. "And you are wrong to teach Shridula!"

Ashish placed his hand on the Bible and held it firmly. "It is not for you to give me orders, Wife," he said to Zia. He didn't sound angry, but his voice was firm.

"The book is dangerous." Now Zia was pleading. "Reading it will only bring trouble down on our heads."

"You do not know, because you were not there with me and the pale English lady. The Holy Book was not a gift to you, it was a gift to me."

"That was long ago."

"You were not the one who sneaked off and hid in the stinking latrine to read it. I was. You did not see me scratch out the words I did not know on a stick of wood, then cower before Master Saji, begging him to read them to me. It was not you he laughed at and mocked and called 'stupid.' Do not speak to me of such things, for you do not know."

Ashish turned back to the open page and traced down with his finger. "Here," he said to Shridula. "Read the next part, too."

"*Rest in the* LORD, *and wait patiently for him: fret not thyself because of him who prospereth in his way, because of the man who bringeth wicked devices to pass. Cease from anger, and forsake wrath: fret not thyself in any wise to do evil. For evildoers shall be cut off: but those that wait upon the* LORD, *they shall inherit the earth.*"

Suddenly the door swung open and a wave of water poured in.

"A curse!" Zia screamed. "A curse! Already it is happening. Do you see, Husband? Do you see what you have done?"

Ashish leapt up and slammed the door shut. "Pounding rain," he assured his wife. "Nothing more."

Shridula closed the book and held it high. But she could not help asking, "Is it talking about us, *Appa*? Will we inherit the earth?"

"No, I do not think so. We are Untouchables. But we will not be evildoers, either."

"Even if we cannot inherit the earth, even if we must be Untouchables," Shridula said, "I still think we should wait upon the Lord."

15

August 1946

*B*rahmin Rama, his *mundu* plastered against him, splashed his way along a river that only a month earlier had been the village road. Rama was not one to curse the rain. Indeed, he prayed for it, and when it came, he rejoiced in it and called it a blessed gift from the gods. But not this day. Not when he was personally forced to endure such a miserable soaking.

Naga Panchami. The fifth day of the bright half of the *Sharvan*—the full moon. Yes, snake pictures, drawn in red sandalwood paste, did decorate wooden boards throughout the village. And yes, clay images of snakes did adorn thresholds, though they had to be tucked away under shelters to protect them from the pouring rain. But this year the village had no *Naga* temple. There was no anthill with a snake in residence that could be decorated and showered with flowers and fruit. They had no place where they could make offerings of milk and honey. And it was all the fault of that wretch of a new landowner. Of that, Brahmin Rama was certain.

Outside the landowner's house, Saji's servant Udit struggled to sweep sheets of water away from the door and off the veranda.

"Send your master out!" Brahmin Rama ordered.

The servant bowed and ducked inside. But he immediately returned. Bowing lower he said, "Master says he is too busy to talk to you."

"Tell him to come out immediately or I will come in and get him!" the Brahmin bellowed. Actually, it wasn't much of a bellow. But no one who heard him could doubt his fury.

The servant scurried back inside.

"Why do you call on me on such a wet day?" Saji Stephen demanded from the doorway.

"Because today is *Naga Panchami*," Brahmin Rama called back. "Because you destroyed the *Naga* temple and desecrated the holy site."

Saji Stephen's face went pale. He desperately wanted to shoot back an indifferent answer, but his tongue wouldn't work in his mouth. Surely, no one had seen him! He was certain of that. Besides, many weeks had passed since that night. He had heard the village gossip about a guilty person, but no one ever mentioned his name.

"Did you think I would not know it was you who destroyed it?" Rama charged. "I am a Brahmin. It is my job to tell the past and to see into the future. Of course I know it was you!"

"You cannot come to my house and make accusations against me!" Saji Stephen insisted—but only half-heartedly, because of course the Brahmin could do exactly that. He had already done it.

"I did not come simply to accuse you. I came to call up the powers of evil against you. I came to put a curse on you, on your family, and on everything you own. Never will you forget the day you lifted your hand against the goddess!"

Saji Stephen dropped to the floor in a dead faint.

By evening, the rain no longer poured down in sheets. And by morning, although the sun rose behind thick, gray clouds, no rain fell. Saji Stephen slogged his way to the settlement in the bullock cart.

"I want the laborers back to work this day!" he ordered.

Dinkar sneaked a glance at Ashish, who stared straight ahead. "But master," he said, "the fields are awash in water."

"I do not care if the workers all drown! I want them out there in the paddies!"

"Even if we force them to go out, what can they do?" Dinkar pleaded. "They cannot weed or hoe."

"Just do it! Do it!"

Dinkar turned an imploring look to Ashish.

"The workers will be back in the paddies," Ashish said. "But they cannot make the rice grow. Pray to your God to do that."

Saji Stephen turned on Ashish, his face twisted in fury. "I do not need to pray. I am the landlord! *I am the master!*"

❧

Hunkered down in the pond that the rice paddy had become, Shridula ran her fingers though the muddy water. "I cannot tell the difference between the weeds and the rice," she complained.

"It is better to leave the weeds in than to pull out the rice," Zia said.

"Then why do we sit in the mud all day? We could sit under a shelter and leave the weeds in just as well."

"We sit in the mud and leave the weeds in because the master commands it of us," Zia told her daughter. "You ask too many questions."

Shridula looked out at the sea of hunched-over women. Each one also dug through the mud, yet each one left the weeds to grow alongside the rice. All except Kashi, a withered slip of a girl. The more the others slowed down, the more frantically she worked.

"Stupid girl! You pull out rice along with the weeds and leave weeds to grow along with the rice," groused a woman with a jagged scar over her eye.

Kashi neither looked up nor slowed her pace.

"You keep working like that and the whole village will starve!" scolded the woman with three teeth.

Plunge, grab, pull. Plunge, grab, pull. Plunge, grab, pull. Kashi worked like a woman possessed.

"The landlord is not here to see you," Zia said gently. "We all get the same handful of rice whether we work or not."

Kashi pulled her hand out of the mud and stared around her. For the first time, it seemed, she saw the other women watching her. She sat down in the muddy water and wept.

☙❧

By late afternoon, Ashish stopped prodding the men and looked up at the sky, the same as he had done countless times before. And he saw the same thing he saw every other time: black clouds, heavy with rain.

"The fields are too flooded to work!" Dinkar insisted. "And at any moment the rain will start again. Let the poor fools go back to their huts."

"The rice is already far behind," Ashish said. "The men must work harder. We all must work harder, or there will be no food for any of us."

"You mean there will be no riches for the landlord. I still live in the first hut, which means I am still the real overseer. And I say the time has come to stop!"

Ashish tried to protest, but the men nearest Dinkar had already heard the overseer's words. As one, they abandoned the paddy and headed for the path to the settlement. For them, the workday had ended.

"Dawn until dusk," Ashish pleaded. "Dawn until dusk until the paddies are free of weeds. Then we can take our rest."

"No!" the young man with the old man's face called out. "We will take our rest right now. If you want the weeds out, you can pull them yourself!"

At that moment, the clouds opened and a torrent of rain poured down.

✿

Days and more days passed before the rain finally slowed to a drizzle. The sun did its best to peek through heavy cloud-banks. But by the time it finally did shine through, the paths and fields were running rivers. When the workers made it back to the paddies, they found healthy weeds towering over stunted rice plants.

"Everyone is well rested!" Ashish called out. "Now we must work as hard as if it were harvest."

Someone shot back, "If it were harvest, we would be rewarded with extra rice and spices, and a great harvest feast!"

"If we do not work hard, there will be no harvest at all," Ashish answered.

As Dinkar led the line of laborers out to the paddies, the landlord's servant Udit came running. "Ashish!" he called.

"Ashish! The master sends for you. You must come with me now."

When Saji Stephen saw Ashish approach, he stopped his pacing. "I told you this was to be the best harvest ever! I allowed you to be my overseer, and I told you to bring me a great harvest!"

The landlord stood at the edge of the water-soaked garden, his face twisted in fury. "I told you exactly what I expected of you. Now I hear that the rice is ruined. What have you done to my paddies?"

There was the rain. More important was the wasted time when the rice seedlings should have been planted. Most important of all was Saji Stephen's lack of direction and discipline for the laborers. But Ashish couldn't tell the landlord that he himself was the one who had caused the disaster in the rice paddies. So he stood perfectly still, looked straight ahead, and kept silent.

"It is your fault!" Saji Stephen yelled. He stamped his feet, and muddy water splashed up, soaking him. "It is the curse! It is the Brahmin's curse that did it!"

Ashish didn't dare move.

"The harvest *will* be a good one! It will be a *great* one!" Saji was shrieking now. "Until the paddies are clear of weeds and the rice is growing tall, the workers will not get even a handful of rice! Not one handful! You tell them that, Ashish. Go back and tell them that!"

Rain or sun, with morning's first light, the workers filed out to the paddies. Carefully they separated the weeds from the growing rice. They pulled out the weeds as best they could, then they cultivated the ground. The men worked, the women worked, and the children worked. Older boys, such as Jyoti's sons Hari and Falak, worked alongside the women. The little ones carried drinking water to the workers. Everyone worked. No one took a break. Only when it was too dark to see the weeds did they file back to the settlement to light their evening fires.

At first, everyone cut down on the amount of rice they allowed their families. More and more water went into the cooking pots and less and less grain. But as the rice sacks grew empty, the men took to digging up roots. The women brought weeds back from the paddy to boil in their pots. Everyone grew thin and wan. Kashi, already shriveled, faded into bones covered by skin.

"Come with me to see the landlord," Ashish said to Dinkar. "We will plead with him together."

But when Saji Stephen saw them coming, he locked his door and refused to meet with them.

When Jyoti stumbled in from the paddy, too weak to boil the weeds she brought, her young son, Falak, said, "I will get food for us."

"No!" Jyoti cried in terror. "Remember what the landlord did to your brother!"

"I know where to get something for us," Falak said. "Do not worry. I will be safe."

The boy sneaked up to the landlord's house, intending to yank a few vegetables from his garden and be on his way. But Saji Stephen, suspecting someone would try such a trick, had arranged for his servant Udit to sleep in the garden and guard it.

Falak made it all the way up to the garden before he heard Udit snoring. He dropped down and crept in among the vegetables. Quaking with terror, he reached out to grab a cucumber. Udit snorted and sat up straight. With a yelp, Falak jumped up and bounded for the path. He leapt over the greens and jumped directly into a chicken's nest. The clutch of eggs crushed under his feet.

All the way back to the settlement, Falak sobbed. No cucumber, no greens. And those wonderful chicken eggs—all crushed under his clumsy feet.

Jyoti lay in her hut, too weak to move. Across the settlement, Kashi lay in hers, nothing in her stomach but weeds.

Falak sat outside his mother's hut and wailed in hopeless despair.

Zia, still lying awake under the *neem* tree, listened to her neighbor. She started to speak, but Ashish shushed her. "There is nothing to do," he warned. "We must each attend to our own affairs."

But Ashish didn't speak for everyone. Certainly he did not speak for Jinraj. "If the landlord will not give us our due, we will take it!" the young man shouted into the night. "Come with me, brothers! We will tear the door off the storage shed and take what is rightfully ours! Tonight we will eat!"

One person after another took up Jinraj's cry. The call echoed from hut to hut to hut until a cacophony of angry voices rose up in one unified bellow. Men and older boys rushed into the night to join Jinraj, who had already started his march to the shed. Small water boys, too young to work in the fields, ran along after, and no one tried to stop them. Old men, swept up in the moment, stumbled behind.

With a roar, the mob rushed the storage shed. Calloused hands slammed against it and determined feet kicked at it again and again. Some men had brought sticks, and they set to work battering the door. Others picked up rocks and pelted the shed until the walls splintered.

Zia sat still and watched the last of the night shadows dance and sway in the eerie glow of dying cooking fires. She heaved a satisfied sigh.

"The landlord will not forget this night," Ashish warned.

Zia nodded. "Neither will we. And for one morning, we will rise up with our stomachs full."

16

August 1946

*A*shish slipped from his sleeping mat under the *neem* tree. The rains had eased, leaving the earth clean and fresh. In front of the next hut, Jyoti moved about, her water pot on her head. Few others in the settlement stirred, but soon they would. Full rice bags made a big difference. Full stomachs even more.

With long strides, Ashish headed toward the first paddy. This day, of all days, he must be hard at work. This day, of all days, must hold the hope of good harvest.

"*Appa!*"

Ashish turned to see Shridula running up behind him. "I like the cool morning," she said.

Ashish smiled and shortened his steps.

Under the rising sun, Ashish stepped up to the maturing rice stalks. "Look at the weeds," he muttered in disgust. "Weeding should have been completed weeks ago. Crops should have been thinned, too."

He raked the stalks through his fingers with the touch of an expert. Looking at the stunted grains in his hand, he shook his head.

"Will it still be a terrible harvest?" Shridula asked.

"Come," Ashish said. "Your *amma* will have porridge on the fire."

∽❧

"No, no! I said no!" Amina's voice grated throughout the landlord's house. "Father-in-law said *you* must watch over the girl!"

"He also said the girl was to watch over your children," Sheeba Esther answered.

"My children have me to watch over them. They need no one else!"

Ten years younger than her sister-in-law, Sheeba Esther was in the habit of backing down whenever Amina shouted orders or issued ultimatums. But not this time. This time the great landlord himself had told them what was to be.

Sheeba Esther glanced over at Glory Anna. The girl looked miserable, as if she were trying to shrink into the corner and disappear.

Rajeev Nathan stepped into the fray. "My wife is right. I do not want that girl in our living area. There is not even room enough for our own family. And my wife does not require Glory Anna's help."

"It is your father-in-law's decision, not mine," Sheeba Esther said to Amina. "If you do not like the arrangement, tell it to him." Her words were strong, but she spoke them in such a soft voice that both Amina and Rajeev Nathan laughed at her.

When Nihal Amos heard the sharp words coming from his brother and his brother's wife, he knew his Sheeba was their target. And he knew, whatever she said in response, her words would be gentle. So he hurried to stand beside her.

In the end, the two brothers took their dispute to their father. "Our wives have no desire to move over and make room for Glory Anna," Nihal Amos said, "nor should they have to."

"And my children should not have to obey the voice of a stranger," Rajeev Nathan added.

Saji Stephen sighed in exasperation. "The girl is here," he said. "What am I to do with her?"

"Is she not to be married next year?" Rajeev Nathan asked. "Why not push the date forward? Why not marry her now and be done with it?"

⚮

Bathed, oiled, and his belly filled, Saji Stephen called, "Udit! I want to go out and check the rice paddies."

His servant stared in surprise. Saji Stephen never went to the fields. He asked few questions about the crops or the workers. Except to shout threats at Ashish, he seemed completely removed from their work.

"Now!" Saji Stephen said impatiently. "This moment! Bring the horse cart around to the veranda for me."

Saji Stephen continued to insist that his overseers bore the responsibility for the crops and harvest. Of course, he eagerly awaited the opportunity to take credit for a successful season. Still, in the months since his brother was murdered, his approach had been to keep his distance from the actual work of the fields.

No one asked questions about his brother anymore. The police had come back one time, but with reassurances from Saji Stephen and his sons, and a generous loan ready and waiting, they seemed satisfied that no one in the landlord's family could possibly have wished Boban Joseph Varghese any harm.

Nor could they find any guilt in the old English missionary. So they simply stopped asking questions, and not one person complained.

Once in the cart, Udit directed the horse along the village road until they came to a pathway that led down between the fields. They passed by an empty rice paddy, then continued on to a second one that was well-flooded. Udit slowed the cart.

"It looks good," Saji Stephen said with hopeful assurance. "Plenty of green in the paddies."

Udit said nothing.

"Green and tall. Most assuredly, I shall have a fine rice harvest. Do you not agree?"

"Those are weeds you see," Udit said.

Saji Stephen, his face burning, glared at Udit's back. He longed to snap out a cutting retort. A snide counter that would inform the Sudra that anything the master didn't know wasn't worth knowing. But he couldn't make his mouth form one coherent word. So he ordered, "Take me back! I have seen enough."

When elderly Uncle Dupak arrived, Saji greeted him with an unnecessarily lavish meal. Uncle Dupak was an extremely important man in the area. He was also "family": the brother of Saji Stephen's sister's mother-in-law, herself from a wealthy and important family. Saji Stephen spoke of the endless rains and bragged about his prosperous rice paddies. He plied Uncle Dupak with a spread of fruits and nuts and platters of sweetmeats.

"My nephew's wife, your sister Sunita Lois, spoke to me about your desire to find a good husband for your daughter," Uncle Dupak began.

"Not a particularly good husband," Saji Stephen quickly corrected. "That is to say, I am of limited means."

Uncle Dupak glanced about him, fixing his gaze on the golden bowl of cashews and the silver platters of fruit. Then he looked down at the luxurious Persian carpet on which Saji Stephen sat. He wrinkled his face and grunted.

"Yes, yes, I realize this all looks to be quite profitable," Saji Stephen said quickly. "But costs are high, you see, and my rice crops are in danger of being choked out by weeds."

Uncle Dupak cleared his throat more forcefully.

"I was counting on a successful harvest to fund the dowry, but my workers have been lazy and my overseers most uncooperative. They shall suffer for it, that I can assure you. But punishment doesn't produce rice, does it?"

Uncle Dupak selected a small red banana from the stalk and slipped off the peel.

"I do have a great deal of prestige in this area, as I am sure you know," Saji Stephen hastened to say. "Power and influence as well. Anyone who marries my . . . who marries Glory Anna, would certainly gain in those most valuable areas. Surely that would be worth a lot to a prospective husband."

Saji Stephen looked at Uncle Dupak and waited for him to speak.

Uncle Dupak wiped the banana from his fingers and helped himself to a handful of cashews. He said nothing.

"Well?" Saji Stephen asked. "Can you find a suitable husband for Glory Anna?"

"Certainly," Uncle Dupak said. "Absolutely."

"Keeping the dowry limitations in mind?"

"Yes." Uncle Dupak helped himself to more cashews. "As a matter of fact, my nephew tells me the dowry is not a problem. It has already been paid."

"Paid?" Saji Stephen asked. "By whom?"

"Your father," Uncle Dupak said. "Years ago."

Saji Stephen's face went pale. Taking care to control his voice, he asked, "How did he pay it?"

"With a fine collection of gold jewelry and gems," Uncle Dupak said. "And gold coins. Most generous, he was! A very fine dowry indeed."

Saji Stephen jumped to his feet. "Father's wealth? Glory Anna's marriage will be paid for with my rightful inheritance?"

"Your father added further terms, too," Uncle Dupak said. "The girl is not to be married before her fourteenth birthday. Which is next year, I believe. Until that time she is to live here in this house, in comfort and in peace."

"But . . . my father had no right to . . . to—"

"Oh, but he had every right. One more thing: Should anything go wrong . . . Should the girl encounter any difficulties or express dissatisfaction with her situation here . . . Well, in such a case this house and all the lands with it would go to your sister's husband to settle Glory Anna's dowry claims and provide for her future comfort."

Saji Stephen shook with fury.

Uncle Dupak reached for another banana.

17

August 1946

*Y*our wife is of a gentle nature, like your mother and grandmother," Saji Stephen told his son Nihal Amos. "Tell Sheeba Esther she will continue to be in charge of Glory Anna."

Saji Stephen sat on the veranda, taking comfort in the coolness of the day. His sons sat with him, one on either side.

"And your wife, Rajeev Nathan . . . she is like your Uncle Boban Joseph. She achieves her end, but everyone suffers along the way. Tell her she is free to tend to her children in any way she wishes. Without assistance."

"Good," said Rajeev Nathan. "Fine."

"With one small room, we have no place for Glory Anna to sleep," Nihal Amos said.

"She will move back into the room she shared with her grandmother. I will secure a personal servant for her."

Nihal Amos looked at his father in surprise. "I must say, you are of an uncommonly accommodating mind today."

"Whatever do you mean? I am at all times a most reasonable man," Saji Stephen said. "Tell Sheeba Esther that her only responsibility will be to oversee the girl and make certain her needs are met. Only until next year, however. I have already arranged a most excellent marriage for her."

"Good," said Rajeev Nathan.

"Fine," said Nihal Amos.

When Udit arrived at the settlement to summon Ashish to the landlord's house, Zia mumbled her displeasure. "Does he think you are still a child?" she grumbled. "Does he think you should sit and wait for him to call you whenever he desires a playmate?"

"I had no choice when I was a child, and I have no choice now," Ashish said. "He is my master."

As usual, Saji Stephen was standing beside the garden waiting for Ashish to arrive. "Come, come!" he called as soon as he saw Ashish coming up the path. Saji Stephen turned away and walked up to the veranda. Ashish followed as far as the patch of dirt.

"You are a fortunate Untouchable," Saji Stephen called down to him. "I give you special attention."

Ashish kept his eyes fixed straight ahead.

"Your daughter," Saji Stephen said. "What is her name?"

"Shridula. Blessing."

"Yes, yes. I remember. She came here to sit with the girl Glory Anna. Now I find myself in need of a personal servant for the girl, and I want it to be your daughter. She will come and live here in this house under the supervision of my second son's wife."

Ashish flinched as though he had been hit with a rock.

"She will have a much better life here than she would in your miserable hut," Saji Stephen said. "I will give her better food. I will permit her to sleep in the barn. She can visit you from time to time—if she wishes."

"No," Ashish pleaded. "Do not ask for my Shridula. It would be too hard on her mother."

Saji Stephen bristled, and his eyes hardened. "You do not understand me, Ashish. I do not ask. The girl belongs to me. I shall do with her as I wish, and I wish her to serve the girl Glory Anna."

"No. Please. If I could—"

"I do you a courtesy to inform you of my intentions," the landlord said. "Were you any laborer besides my playmate Ashish, I would simply send someone to bring the girl to me. Willingly or by force."

"Landlord . . . Saji . . ."

"*Master* Landlord!" Saji Stephen's words were clipped and brittle.

"Master Landlord, I beg of you, allow my daughter to come to your house in the morning and return home in the evening. Please . . . master."

A smile creased Saji Stephen's face.

"Go back to work," the landlord said. "At sunup tomorrow, your daughter is to be waiting at the edge of my garden. She will stay here day and night, for as long as I say."

☙

"No!" Zia screamed when Ashish told her of the landlord's command. "No, not my Shridula!"

"Saji Stephen is not like his brother," Ashish explained, for he knew the terrors that must be running through his wife's mind. "She will be a servant for the girl. The girl's auntie will watch out for them."

"No!" Zia cried. "Shridula cannot go! Why did you agree to such an arrangement?"

Ashish reached out and touched his wife's leathery arm. "It is not for us to say," he said softly. "Saji Stephen is our master."

Shridula sank down in the corner and buried her head in her hands. No one had ever considered the possibility that she might have an opinion.

"How long does he want her to work in his house?" Zia asked.

Ashish shrugged his shoulders. "He said she could come back and visit us."

Zia tossed her *pallu* over her head and wept.

"He said she would have plenty of food," Ashish said. "Maybe our Shridula will come back to us plump like a rich lady." Even Zia, in her anguish, had to smile at that possibility.

The monsoon season was not willing to retreat without one last drenching downpour. It started in the hours after midnight and refused to let up. By the first light in the eastern sky, Shridula pulled the end of her *sari* over her head and hugged her mother good-bye.

"I will walk with you," Ashish said.

"No," Shridula told him. "This is for me to do."

Shridula picked her way to the landlord's house through the flowing mud and the pouring rain. By sunup, she stood waiting at the edge of the garden.

In the rainy gray of full morning, as she continued to wait, a cool breeze blew from the west and plastered the girl's wet *sari* against her reed-thin form. She shivered in the downpour and continued to wait.

The sun kept rising—Shridula could feel its heat even though clouds blocked its light—and fear began to well up inside her. What if she had done something wrong? What if the landlord punished her father for her stupidity by sending *thags* with clubs to beat him up? Tears tumbled down her cheeks and mixed together with the steadily falling rain. But still Shridula waited.

When the sun reached its zenith, it finally broke through the clouds. Sheeba Esther, a small woman with the face of a girl, peeked out from around the veranda.

"Oh!" she cried in surprise. "You must be Shridula!"

Shridula folded her hands and bowed her sopping-wet head.

"Come, come! I did not expect you in all this rain!" Sheeba Esther pulled Shridula over to the corner of the veranda and threw a sheet over her. "You poor child! Wait here while I get dry clothes for you."

"I can work in the garden," Shridula suggested to Sheeba Esther. She looked doubtfully at her fresh sari. "But not in this."

"You are not here to work as a gardener," Sheeba Esther said. "You are to serve Miss Glory Anna and keep her company."

But Shridula had not the first idea how to serve someone of upper caste birth. And she certainly didn't know how to keep such a one company. So for most of the day she sat on a stool and stared at her hands.

At long last Glory Anna said, "Shall I teach you to make tea for me?"

"I do not think so," Shridula said. "I am Untouchable and I will pollute you."

"I am a Christian," Glory Anna said. "We do not have those same rules."

Shridula looked up at her. This could be a trick.

"Really," Glory Anna said. "My grandmother told me. Come, I will teach you to make tea."

18

September 1946

*G*o ahead," Glory Anna urged Shridula. "I want you to brush my hair." She pointed to the intricately-patterned silver hairbrush that sat alongside the matching comb and mirror.

Shridula didn't move.

"Hurry!" Glory Anna picked up the brush and, with growing impatience, thrust it toward Shridula.

But Shridula shrank away. "I must not," she mumbled. "I am an Untouchable. Untouchables are not allowed to touch metal."

"Such tiresome rules!" Glory Anna heaved an exasperated sigh. "The landlord says you are to be my servant. That means you must obey me, and I say you must brush my hair." Again she thrust the brush toward Shridula. "Hurry now. Do as I say."

Shridula reluctantly took the brush. How cool the silver felt against her fingers! How smooth! She rolled the handle back and forth in her hand.

"Brush my hair!" Glory Anna demanded.

Slowly, taking great care to be gentle, Shridula pulled the brush through Glory Anna's glistening black hair.

Imagine, her Untouchable hand grasping metal. Silver! Imagine, Glory Anna dressing her in a *sari* made of real silk! Imagine, washing her Untouchable body with fragrant *soap*! So many new things!

Every day with Glory Anna opened fresh doors of experience for Shridula. Her most well-worn words became: *No, no, I must not!* Glory Anna's refrain remained: *Oh, but you must!*

The first night and the second, after her evening chores— brushing out Glory Anna's long hair, folding Glory Anna's *sari* and laying it in the chair—Shridula headed for the barn to make herself a bed in the hay. On the third night, as Shridula prepared to leave, Glory Anna said, "If Sheeba Esther got a sleeping mat for you, you could sleep on the floor here in my room."

Which is how, in the dark of the night, Shridula came to be lying on a mat squeezed between the cupboard and Glory Anna's bed, wishing with all her might she could see the stars overhead. Wishing she could feel the breeze blow through the branches of her father's *neem* tree, which he had planted with his own hands. Wishing she could listen to her *amma* and *appa* whisper to each other as she fell asleep.

"I am sorry you were born an Untouchable," Glory Anna said. "And a girl, too."

"I am a blessing to my parents."

"I am a blessing to no one," said Glory Anna. "On the day I was born, not one person rejoiced. My father thinks I killed my mother—I know he blames me. Maybe if I had been a boy . . ."

"They did not put you in a pot and bury you," Shridula said. "They did not leave you out in the field to die."

"Only because my grandmother would not let them."

"Well, then, maybe to her, you *were* a blessing."

Glory Anna said nothing. Shridula stretched out on the sleeping mat and let her eyes drift closed.

"Maybe so," Glory Anna whispered. "Maybe I was a blessing to my grandmother."

"What are the fluffy white cakes?" Shridula asked as Sheeba Esther laid a platter before the girls on the veranda.

"*Idli*," Glory Anna said. "Rice cakes. Have you never eaten them?"

Shridula had not. Nor had she tasted *dosa*, the big pancakes. Glory Anna showed her how to eat those with spiced vegetable stew. Certainly Shridula had never poured *ghee* over her food before. "Not so much!" she cried to Glory Anna, who poured it on like a golden river. Glory Anna laughed and poured out another dollop.

Saji Stephen frowned when he saw the girls sitting together on his veranda. He had warned Sheeba Esther to keep the Untouchable out of sight. But since the landlord was supposed to be away all day, she had given them permission to enjoy the pleasantness of a cooler day.

Shridula was the first to hear the angry shouts.

"Just some men," Glory Anna said. "They are down by the road."

Shridula scrambled to her feet. "I should not be here."

But Glory Anna caught her by the arm. "Never mind them. Some villager is always angry and yelling at another. It has nothing to do with you."

Shridula, hesitating, shot a nervous glance down at the road.

"Sit down," Glory Anna insisted. "Here, take another *idli*."

But as Shridula reached for the rice cake, a rock crashed through the pepper vines and smashed the platter to pieces.

"Unrest is what it was," Rajeev Nathan declared as he stomped past his father and across the veranda to where his brother sat. "Political unrest. It had nothing at all to do with Glory Anna or with that Untouchable servant girl of hers. It had everything to do with me!"

"Ridiculous," Saji Stephen said. "Stop pacing and sit down."

"Can you not see, Father? It is not the Untouchable that upsets them. It is the fact that I have a Muslim wife!"

"You are a Christian, she is a Muslim, they are Hindu. It is ideal. You said so yourself. You are the model of the new India. Is that not what you always told us?"

"The problem is, they do not *want* that kind of new India. They want two nations, one for Hindus and one for Muslims."

"And where would you fit into that?" Saji Stephen asked. He made a thinly disguised effort to suppress his laugh.

"I do not fit into it at all, Father! That is precisely the point!" Rajeev Nathan's raised voice quaked. "Two weeks ago Muhammad Ali Jinnah proclaimed Direct Action Day. To peacefully demand a Muslim homeland in British India is what he said, but look what happened—Riots in the north! Thousands dead in Calcutta alone! The disruption and violence have spread all over India, and now here they are in the south. Riots right in Malabar!"

Saji Stephen stared at his son. "What a lot to imagine from a single rock smashing our *idli* platter."

"Really, Rajeev Nathan," Nihal Amos said with a sigh. "You can take so small an event and cast it into the most dramatic light."

"Do not call me Rajeev Nathan! Do not call me by any Christian name! From this day forward I am simply Rajeev the Indian!"

✍

On an especially lovely morning, on a day fresh and cool, Rajeev made a trip alone in the horse cart. Switch in hand, he urged the horse to move faster, to pull the cart quickly past the high caste settlements and on toward the Sudras' fields.

Sudras, their *mundus* tied high and short, their bare legs showing for all to see, sweated as they worked in their small paddies. They did their own planting, their own growing, and their own harvesting, their wives at work alongside them. Their children worked, too. Even the small ones, who ran back and forth toting water to the paddies and lugging sheaves of cut rice back with them. But Rajeev refused to look at the Sudras. He kept his eyes fixed on the road ahead.

Rajeev arrived at the English Mission Medical Clinic before noon. He clambered out of the cart, hurried to the front door, and pounded on it with his fist.

✍

"My grandmother told me how the white men came to India," Glory Anna said to Shridula. "All the way from the other side of the world. It was God's will they should come and govern India and take away our riches."

Shridula wrinkled her brow.

✿154✿

"My grandmother said that at the end of India's land, where the sun sets, is a great sea. One day when the Indian people went to bathe in that sea, they saw a strange creature standing on the beach. His hair was red like fire, his face very pale, and his eyes as blue as the sky. The creature could not speak the Indian language, so no one understood what he said. After that day, many of this kind swarmed all over the seashore."

"How did they get there?" Shridula asked.

"No one knows," said Glory Anna. "They were just there. They came and they never left."

Shridula stared at Glory Anna's silky-smooth skin, so creamy pale. Her eyes were not colored like the sky—except perhaps when the sky is black with monsoon clouds—and not a spark of fire could be found in her hair. Even so . . .

Slowly Shridula raised her own dark arm and examined it.

"Are you one of them?" Shridula asked.

"No!" Glory Anna said. "Only . . . Well, I think maybe they were Christians, too."

"What about the Brahmin? He is not a Christian, but his skin is even paler than yours."

"He is not like me, though," Glory Anna said. "Brahmins are not like us!"

Shridula studied her own dark arm. "I want to see my family," she said. "The landlord said I could see them. I want to go home."

19

October 1946

ℋarvest!" Ashish called.

The sun had barely begun to rise pink and gold on a near-perfect morning. Not a cloud marred the dawning sky.

"Harvest!"

For as many years as Ashish could remember, it had been Boban Joseph Varghese who had called the workers to harvest. But Boban Joseph was gone now, and the call was long overdue. The paddies hung heavy with ripened rice that had known far too much rain. It must be brought in quickly, before it rotted Already settlement carpenters had sharpened the scythes at the whetting wheels so that workers' cuts would be swift and clean. Harvest tools lay in piles, water jars stacked next to them.

"Harvest!"

Laborers, sluggish and reluctant all season long, caught Ashish's excitement. Chattering excitedly, they snatched up their assigned tools and moved out toward the paddies.

"Huh! Rice in even this best paddy is stunted," Dinkar complained to Ashish.

"Hush!" Ashish warned. "We will do what we can and express no regret over what we cannot do."

✐

"India for Indians! No more British domination!" shouted Wafi, Rajeev's six-year-old son, as he marched around the landlord's house.

"Amina! Stop your son this instant!" Rajeev called to his wife. To Saji Stephen he complained, "Do you see, Father? My own son—hardly more than a baby but a Communist already! I will not have it!"

Self-rule and communism. Violence and riots. A Muslim daughter-in-law under his roof and a chanting grandchild marching around it. How could Saji Stephen think about the rice harvest with all that chaos weighing him down? And always, always, his two sons' never-ending arguments.

"That Muslim Jinnah will not let up on his presumption of two nations," Rajeev stated. "*Hinduization*, that is what he says. India is not even independent, and already he must pronounce it a failure."

"Already, you say?" Nihal Amos countered. "Your friends, the British, could at least have attempted to find a solution that would keep India as a British protectorate."

"It was Jinnah who provoked the riots with his call for Direct Action! No one can deny that!"

Saji Stephen tried to interrupt the argument, but Nihal Amos jumped to his feet and shook his fist in his brother's face. "It was nothing but a peaceful demonstration until the British went and changed it into a riot! The British turned guns on innocent Indians and started murdering them!"

"But the Hindus were the ones who—"

"Stop it!" Saji Stephen cried. "Both of you, stop! Look at yourselves. This is why there will never be a united India!"

The entire village depended on the Varghese rice harvest. Whenever a villager passed a member of the Varghese family, the accepted greeting was to touch one's forehead, bow, and ask after the crops. But this year was like no other. The Brahmin went through the ritual of blessing the crops, but few paid him any mind.

In the days of Saji Stephen's father, Mammen Samuel Varghese, a spice merchant by the name of Prem Rao was one of those who always paid careful attention to the harvest. And not just to the landlord's rice; his pepper vines and spice trees were of even greater interest to Prem. But along with Mammen Samuel, old Prem had long ago passed from this life.

Prem Rao left behind a proud legacy: his two sons, Babar and Irfan. Prem Rao had assumed the boys would follow him in his business. But unlike their father, the two young men did not consider village life as merchants the only possibility for them. Instead, they grew their moustaches full and bushy and joined the Indian army. So when Japan invaded Burma in 1942 and captured Indian territory, the Rao brothers marched off to fight. To fight for not Britain but for India.

The Burmese campaign was long and hard, especially for the Indian troops. Though they fought valiantly, the British commanders still considered the Indians expendable. And when battles pressed in closer to home, British soldiers were pulled away from Burma and reassigned to Europe. Arms and munitions, food and supplies, followed the British boys, leaving the beleaguered Indian troops on the Burmese front desperate.

On one particularly cold night, Irfan worried over his sick brother. He gave Babar his last morsels of food and the rest of his water, then tucked his own blanket around him. Babar died that night. After that, Irfan forced himself to survive for three reasons: his two sons, and his brother's boy, who no longer had a father.

Irfan Rao arrived home in 1945 to find his sons and his nephew all card-carrying members of the Communist Party.

"What is the meaning of this?" Irfan demanded of Nihal Amos. "You are the landlord's son. Why could you not leave these boys alone? Why could you not let me and my brother be proud of them?"

"Would you be prouder if your sons and nephew had died fighting battles for the British?" Nihal Amos asked.

Irfan Rao's face clouded and he ran his hand over his bush of a moustache. His lower lip curled down in the same way his father's had done. "It is not my fault the British declared us belligerents against the Axis powers," he said. "They never even bothered to consult the Indian Congress."

"That is not what I meant," Nihal Amos said.

"It is not my fault the Japanese invaded Burma, then pushed their way into India. It is not my fault the British had more important matters to tend to than us. It is not my fault that my brother died."

"The British only care about the British," Nihal Amos said. "Why does it bring you pride to die for them?"

Irfan, grunting, waved Nihal Amos away. "You Communists, with your strikes and trade unions! It's you who have brought the fight to us."

"*American Modal Arabi Kadalil!*" Nihal Amos recited. "Our slogan: *American Model into the Arabian Sea!* Do you understand? We will do whatever is required to achieve our goal.

Anything! We will fight the police, if we must. We will even fight the army!"

"Then the army will kill every one of you," Irfan said. "My sons and nephew, too, I fear."

Nihal Amos looked the older man in the eye. "I tell you the truth, Irfan Rao. The fight is not over. What we have seen is only a rehearsal for the real revolution. We will have a Communist India!"

Irfan pulled himself up to his full height. "I am an Indian!" he said. "I am proud to be a respected member of a respected family of the respected Vaisya caste. You are higher caste than I, but I am higher caste than the multitudes around me. You, Master Landlord's son, have no right to take my standing away from me—nor from my family!"

❦

The field laborers moved across the rice paddy in a long line, all swinging their scythes in rhythm with one another. Step, swipe! Step, swipe! Step, swipe!

"Hari, pick up the pace!" Dinkar ordered.

Hari moved his skinny legs faster, swung his bony arms wider. But his rhythm wasn't there.

"You are doing fine!" Ashish called to the boy. "Keep swinging that scythe!"

Dinkar mopped his face with the edge of his *chaddar* and scowled at Ashish.

"This is his first harvest on the cutting line," Ashish said to Dinkar. "Everyone has to learn."

The women came along behind to gather up the stalks of rice and tie them into bundles.

"Pick up the pace!" Dinkar shouted to Hari. "If you cannot keep up, you can go back to carrying water with the small boys!"

Hari stepped more quickly and swung his scythe faster, and as he did so he clenched his teeth and hardened his face.

❧

By the time Jyoti came in from the paddy, Zia's cooking fire was already hot and her rice boiling. "I threw in an extra-large handful," Zia called. "Bring some of your chili peppers. You and your boys can share our pot tonight."

"You still have rice?" Jyoti asked in amazement.

"Some. Shridula's allotment."

Jyoti hurried her bony frame over to the chili plant beside her hut and pulled off two peppers.

Zia stirred in three pinches of curry and Jyoti's chilies. When they had cooked into the rice, she spooned out a dish full of spiced rice for Ashish. After he settled himself, she dished out bowls for Hari and Falak. The younger boy grabbed his share, scooped up a bite in his fingers, and shoved it into his mouth before he even sat down. Hari took his and moved off alone.

The women sat down to wait their turn to eat. "Everyone's rice bags are almost empty again," Zia said to Jyoti. "All of us are hungry. But the harvest is almost over. Soon our bags will be full again."

When Hari finished eating, he spread sleeping mats out close to the pepper plants for his mother and brother, the same as he did every night. But not his. His sleeping mat he laid out on the opposite side of the hut, away from everyone else.

❧

As the first shards of pink and gold streaked across the sky, as the sun prepared to rise on another cloudless morning, Jyoti dragged her stiff body off her sleeping mat and started the cooking fire. She took out what remained of her package of wheat flour and prepared a pot of watery porridge.

"Falak!" she called out to her younger son as he came from around the hut. "Where is Hari? Your meal is almost ready."

Falak didn't answer.

"What is wrong?" Jyoti demanded.

"Hari is gone."

Jyoti stared at her son. "What do you mean *gone?*"

Falak still didn't answer.

"Never mind," Jyoti said. "He will be back directly. Maybe he took a quick trip to the woods."

Falak's eyes filled with tears. Jyoti grabbed him by the arms and demanded, "Where did he go? You know something! What do you know?"

Tears ran down Falak's face. "He joined the Communist fighters, *Amma*. Hari is not coming back."

20

November 1946

*S*hhh . . ." Glory Anna cautioned. She moved out of the room and edged around the corner toward the open veranda door. When no one looked her way, she glanced back and beckoned for Shridula to join her.

" . . . because its treasury is all but empty." Rajeev speaking. "No mandate in England, not after the war. And the British know we Indians will not support them any longer."

"So what will they do?" Nihal Amos. Glory Anna couldn't see him, but she knew his voice.

"End British rule in India, of course." Rajeev again, strong and cocky. "They have no other choice. The decision has already been made!"

Shridula gasped.

"Shhhh!" Glory Anna grabbed Shridula's arm and dragged her away from the veranda door.

What Shridula and Glory Anna heard from around the veranda corner, every person passing along the road heard as well. And what one person heard, he quickly passed along to two other people, and those two to six more. "Did you get the news? It came from a most reliable source. British rule of India is coming to an end!"

Soon the entire village buzzed with the gossip.

✣

Brahmin Rama started his morning the same way he started every morning: he worshipped Brahman, the great World-Spirit, by reciting the Vedas. After that he worshipped his ancestors by partaking of ritual water drinks, and then he worshipped the gods and goddesses by pouring *ghee* on the sacred fire. He worshipped all living things by scattering grain on the threshold of his house for the benefit of animals, birds, and roaming spirits. Yet even he heard the talk. So after he completed his morning rituals, he settled himself perfectly still before an idol. He sat with legs crossed and eyes fixed straight ahead. With his hands resting on his knees, palms up, he recited still more mantras—punctuating his words with ritual gestures.

Independence. What would it mean?

After his prayers, Brahmin Rama stopped by the kitchen and told his servant, "Cook *chapatis* for me and pack a few supplies. Tomorrow I shall leave on a spiritual journey."

✣

Shridula, careful to keep her eyes averted, gathered the courage to ask Glory Anna the question that had plagued her for so many days: "If the British end their rule of India, will you still live here?"

"I do not know what will happen to any of us," Glory Anna said. "Maybe everything will be different. Maybe it will be the end."

"Maybe it will be the beginning," Shridula suggested.

Glory Anna stared at her.

"What I meant, of course, is it may be the beginning for you," Shridula hastened to say. "I am what I am. I know that."

In order to get an early start, Brahmin Rama started his morning rituals long before dawn. He dressed in a simple cotton *mundu*, slipped sandals on his feet, and picked up a light pack tied together in a white *chaddar*.

When the Brahmin passed by the landlord's house, Saji Stephen looked up from his veranda. "Where are you going?" he called.

"To Benares, the sacred city," Rama called back. "To walk the *Panch-kos* road and wash in the holy Ganges. To make sacrifices and say prayers at the Golden Temple."

"For us all?"

"For us all."

Moving past the landlord's house, Brahmin Rama picked up his pace. He held his head high, puffed out his skinny chest, and acted as though he truly was prepared for whatever might be ahead.

"I am waiting for you to brush my hair, Shridula!" Glory Anna sighed in exasperation. "What is the matter with you?"

Shridula took the brush and pulled it through Glory Anna's thick hair. "My *amma* and *appa*," she said. "Everything in the world will change and they do not even know anything about it."

"Of course they do," Glory Anna said. "Everyone knows."

"Not in the laborers' settlement," Shridula said. "I do not think so."

Glory Anna's hair shined as Shridula pulled the brush through it, stroke after stroke after stroke.

"Maybe you should go see them," Glory Anna said.

"When?"

"Tomorrow."

❦

Great mountain peaks of the Western Ghats shadowed the midlands of Malabar where rolling hills and sloping valleys pushed their way clear through to the sea. Brahmin Rama marveled at just how vast landlord Varghese's holdings were.

Two different times, drivers of bullock carts stopped to offer the Brahmin a ride. But since Rama could not be certain of the drivers' castes, and since he was unwilling to risk pollution, he thanked each one kindly and declined.

In the late afternoon, a brown *chital* sprang across his path. Brahmin Rama stopped and smiled at the sound of the graceful animal's high-pitched coo. Had he not lived his life confined to the village, the Brahmin might have known that cry was the spotted deer's warning that a tiger lurked nearby. But since he didn't know, Brahmin Rama stood in the road and smiled in blissful ignorance after the fleeing animal.

As he passed by a small village, Brahmin Rama spotted a man sitting beside the road, his twig-thin legs bent and twisted. "Alms," the man called, reaching out his shaky hand. Rama undid the strings of his purse and pulled out two *annas*. Without slowing his pace, he tossed them toward the man.

This way I show my reverence, he thought. *When I get to Benares, the gods will look upon me with special favor because of my kindness.*

It was the Brahmins' way. Even beggars served to enhance their standing as the revered highest caste.

⁂

Jesus loves me when I'm good, When I do the things I should.
Jesus loves me when I'm bad, Though it makes him very sad.
"What are you singing?" Zia asked her husband.

"The pale English lady used to sing that song to me when I was very little," Ashish said. "I have not thought about it for so long."

"Those are English words? What do they mean?"

"It is about the Jesus God," Ashish said. "He loves me even if I am not good enough. That is what the Holy Book teaches."

"I do not think that can be right," Zia said. "If there was a real God, and if he truly did love us, he would not have turned his back on us."

⁂

Brahmin Rama, who steadfastly refused to begin his daily prayers before he performed his morning ritual bath, stood up from his first night of sleeping in the wild and blinked around him in a confusion that bordered on panic. How was he to bathe himself?

Like most high caste Indians, Rama suffered from an absolute terror of pollution. It was this very matter, in fact, that so disgusted him about Englishmen. In their health clinics, they insisted on abiding by every minute health rule ever designed by man, claiming they only desired to protect themselves from all forms of contamination. Yet they turned up their aristocratic noses at the Indian's daily cleansing. They preferred their own weekly bath in a tub of water contaminated by their own dirty bodies. Furthermore, they washed their faces in basins that had been spat in and gargled over. Absolutely disgusting!

Rama pulled together a few twigs and, after some effort, managed to start a cooking fire. He took flour and oil out of his pack and kneaded it into dough, which he fried as cakes in his own skillet. He had no choice. It was the only way he could be certain his food was completely pure.

✦

"Your Shridula," the woman with a scar over her eye called out as she passed by Ashish's hut. "She is coming down the road."

"Shridula is on her way," Dinkar announced.

"She is almost here!" Jyoti called out.

Ashish hurried out to the path to meet his daughter. Zia waited for them, stirring up spiced rice, and laughing out loud as she stirred.

✦

Brahmin Rama didn't count how many days he walked, how many lean-to shelters he threw together, how many *chapati* cakes he fried in his skillet, how much rice he cooked over outdoor fires. But one night, after he started yet another fire for yet another evening meal, a traveling holy man sat down close to him and called out a greeting. Brahmin Rama nodded in reply.

"Where are you going?" the holy man asked.

"To Benares," Rama said. "To the Golden Temple beside the holy Ganges. I am on a pilgrimage."

"To walk all that way and back again will take you most of a year," the holy man said.

Brahmin Rama stared in disbelief. Could it truly be so far? Rama passed half of his evening's rice to the holy man, then he moved over closer. The two talked long into the night. The next morning, Brahmin Rama wrapped his belongings up in the white *chaddar* and turned his steps toward Cochin.

"You will suffer enough once you arrive in Benares," the holy man called after him. "It will not add to your sins to arrive in a railroad car."

*

"*Appa! Amma!* Do you know what is about to happen?" Shridula asked. "Have you heard?"

"Sit, Daughter," Ashish said. "Catch your breath. Then you can tell us the news from the village."

Clusters of men squeezed in close. They pretended to talk to one another, but everyone knew they were actually listening to what Shridula had to say. Women deserted their cook fires and edged over, too. The children simply pushed their way through to the front.

"The British are going to end their rule in India," Shridula said.

"They will leave the land?" Dinkar exclaimed. "Are you certain?"

"Everyone at the landlord's house says so."

"What does that mean for us?" a man called out.

"I do not know," Shridula said.

"Will we still be the landlord's slaves?" asked another.

"I do not know. I have not heard that."

"What of the Communists?" Jyoti called out. "What of my Hari?"

"I do not know."

"What will happen to the village?" demanded the young man with an old man's face.

"I do not know," Shridula insisted. "I do not know!"

Brahmin Rama jostled his way through the crowds of pilgrims that thronged *Panch-kos*, the road that circled around Benares. His father had always talked of walking this road, though he never did. It was the great ambition of every true Hindu. Brahmins surrounded Rama on every side, and holy men, too. Of course there were also the beggars who swarmed after them. And lepers. Lepers everywhere. Their fingers and toes gone, they reached out to Rama with stubs of hands.

Someone pulling a cart with a man inside pushed up against Rama. The Brahmin tried to step aside, but a skinny man staggered up on the other side, his old mother clinging to his back. So many sick heading for the holy waters of the Ganges. Or perhaps just to this road. For it was believed that anyone who should die on *Panch-kos* would immediately be admitted to Shiva's heaven.

Clanging cymbals punctuated a wild clamor of voices. Brahmin Rama knew what that meant; a temple up ahead. People clogged the road, their shouts deafening him. Rama tried to pull back, but the crowd forced him forward. When he caught sight of a small alley, he lunged for it.

Immediately Rama regretted his impulsive move. The alley was dark and narrow. If he stood in the middle and reached out with both arms, he could touch walls on each side at the same time. Where it led, he had no idea. He must force himself back into the flood of people.

Then the Brahmin looked up. Towering before him, its gilded domes glistening in the sun's rays, was the Golden Temple. Brahmin Rama folded his hands in prayer and raised them toward heaven.

Rama joined the worshippers who crowded through the alley, and he moved toward the entrance. On the temple's threshold, he fell down and lay prostrate. Then, rising with some difficulty and pushing past the myriad of tramping feet, he scooped up water from a dirty puddle and splashed it over his forehead, his eyes, his lips. He raised the last holy drops to his tongue and swallowed them.

✑

Shridula hunkered down small on the dirt floor of Ashish's stifling hut. "I want to come home," she begged.

"Is the landlord cruel to you?" Zia asked her.

"No, but I want to be with you."

Ashish touched his daughter's arm. "He is the landlord, and we—"

"I know what we are!" Shridula snapped. "Untouchables! And I know the landlord owns us. Everyone tells me it cannot be helped. Everyone tells me it is my *karma*. I do not want to hear it anymore!"

Ashish pulled his hand back and said nothing.

"You say you do not believe in *karma*," Shridula said to Ashish.

"No," he said.

"Then why does everything bad happen to us?"

Ashish took Shridula's hand in his. "It does not, Daughter," he said. "Some bad happens and some good happens. We miss having you here . . . but you are not far away. We have very little rice . . . but you have so much that you share with us. We do not know what will happen . . ."

" . . . but we can hope," Shridula finished.

※

Brahmin Rama wove his way through countless women seated beside the road, all calling out promises of good luck for the price of a garland of marigolds. A holy man in front of Rama—long-bearded and wild-haired, with the white ash mark of Vishnu on his forehead—tossed a coin to a wrinkled old woman. He chose a garland from her basket and hung it around his neck. Rama stepped up behind him and did the same. Just beyond the woman, Rama stepped aside, knelt down in a line with other Brahmins and, like them, leaned forward. A Brahmin-approved barber moved along the row and shaved each head. When he finished shaving Rama, the Brahmin raised his folded hands and recited a mantra. He handed the barber an entire *rupee*, and left still more righteous than he had come.

No longer was the road open or the air fresh. Huddled wooden buildings, weathered and sun-brittled, lined the last stretch before the road reached the bank of the holy river. Brahmin Rama wrinkled his nose against the dank smells of sweat and grime and bodies crowded too close together.

The sun beat hot on Rama's shaved head as he stepped down the wooden bathing-steps to the Ganges River. Mud, mud, and more mud. Even the steps seemed to be made of mud. A cloud of flies billowed up and swarmed over him. Brahmin Rama swatted at them as he stepped down into the flowing grime.

※

"The landlord will take care of us," Zia said to her daughter. "He needs us. He will see that nothing bad happens to us."

"He talks about protecting his crops and he talks about protecting himself, but he never speaks of protecting us," Shridula said.

"Everyone has his position," Zia answered. "Our position is a quiet and submissive one. It is not a happy one, but it is our position. Those above us—the Brahmins and the landowners—their position is to protect us." She looked at her husband with pleading eyes, but he said nothing.

"No, *Amma*," Shridula whispered. "We must take care of ourselves."

✑❧

"The Mahatma," stated a stocky Brahmin who traveled with his small son. "The one called Gandhiji." He leaned in and poked at the fire. "He is a real Indian."

"What do you mean?" Brahmin Rama asked.

"Have you not heard? He was willing to fast to his death in order to bring down the opposition. That is the Hindu way. Gandiji is like a creditor sitting *dharma* at his debtor's door."

"I heard him give a speech in Delhi," said another in the group of Brahmins gathered around the fire, an old man with cinders rubbed into his hair. In the light of the fire, his hair sparkled, a muddy gray. "Gandhiji said, 'This city is not India. Go to the villages; that is India, for therein lives the soul of India.'"

"Indian people *like* that sort of talk," another said.

"I do not like it," Rama said. "If the Mahatma has his way, what will happen to our position as Brahmins?"

No one answered.

"The landlord in my village thinks he can be a good Christian and mix in enough Hinduism to satisfy everyone. He satisfies no one. Mohandas Gandhi thinks he can be a good Hindu and mix in enough Christianity to satisfy everyone. He will find himself at the same end. No one will be satisfied."

"Gandhiji will lead us to freedom!" the stocky Brahmin insisted.

Brahmin Rama shook his head. "If we do not stop him, he will lead us to destruction."

Late into the night, long after Shridula had returned to the landlord's house, Ashish lay awake staring up at the stars. Zia lay next to him, her breathing steady and deep. Ashish closed his eyes and sang softly into the dark:

Yes, Jesus loves me! Yes, Jesus loves me! Yes, Jesus loves me! The Bible tells me so.

21

December 1946

*T*errible harvest!

Ashish kicked his way through the paddy stubble. Even those stumps of grain stalks were wrong. They stood far too high. "Chop it low to the ground," he had said again and again. Yet the stubble reached almost to his knees. Time to prepare the fields for the winter crop, and all this extra work to do.

Actually, the winter planting should already have been done. They need not worry about rain, of course. Not in December. The days were still cool and comfortable, though they wouldn't stay that way for long. But hot or cool, wet or dry, the planting-growing-harvest cycle must go on.

Cursed land!

Ashish's stomach ached with hunger. The same pain plagued everyone in the settlement since the landlord cut their food ration in half. Punishment for a poor crop, he said. Visits from Shridula cheered her parents, of course, but not only them. For whenever Shridula came, her arms overflowed with vegetables from the landlord's lush garden. And when she finished handing those about, she pulled out treats from hidden folds of her *sari*. "From Landlord Lady Sheeba Esther," Shridula would say. "She told me I could bring these to you."

Selfish Master Landlord!

No help ever came from him. He didn't even give the laborers their harvest feast. That feast was their rightful due, yet the landlord gave them nothing but a small measure of rice to keep them alive and working. No extra grain, no spices, and no feast. "That fool Saji Stephen!" Ashish spat. "Spoiled brat of a landlord!"

Even so, the new crop must go in or everyone would soon be much hungrier.

The rice stubble rustled softly . . . paused . . . then rustled more violently. Ashish stopped to listen. "Rats!" he said. *Well, fine. Surely enough rice kernels littered the field to satisfy many rats.*

But rats weren't the only creatures that rustled through field stubble. A sleek body popped out and skittered past Ashish. It paused, turned its beady eyes back on him, and sniffed the air with its pointed snout. A mongoose. Out for a meal of plump rats, no doubt.

Reaching his arms out wide, Ashish said with a grin, "For you, *Appa!*"

Ashish's father had always had a special affection for every mongoose that skittered through a field. It wasn't that Virat had particularly liked the cunning little animals. It was that they had no fear of cobras, and cobras terrified Virat. A mongoose would tease . . . and nip . . . and dance . . . and force the agile cobra to strike. That's when the mongoose would shoot out its skinny head and snatch the cobra's head in its mouth to drag it off for dinner.

Clever, clever mongoose.

Several times, Virat had summoned young Ashish to watch a mongoose and a cobra engaged in their deadly dance. Every time the mongoose won.

"Be like a mongoose," Virat told his son. "Others will come after you with poison, but if you keep your wits, you can prevail."

✍

"Do you think the laborers are helpless, Father?" Nihal Amos exclaimed in exasperation. "They are not! No, they most assuredly are not!"

"You are not the landlord in this house," Saji Stephen reminded his son. "I am the landlord, and I will deal with my laborers in my own way!"

"You cannot starve them," Nihal Amos insisted. "You withheld their harvest feast, even though it was their due. Now you have cut even their small food allotment in half. It is not right. It is not Christian."

"Do not dare to tell me what is Christian!" Saji Stephen ordered. "The workers have already gotten more than they deserve. The disastrous harvest was their fault."

"The Communists say—"

"I do not care what those subversives of yours say! I do not care what the Hindus say and I do not care what the Muslims say. I do not even care what the British say."

"It is only that—"

"And I certainly do not care what you say, Nihal Amos. Get out of my sight!"

✍

"Hoe the stubble clear down to the ground!" Ashish ordered. "I want the field clean."

The workers stood together, raised their hoes, and chopped in unison.

Ashish gazed across the field and shook his head. He ran his hand through the gray stubble on his craggy face and groaned. The laborers worked, but it wasn't enough. The trenches should be open by now. They should already have flooded the field.

"Faster!" Ashish called. "Chop faster!"

Hoes swung high and landed hard. Up again, then down again. Up, then down. The line moved forward step by step.

A scrawny man with bowed legs swung his hoe . . . but not as high as the others. He chopped down . . . but not as hard. He stepped forward . . . but not as far.

"Binoy!" Ashish called. "Keep up!"

The scrawny man lurched forward and swung his hoe . . . but not straight. The man in line next to him ducked and yelled.

"Move!" Ashish ordered. "Go!"

Hoes swung high. Hoes landed hard. Up again, down again. Once more the line moved forward. Scrawny Binoy, with his bowed legs, panted and sweated as he struggled to keep up. He raised his hoe high . . . sort of. He chopped down hard . . . but not straight. The man next to him shoved him away. Binoy lurched and fell just as the man on the other side brought his hoe down.

Binoy shrieked, and the line stopped.

Ashish pulled the *chaddar* off his head, squeezed his eyes closed, and wiped his face. "You two," he called to the men on either side of Binoy. "Take him to the edge of the field. I will go to the landowner and get help."

Dinkar ran up behind him. "Forget that bent-up old man!" he ordered. "He will not be alive when you get back."

"I will run all the way," Ashish said.

"Forget him. He is not even a good worker."

"Find shade and lay him out," Ashish ordered the two men. "I will get help and be back as quickly as I can."

Dinkar glowered at all of them. "Get back to work!" he insisted. "You too, Ashish!"

Ashish's face hardened. "No! You men will carry Binoy back to his hut and I will go for help." He turned away and loped across the paddy. Ignoring Dinkar and his protests, the two men picked up Binoy and headed across the field toward the path that led to the settlement.

"I will show you the meaning of helpless," Saji Stephen said to Nihal Amos. He settled himself on his Persian carpet and called to his servant, "Udit, bring my book of accounts."

"You do not need to read me the names of your laborers," Nihal Amos said with a sigh.

"Oh, but I do. Someone must be landlord after me. It certainly cannot be one who bestows power on slave laborers."

"Rajeev is your firstborn. He is the one who wants the power."

"My brother Boban Joseph was the firstborn, yet here I sit."

Udit hurried out and laid the book of accounts in his master's hands. Saji Stephen opened the leather cover and turned to the first page. As he ran his finger along the ink markings, a smile crossed his face.

Ashish ran across the paddy and on to the path between the fields. His breath came in great gulping gasps, yet he refused to slow his pace. When he could run no more, he slowed to a fast walk, but as soon as he could pant evenly, he broke back into a run.

With the landlord's garden finally in sight, Ashish fell to his knees. He gulped several deep breaths and struggled back to his feet. He could no longer run. As he walked toward the garden, he heard Saji Stephen's crowing voice: ". . . whose name was Anup. We owned their family for three generations! Ha!"

Ashish slowed his pace. Anup was Zia's father. The landowner was talking about his wife's family.

"And look at this one: Virat, the *chamar*. He came to my father forty-eight years ago with a half-blind wife and a beaten son. The son is now my overseer, Ashish. When we were both little boys, my father gave him to me for a plaything. We got him and both his parents for a tiny loan. Look at what is written about them."

Ashish, just around the corner from the veranda, stopped still.

"Sixty percent interest. We added that amount every month. More charges for food and a place to sleep, of course. More for the English medical clinic, even though it cost my father nothing. More added for clean clothes. Look at this . . . my father added to the debt every time Ashish was summoned here to play, for the food he ate and for my old clothes he was forced to wear."

Nihal Amos murmured something under his breath. "What is the amount of their debt now?" he asked.

"Over two thousand rupees! Even better, Ashish is mine, his daughter is mine, and her children and grandchildren and great-grandchildren will belong to my children and grandchildren."

Nihal Amos said something else, but too softly for Ashish to understand.

"Because the slave Ashish is helpless," Saji Stephen responded, "all the workers are helpless."

Ashish sank to his knees and buried his head in his hands.

$\mathscr{L}$

"I should not have told you," Ashish said to Zia as they sat together in the dark of their hut.

"I already knew," Zia said. "It is why I never could blame my father and mother for getting away. Because they knew, too."

"I wish I did not know," Ashish said. "I wish I could still believe I work for a purpose. I wish I still had hope."

Zia said, "You are alive, Husband. There is always hope."

"If the English ever leave India," Ashish wondered, "will they take their God with them?"

22

December 1946

ook at this, Shridula." Glory Anna held up her painting. "What do you think?"

Shridula looked up from where she sat in the corner of the great room. She leaned her head to one side and scrutinized the green stripes accented with brightly colored drippy spots.

"It is bright," Shridula offered.

"Leaves of a mango tree," Glory Anna explained. "With ripe mangoes showing through. That is what it is."

"Yes." Shridula nodded and smiled. "Very colorful."

When Glory Anna tired of painting, she instructed Shridula to clean up after her. Glory Anna got out the sitar, carefully balanced it on her shoulder, and began to pick a whining refrain.

"My grandmother taught me to play this," she said.

Shridula sank back down into her corner and pasted a smile on her face.

"Enough of that noise! Enough!" Saji Stephen bellowed from the veranda.

Glory Anna sighed. She untangled herself from the sitar, carefully set the instrument back up in the corner, and headed for her room. Shridula got up and followed her.

"I have never had a friend before," Glory Anna said.

Shridula sat in her place in the corner and sank her head into her hands.

"Do you want me to read to you?" Glory Anna asked. "My grandmother taught me." She reached behind the cupboard where she had hidden Parma Ruth's leather-bound Bible. "It is written in English, though, so first I will read it and then I will tell you what it means."

Glory Anna opened to the beginning, Genesis. She flipped a few pages until she got to chapter six. "*And it came to pass, when men began to multiply on the face of the earth, and daughters were born unto them . . .*"

When she finished the chapter, Glory Anna told Shridula, "It said that everyone in the world was really wicked except for one man named Noah. So God told Noah to build an ark, which is another name for an enormous boat, because monsoon rains were coming and they would flood the entire world, but Noah would be safe in the ark."

"What I do not understand is how Noah got all the animals to go into the boat," Shridula said. "When the monkeys saw the tigers, why did the monkeys not run away? Because the tigers would eat them. Would they not?"

Glory Anna stared at Shridula. "I did not say anything about the animals."

Shridula flushed red and looked away.

"Hindus do not have this story," Glory Anna pressed.

Shridula picked at the edge of her sari and twisted it between her fingers.

"How do you know the story of Noah and the ark?"

Shridula sat in terrified silence. She didn't dare to look up.

"Tell me!" Glory Anna ordered. "You are my servant, and you have to obey me!"

"The pale English lady . . . at the mission clinic . . ." Shridula stammered.

"You know her?"

"No. She told the story to my father when he was a little boy, and he told it to me."

"How could he understand her?" Glory Anna demanded. "They speak English at that clinic. Did she tell him the story in English?"

"Maybe . . . I do not know."

When Glory Anna didn't respond, Shridula pleaded, "Please, do not punish my *appa!* He did not mean to do anything wrong. Please, do not tell the landowner!"

"I will not tell anyone," Glory Anna said. "Did you ever see the pale English lady?"

"No," said Shridula. "But I wish I could. Maybe someday I will."

"Maybe Sheeba Esther could take us to see her," Glory Anna said.

"Do you think so? Do you think she really could?"

⟨⟩

"Sit beside me," Glory Anna said to Shridula. "I am going to teach you to read."

Shridula fixed a well-practiced blank look on her face and stared at the open Bible. It looked very much like the Holy Book she had so often read with her father, but of course, she said nothing about that.

"These are called words," Glory Anna said—slowly and carefully, as though she were talking to a young child. Shridula nodded. "I will point out easy words and you try to say them after me."

Shridula took great care to stumble on even the easiest word and to make mistakes. Over and over. Each time they read together. Morning and afternoon. One day after another day after another day.

When they came to the book of Exodus, chapter twenty, Shridula forgot herself and read all the way down to verse eighteen.

"You are learning so fast!" Glory Anna exclaimed. "I must be an exceptionally good teacher!"

"I do not understand this part, these commandments," Shridula said. "There are no idols in your house, and Master Landlord says the laborers should not work on Sunday. Those are the first commandments. But look at these other ones. *Thou shalt not kill.* Everyone believes your father killed his brother. *Thou shalt not steal.* My father knows about the landlord's book. Everything my father earns the landlord steals from him. *Thou shalt not bear false witness against thy neighbor . . .*"

Shridula paused, but Glory Anna pressed, "*What?*"

Shridula took a deep breath and chose her words carefully. "Lying. My *appa* grew up playing with your father. My *appa* suffered always because of lies your father told about him."

"Yes," Glory Anna said. "I know."

"I do not understand. If these are the Christian commandments, and if this is a Christian house, why is everything so wrong?"

"Everyone here is Christian because their ancestors were Christians and not Hindu—well, except Amina, Rajeev's wife, of course. She is Muslim. But even though everyone says they are Christians, no one really is, because no one really follows the Christian God. That is what my grandmother said. No one except my grandmother and me. And Sheeba Esther. And maybe your *appa*."

"Appa does not like the Hindu gods," Shridula said, "but I do not think he follows the Christian God, either."

Glory Anna forgot about her paints stacked under the table in the great room. She didn't get the sitar out of the corner anymore, either, for which everyone in the house gave great thanks. Instead she spent almost all her daylight hours sitting with Shridula, reading the Holy Bible.

&

"Come, come," Sheeba Esther called to Glory Anna. "You spend too much time closed in your room. Play the sitar. What sort of wife will you be, able to do nothing but make that beautiful instrument suffer and squawk?"

"I cannot play it," Glory Anna said with a pout.

"Come, I will teach you."

Sheeba Esther took out the polished rosewood sitar and balanced it delicately between her dainty left foot and her knee.

"Pluck the tune on these seven main strings," she said. "These other strings—" she pointed to the eleven strings under the frets, "they are sympathetic strings. Listen now when I play the accompaniment on them." Her pale, smooth fingers brushed over the strings and started the buzz of the *jiwari*, the music of the sitar.

Shridula, who sat quietly in the corner, closed her eyes as the soft warmth of the tune enveloped her.

"I wish I could play like that," Glory Anna said.

"No one starts out playing well. It takes much practice. It is said that one must spend twenty years learning, twenty years playing, and twenty years teaching in order to truly appreciate the sitar."

"How old are you?" Glory Anna asked.

"Not even twenty years. But I started practicing when I was very small. I cannot even remember back so far."

She would do exactly as Sheeba Esther said, Glory Anna promised. She would practice every day.

"Sheeba Esther," Glory Anna suddenly asked, "Will you take us to the English Mission Medical Clinic?"

The music stopped with a harsh plunk. "I will not! Why would you ask such a thing of me?"

"Because I have never seen an English lady," Glory Anna pleaded. "And I have never even heard a real English lady talk. I know she lives at the clinic, and I know she is very old. And I thought . . . I told Shridula—"

"How very foolish you are!" Sheeba Esther exclaimed. She stood up and carried the sitar back to its place in the corner of the great room.

✍

When Sheeba Esther handed her husband his bowl of rice and *sambar*, she said, "What does get into the head of a young girl? Today Glory Anna and her servant girl asked me to take them to the English medical clinic so they could see a real English lady! Can you imagine anything so foolish?"

Later that evening, as he sat on the veranda, Nihal Amos said to his father, "Whenever the British leave India, it cannot be too soon. Why, that Glory Anna of yours had the audacity to ask my wife to take her to the English medical clinic because she wants to see a real English lady!"

"Women talk too much," Saji Stephen said. "You should have told her—"

Rajeev stood up abruptly. "I have much to which I must attend, Father," he said. "Do excuse me this evening."

In the early hours of morning, when no one except the servants stirred, Shridula, who had already started her morning chores, headed back to Glory Anna's room, her arms loaded down with fresh *saris* for the cupboard. She nudged the door open with her foot.

"It is about time you got back!" Glory Anna whispered. "We must hurry! Dress me in a clean *sari* and brush my hair. Rajeev Nathan has the cart ready to take us to the English clinic!"

Shridula almost dropped the pile of clothes.

"Come, come! Do hurry. You and I are going to meet a real English lady!"

As the girls climbed into the bullock cart, as they settled themselves—Glory Anna on a plank behind Rajeev and Shridula on another propped against the back of the cart— Rajeev said not one word. He urged the animals forward until the sun was full overhead. Hour after hour, as they bounced along in silence, Shridula tried to imagine her grandmother Latha and grandfather Virat walking that same road in the days before they belonged to the landlord.

The bullocks lumbered past weathered houses of wood, sheltered by leafy *neem* trees—not great houses like the landlord's, but small, friendly places. Past fields where Sudras worked, their *mundus* hiked high, their legs bare and muddy. The bullocks pulled the cart across a bumpy bridge, to the other side of the river where the outcastes lived. Past mud huts on barren ground surrounded by nothing but dusty brush.

Past Untouchable land.

Past the land of Shridula's people.

When the bullock cart finally reached the English Mission Medical Clinic, Rajeev jumped down and headed directly for the main door. "Doctor!" he called. "Dr. Cooper!"

"You have returned yet another time?" Dr. Cooper sighed impatiently when he saw Rajeev. "Whatever do you want?"

"These young women." Rajeev gestured to the bullock cart where Glory Anna and Shridula still sat. In his best English he said, "They are being eager for visiting with the aged English lady. I am to be thinking you and I be having the proper time to be taking further action on matters in both our interest."

"I cannot imagine any matters that could possibly be in both our interests." Dr. Cooper made no attempt to disguise his disdain for the Indian.

"That is to be depending," said Rajeev. "Is your desire to be staying in India, or is it to be leaving in safety?"

"My, my, my!" Miss Abigail Davidson exclaimed in the Malayam language. Her hands flew to her wrinkled cheeks. "You are that sweet child's daughter? Oh my, oh my!"

She grabbed Shridula in an embrace and rocked her back and forth. "Blessing, that was his name. And you say it is your name as well? Two Blessings in one family! Oh my, oh my, oh my!"

Miss Abigail kept Krishna and little Lelee running back and forth to the main house, carrying cups and teapot, and fetching biscuits and bananas.

"Sit, sit!" Miss Abigail said to the girls. "Tell me all about your father, my child. Tell me about you—both of you!"

Because she knew her place, Shridula kept her head down, her hands folded, and her mouth closed. Glory Anna did the talking.

"Let me show you something," Miss Abigail interrupted. She opened her cupboard and dug through the containers on the top shelf. From the bottom of the stack, she pulled out a dusty box.

"Here, look at this." Carefully, almost reverently, Miss Abigail unfolded a thick layer of faded paper. Inside was light blue fabric. First, she unfolded a long skirt, then she pulled out a matching old fashioned top with long sleeves puffed out at the top, and trimmed with intricate lace insets. "My favorite dress," Miss Abigail said. "I was not always an old lady, you know!" She laughed out loud. "I only wore this dress on the most special of occasions. Which, as you can see, did not come my way often enough."

Tenderly, Miss Abigail ran her fingers over the lacy sleeves.

"The last time I wore it was when I took your father back to the workers' settlement," she told Shridula. "Such a sad day that was. Oh, I did not want to let him go! I wanted him for my own, you see. But that would not have been right, would it? He wanted to be with his real parents."

"He told me about you," Shridula said.

"Did he now? How nice of him to remember."

"It is a lovely dress," Glory Anna said.

"Tell me," Miss Abigail said to Shridula, "did your father keep my Bible?"

Glory Anna stared at Shridula. "Your father had a Bible?"

Shridula shifted uncomfortably, taking care to avoid Glory Anna's eyes. "Yes, Miss Abigail," she answered. "He learned to read it, too. He hid in the latrine pit where no one could see him."

Miss Abigail threw back her head and laughed out loud.

"Tell me, child, is your father a follower of Jesus?"

"I do not think so," Shridula said. "He thinks Indians have too many gods already."

"I was determined to make a convert of him," Miss Abigail said. "Oh, how much I did not understand back then! How much we all did not understand."

23

"*D*o not put extra rice in our pot for that scavenger woman and her son to eat," Ashish told his wife as they prepared to head back to their hut.

Zia wiped the mud from her face.

"But, Husband, her rice bag is empty. They have nothing to eat but wild roots!"

"Look to your own rice bag," Ashish said. "If you do not stop giving away what little we have left, we too will be digging up roots. Then we will not have strength enough to do our work."

"Jyoti's bones stick out like branches on a tree," Zia pleaded. "And her Falak can hardly carry a full water jug out to the fields."

"I am sorry for them, Wife," Ashish said. "But we have nothing to spare. When Shridula brings us extra from the landlord's house, you can give some of that to Jyoti. But what rice we have left in our bag will be for you and me, and no one else."

Ashish had spoken his piece, and Zia should accept it. But she could not help herself. "Can you not go to the landlord once more? Can you not plead with him one more time to give us more food?"

Ashish wiped his filthy hand across his equally filthy face. "I have pleaded and pleaded and pleaded. The last time I went, he would not even talk to me. He sent his servant to throw rocks to drive me away."

"It is not right," Zia said.

"Much is not right. Go to the hut and cook rice for us, Wife. For you and me and no one else."

Ashish had just settled himself under the sheltering limbs of the *neem* tree, his small bowl of rice and chopped chili peppers clutched in his hands, when Dinkar called out to him, "You stand watch in the field tonight."

"Why must it be me?" Ashish asked. "Why not a younger man?"

"Because the landlord sent word that he wants you for the watchman. He said maybe that would take your mind off begging him for rice."

Ashish grunted but said nothing.

ᴥ

The night was moonless and dark. For a long time Ashish lay on his back on the raised wooden platform in the middle of the rice paddy and watched the stars. He tried to remember his father—gentle face, furrowed and leathery, teeth that stuck out too far. Strong hands, calloused and rough.

He could see his father in his mind, but he couldn't quite picture his mother. Why was that? Perhaps because of her face. From one side, it was pretty, even after the rest of her had grown old and stooped and gray. But scars streaked the other side, circling around her blind eye. Quite like the boy Krishna at the English Mission Medical Clinic, whose aunt had thrown boiling water in his face. Except that the boy's entire face was scarred, not just the one part. What happened to his mother? Ashish had asked, of course, but she always insisted she couldn't remember. It seemed an extraordinarily strange thing to forget.

Ashish jerked awake. He sat up straight on the wooden platform and looked around. Danger lurked in the night. Thieves, perhaps? No, not until the grain was mature. Wild animals, most likely. The settlement still talked about the killer tiger that had once picked off workers. Ashish was very young then, but he remembered the horror of it.

Ashish climbed down from the platform and walked across the paddy field. He moved toward the path, in the direction of the next field.

Nothing. Ashish was ready to turn back when something caught his eye. Just a movement—or maybe nothing at all. He squinted and stared hard. Certainly not a thief, for it was on the other side of the path, outside the field. A small animal, perhaps?

For a long time, Ashish stared into the darkness.

Nothing.

He rubbed his eyes and moved farther down the path.

Nothing.

He shrugged, ready to turn back to the raised platform, but then he saw it again. A flash of something. No doubt about it this time.

Ashish ducked down. Yes, yes, someone moving toward the storehouse.

Staying close to the ground, Ashish crept forward—slowly, slowly, slowly—all the way to the storehouse. Then he hunkered down to wait. Soon a shadow slipped toward him. Ashish waited until it was close, then he leapt out.

The shadow didn't put up even the pretense of a fight. Ashish struggled through tangles of ragged silk to grip a pair of bony wrists. He forced the intruder to her feet and peered close.

"Jyoti!" he gasped.

But the scavenger woman wasn't looking at him. Her eyes were fixed somewhere in the darkness beyond. "Run!" she cried.

A frantic scramble erupted behind the storehouse, followed by quick running steps. Then silence.

Ashish sighed. "What is the matter with you? If I turn you over to the landlord, you know what he will do to you—and to your son."

Jyoti's face hardened.

"Why would you risk both your lives on such a foolish attempt at thievery?" Ashish demanded.

Jyoti's eyes flashed with defiance. "What choice do I have? My son and I are starving!"

Ashish loosened his grip on the woman's wrists. "If you steal the landlord's grain, we will all be beaten. Go home. I will not speak of tonight."

Jyoti fell to her knees and grabbed hold of Ashish's feet. "We still have no rice," she cried. "What am I to do?"

"I am sorry," Ashish said. "But I can do nothing."

"Give me one handful. Please, just one handful."

"I cannot," Ashish said. "Go home."

⟋♥

The next morning, Ashish, who usually led the assembly of workers to the fields, held back at the settlement.

"What are you waiting for?" Zia asked him.

"Nothing," Ashish insisted. "Today I will be at the end of the line for a change."

Zia shot him her look that said *You do not fool me one bit!*

Ashish didn't care. After a night of guilty sleeplessness, he decided he could find one handful of rice for a starving woman and her son.

But Jyoti didn't come out of her hut, and neither did her son.

When Ashish could delay no longer, he reluctantly followed the line of workers out to the field.

⁂

After a long day, Ashish shaded his eyes and, looking toward the setting sun, gazed across at what the workers had accomplished. A satisfied smile spread over his face. "This paddy is clean," he said to Dinkar.

"If we open the trenchers this evening, by tomorrow the field will be well flooded," Dinkar said.

"The rice should already be planted and growing," Ashish lamented. "Still, it is not too late to produce a good harvest."

"If the gods smile on us."

The smile faded from Ashish's lips. He said nothing.

Up ahead, something moved in a pile of dry stubble. Ashish stopped to watch. He was ready to prod at it with a stick when a familiar sleek brown head poked out.

"My friend, the mongoose!" Ashish exclaimed.

The mongoose fixed its beady eyes on Ashish and stared back.

"He does seem to recognize you," Dinkar said with a laugh.

Ashish grinned. "I will take six or eight of the young men with me and get those trenchers open," he said as he started back across the field. "Once the last of the workers has finished—"

A scream ripped through the air.

"No, no!" Jyoti shrieked. She waved her hands frantically about, then grasped her head. "Zia! No, no!"

⁂

Ashish bent over his wife who lay on the ground. Tenderly he pulled her muddy *sari* down from her arm. Two bright red spots below her shoulder showed where the cobra's fangs had pierced her. Already her arm had begun to swell.

"I did not even see . . . did not see the . . . see the . . ." Zia mumbled.

"We will send for the herbal man," Ashish told her. He tried to swallow back the terror that welled up in him.

"I knelt down . . . to pick up the water jug. Falak left it and . . . I never saw the snake."

"I will get the landlord to take you to the English medical clinic. The pale English lady will fix you." Ashish shivered uncontrollably, even as he dripped with sweat. He wanted to pick Zia up and run with her to the landlord's house, but his muscles wouldn't work. They felt as though they had melted into a pile of mud.

"I deceived you, Husband," Zia whispered.

"Shhhh! Shhhh!" Ashish hushed her.

"I have been helping Jyoti . . . I helped her steal . . . to steal the rice."

"It does not matter!"

"I could not let her starve! And her boy . . . he would die, too. I could not . . . could not . . ."

"You are a good woman, Zia."

Zia clutched at Ashish. "A long cobra . . . Huge head . . . But to me, invisible." She gasped for breath. "Why could I not see it?"

As Ashish and Dinkar carried Zia from the field, Falak ran to the landlord's house. He gasped out what had happened, and begged, "Ashish said, please, would Master Landlord take his wife to the English clinic in his fast cart. Please, Master Landlord can add double the cost to his debt."

But Saji Stephen refused to come out and hear the boy. Instead, he sent a servant out with his answer: "Ashish is not the master and I am not his slave. I will not obey him."

"Go to your father!" Sheeba Esther told Shridula. "I will send for a healer."

⟡

Long into the night, Ashish and Shridula sat together beside Zia as the healer chanted one mantra after another. Then he suddenly stopped. "No more," the healer said. "The poison is too stubborn. She will leave this life."

Shridula threw her *pallu* over her head and sobbed. Ashish longed to console her, but he had no words of comfort in him.

"Your mother was good and kind," Ashish finally managed to say. "If there is any rebirth, she will live again as something good." His voice broke. He pulled off his *chaddar* and sobbed into it.

"I do not want her to be reborn," Shridula insisted. "I want her to go to heaven and live with God."

Ashish shook his head. "I cannot understand. She helped the scavenger woman take rice from the storehouse, yes. But not for herself. She took it for the starving woman and her son. Even so, a sin is a sin. An Untouchable must never steal from a high caste landlord. Did the gods send the cobra to punish her?"

"No, *Appa*. No!"

"But the landlord could not put an evil spell on us . . . Could he? He is not even a Brahmin!"

"Please, *Appa!*" Shridula pleaded.

Ashish picked up his *chaddar* and wiped his red eyes. "I will go to Master Landlord and demand that he tell me what he did. And if he will not tell me, I will—"

"*Appa*, be careful," Shridula pleaded. "Maybe it is better not to know."

24

February 1947

"*I*t is the Muslim League and the Indian Congress, too," Glory Anna told Shridula. "Both are insisting that all the castes should be equal."

Shridula, who had gotten up early from her sleeping mat to gather twigs and tie a new broom, was too busy sweeping out the room to pay much attention to Glory Anna's chatter.

"Do you understand what that means, Shridula? No difference between you and me!"

Ignoring the splinters in her hands, Shridula swept the dust out the door.

"I told you to lay out my yellow *sari*, not this blue one!" Glory Anna called after her.

Shridula hurried back inside, apologizing all the way. She scooped the fresh folds of blue silk from the bed and refolded it, hurried it back into the cupboard, and took out the yellow *sari*.

"You can finish that tiresome sweeping later. I want you to brush my hair and dress me."

Shridula set the broom aside and took up the silver brush. Gently she pulled it through Glory Anna's long hair, taking great care not to pull too hard.

"Untouchables should be an equal part of Indian society the same as the rest of us," Glory Anna stated. "You should be able to go everywhere I go and do everything I do. Would that not be good?"

Shridula smiled a patient smile. Of course, it would be good. But who would sweep the floor? And care for the clothes? And brush the mistress's hair? If all castes were the same, masters couldn't be masters any longer, for who would be their servants?

***

Brahmin Rama sat cross-legged on a straw mat spread out under the mango tree in front of his house. He pushed his wire-rimmed spectacles back on his nose and called out in a loud voice, "My spiritual journey to the holy Ganges proved to be a time of immense enlightenment. I learned many things of great importance to all of us who share this village. In fact, I have an entirely new understanding of matters vital to all who will share the new country of independent India!"

Several men slowed their steps along the road, then stopped to listen. Spice merchant Mani Rao, eldest son of Irfan Rao, closed up the tops of his sacks of spices and edged over as close as he dared. Other Brahmins in the settlement called to their sons and nephews to come and hear the words of the wise Brahmin who had personally walked the *Pancho-kos* road, recited mantras in the Golden Temple, and dipped his head into the sacred water of the Ganges.

"In the new, independent India, there will be room for everyone—all castes and all religions."

"What are you saying?" a man called out from beside the road. "I do not eat meat! Why should I mix with men who do?"

"I will not even eat vegetables grown in the ground," shouted another. "How many others can claim such purity?"

"My clothes are spotless," an aged Brahmin intoned. "And my mind is as clean as my clothes."

"Yes, yes!" Brahmin Rama quickly agreed. "A Brahmin must unfailingly uphold the code of purity. Clean and unclean can never be one."

"Not just Brahmins!" shouted the spice merchant.

Brahmin Rama cleared his throat. "No, certainly not. All upper castes." He looked at the raised eyebrows on the Brahmin next to him. Rama took a deep breath and pushed the spectacles back up on his perspiring nose. "But led by the Brahmins, of course. Yes, led by the Brahmins, all upper castes will uphold the code of purity in the new India where there will be room for all."

"There is room for all right now," the Brahmin next to him said. "Each caste has its own place. The system has worked quite well for thousands of years."

"Once the British are gone, it will work even better," Brahmin Rama said. "It is up to us, the upper castes, to see that it does."

⚮

"The Punjab, Husband! You know nothing of that province. It is my people who know it because it is their land!" Amina's voice echoed loudly throughout the landlord's house.

Glory Anna didn't hurry to close her door the way she usually did when Amina and Rajeev raised their voices to each other. Instead, she pushed the window shutters wide open so she could hear more clearly.

"What I do know is that the Muslim League is doing all it can to gain power there," Rajeev said. "While true Indians sacrifice everything for a free and united India, the Muslim League stirs up division. Muslims against Hindus. Muslims against Sikhs—"

"And everyone against Muslims!"

"Do you not see, Wife? The League's demands will be the death of a united India!"

Stomping . . . slamming . . . but no more shouted words.

Glory Anna looked at Shridula and made a face. "Ha! A Christian and a Muslim in a Hindu country. Rajeev and Amina were supposed to be the picture of a new, united India."

Shridula said nothing.

In the cool of the late afternoon, Brahmin Rama looked around him at the small clutch of Brahmin boys who sat at rapt attention under the mango tree. "With my own eyes, I saw Mahatma Gandhi," he told them. "With my own ears, I heard the Great Soul speak."

The Brahmin spoke in an unusually loud voice, glancing up periodically to see if more villagers would come back and linger behind the boys to listen.

"Imagine!" exclaimed one of the few men who had stopped. "In our own village sits one who saw the great Gandhiji! One who heard words of wisdom straight from the Mahatma's mouth!"

Brahmin Rama, flushed with pride but pretending not to hear, continued to speak: "Of course, I would not presume to touch the Mahatma. He is only a Vaisya."

A hushed silence fell over the small assembly. A thin man near the front, a merchant and himself a member of the lesser Vaisya caste, ventured, "Even so, he is the great Mahatma."

"I fear that Mahatma Gandhi understands little of India's true history, and even less of the ancient texts," Brahmin Rama said.

The entire group caught its collective breath in a shocked gasp.

Rama quickly added, "Not from caste alone, you understand. No, mostly from living too long among the British."

"But, Brahmin," the thin man pushed, "we hear it said that all of India follows the Great Soul."

With a nervous hand, Brahmin Rama wiped perspiration from his forehead and once again pushed at his spectacles. "Mohandas Gandhi entreats us to accept outcastes as our equals," he said carefully. "The very same outcastes he describes as social lepers. When you say all of India follows him I must ask you: follows him where?"

"Do not tell me what you will do or where you will go!" Rajeev's angry words rolled from the back of the house, under Glory Anna's door and through her open window. "You are my wife. You will do as I say and you will go where I send you!"

"Maybe I do not want to get married," Glory Anna said quietly to Shridula.

"Maybe a new India put together like Rajeev put his family together would be even worse than the old India," Shridula suggested.

The voices stopped abruptly. Only the wail of a child echoed through the window.

"Everyone the same . . ." Shridula mused. "How could that work? Amina is a Muslim and a woman. Of course she wants to be equal to her Hindu husband. But Rajeev has all the power. He would not want to give that up. How can the weak be equally strong unless the strong agree to be equally weak?"

"Yes," Glory Anna mused. "I would not mind if you lived like me, but I would never want to live like you."

***

More villagers pressed in around Brahmin Rama, each with a question on his lips. Did the Mahatma really dress like a poverty-stricken Indian peasant? Was it true that he walked the width and breadth of the country? Would he come to Malabar? Did he say how soon he would force the British to leave India? Always, after each question, the people called out the same refrain: *Give us the answer in Gandhiji's exact words!*

To Brahmin Rama's troubled amazement, the villagers did not echo his criticisms of Mohandas Gandhi. Whatever the Mahatma's words, the villagers insisted their own opinion matched it exactly.

"So, then, does the Mahatma really say all castes should be considered equal?" a merchant near the back called out.

Brahmin Rama took a deep breath. "No, no! Not that way. The Great Soul says a scavenger must forever do the work of a scavenger, which is precisely my opinion." Rama straightened his back, and, with a voice now strong and even, declared, "I heard the Mahatma speak, and I can tell you honestly that in every way he is a Hindu of Hindus."

From the back of the crowd, next to the road, a voice challenged, "Is that so? Even with all the influence of the West on him?"

A startled look crossed Brahmin Rama's face. He searched the growing clusters of villagers for the speaker.

"Would a 'Hindu of Hindus in every way' insist on loving the most impure and cursed of creatures?" the speaker asked.

Ah, yes. Brahmin Rama clearly recognized the rude speaker as none other than Rajeev, son of landowner Saji Varghese. But before the Brahmin could fully piece his thoughts together and come up with a coherent response, Rajeev started in again: "Care for the poor. Respond to violence with nonviolence. All this sounds much more Christian than Hindu."

"Ridiculous!" Brahmin Rama sputtered. "Impossible!"

But Rajeev wasn't finished. "What of his push to open Hindu temples to all castes? Even Untouchables. I ask you, Brahmin Rama, would a Hindu of Hindus allow such a desecration of their holiest places?"

At first, the crowd fell silent and stared aghast at Rajeev. But then their eyes turned to the agitated Brahmin.

"The Mahatma and I think as one," Brahmin Rama said as forcefully as he could. "No Hindus must be allowed to convert to other religions. Not one man and not one woman! India is for Indians, and Indians are Hindu!"

25

March 1947

"Mahatma Gandhi is a Hindu," Shridula stated. "An Indian and a Hindu."

"I know that," Glory Anna said. "But he did live in England. That is where he heard the teachings of Jesus. He liked them so much that he took them as his own."

"You are making that up. The Mahatma is a Hindu."

"I have heard Rajeev say it again and again. Gandhiji especially liked the part of Jesus' teachings called the Sermon on the Mount."

Shridula looked doubtful. "What does that part say?"

"Well, I do not know," Glory Anna admitted. "Not exactly. But we could find out." She took her grandmother's Bible that now lay on the lowest shelf of the cupboard and flipped through page after page after page. "Here," she said. "This is the part about Jesus."

Glory Anna turned the page and read: "The Gospel according to Saint Matthew. Chapter one." Slowly she started to read: *The book of the generation of Jesus Christ, the son of David, the son of Abraham. Abraham begat Isaac; and Isaac begat Jacob;*

and Jacob begat Judas and his brethren; And Judas begat Phares and Zara of Thamar—"

"This does not make any sense!" Shridula interrupted. "Why would the Mahatma take any of these words for his own? I do not believe he did!"

For hours on end, Saji Stephen sat on his veranda and watched the road, all the while making a great pretense of tending to his business affairs. Morning after morning, as the sun climbed in the sky, he settled himself on the fine Persian carpet under the fragrant new blossoms on the jasmine vines and loudly called for his leather-bound accounting book. For the remainder of the day, he sat alone with the book open in his lap. He watched the road until he saw someone approach, at which time he focused his eyes on the book and made a great show of tracing his finger down the page while mumbling to himself.

"Fine morning," a hunched-backed man called out as he reverently touched his forehead. Saji Stephen bent lower and squinted at his accounting book, completely ignoring the man.

Two young Brahmins passed by, deep in conversation. They never turned their eyes to the landlord at all. Although Saji Stephen's face hardened and his jaw clenched, he pretended not to notice the slight.

All day long, travelers passed along the road, their possessions tied to their backs or balanced on their heads or piled into bullock carts. Especially merchants, who were inevitably laden down with wares destined for the market in the next village. People hurried by on their way to tend to business, and so did people who hoped to look as though they had business to which they needed to attend. Some called out greeting to Saji Stephen. A few respectfully touched their foreheads. More than a few paid him no mind at all. Saji Stephen did not acknowledge any of them.

"Father, I—" Nihal Amos began as he stepped out onto the veranda.

But Saji Stephen cut him off. "Go away! Can you not see how busy I am?"

For three days, from midmorning until the sunset, Saji Stephen passed his time in that way. On the fourth day, as evening approached and a cool breeze stirred the air, Saji Stephen finally spied Brahmin Rama's skinny frame heading up the road. Quickly he bent low over his book of accounts and wrinkled his brow in a great show of concentration.

Brahmin Rama drew near, but Saji Stephen huddled down lower still. When the Brahmin approached close enough to be heard, he called out, "You sent your son to embarrass me, Landlord!"

Saji Stephen looked up in feigned surprise. He replaced the absorbed look on his face with one of pained offense and said, "Please, Rama, I know nothing of such an embarrassment."

Brahmin Rama quickened his steps. "The Great Soul Gandhi and I are of one mind."

"Is that so?" Saji Stephen's eyebrows shot up in mock surprise. "You agree with the Mahatma that all castes should be equal? My, my, that does astonish me."

The Brahmin, his lips pursed tight and his eyes defiant, stepped up beside the landlord's veranda.

"You agree with Mohandas Gandhi that Hindu temples should be open to all, including Untouchables? How enlightening that must be to your Brahmin brothers." A smile teased at the edges of Saji Stephen's mouth. "Do come up and sit beside me. I would be most interested in hearing about your drastic change of mind."

Brahmin Rama didn't waste time pretending to protest. Instead, he stepped up, arranged his *mundu* around him, and sat down. Carefully he removed his spectacles and swiped at the perspiration-spotted lenses with the corner of his fine linen garment. "The Mahatma and I are of one mind on *most* things," he said. "On those that remain in question, Mr. Gandhi simply requires further instruction."

"In order for him to become the 'Hindu of Hindus in every way' you claim him to be?" Saji Stephen's small smile broke into an unabashed grin.

The Brahmin replaced his spectacles on his nose and wrapped the stems over his ears. "No," he said. "To overcome the contagion he received from his time with the British."

"*And seeing the multitudes, he went up into a mountain: and when he was set, his disciples came unto him: And he opened his mouth and taught them, saying* . . . Yes, yes!" Glory Anna said. "Here is the Sermon on the Mount, in chapter five of the book of Matthew!"

Shridula's eyes narrowed.

"*Blessed are the poor in spirit: for theirs is the kingdom of heaven.*

Blessed are they that mourn: for they shall be comforted.

Blessed are the meek: for they shall inherit the earth.

Blessed are they which do hunger and thirst after righteousness: for they shall be filled.

Blessed are the merciful: for they shall obtain mercy.

Blessed are the pure in heart: for they shall see God.

Blessed are the peacemakers: for they shall be called the children of God.

Blessed are they which are persecuted for righteousness' sake: for theirs is the kingdom of heaven.

Blessed are ye, when men shall revile you, and persecute you, and shall say all manner of evil against you falsely, for my sake.

Rejoice, and be exceeding glad: for great is your reward in heaven: for so persecuted they the prophets which were before you."

"The Mahatma really teaches all that?" Shridula asked.

"I suppose so," Glory Anna replied. "That is what Rajeev says."

❧

Saji Stephen stared straight into the Brahmin's face. "Right now Dr. Ambedkar is busy stirring up the Untouchables, urging them to refuse to be Hindus. But of course this is not news to you."

"Certainly not," Rama replied. "But why should the words of so insignificant a fool make any difference to you?"

"Because that insignificant fool commands great respect among the hoards of Untouchables."

Brahmin Rama shrugged dismissively. "Hindus follow the Vedas. No other religion that—"

"There! That is precisely Dr. Ambedkar's point, is it not?" Saji Stephen interrupted. "He says Hinduism is not rightly a religion at all, but only a political scheme crafted by the upper castes to make it possible for them to rule India."

"Foolishness!"

"If so, then it is foolishness that grows more popular by the day."

Brahmin Rama sniffed. "Where is the problem in that, anyway? The upper castes *should* rule India!"

"*Blessed are the poor in spirit,*" Glory Anna read. "Well, that is not this family. We are not poor in anything."

"We are poor in everything," Shridula said. "Maybe the kingdom of heaven is for Untouchables."

"*Blessed are they that mourn,*" Glory Anna read. "Mourn. Hmmm. . . . Is mourning like complaining? Everyone here complains."

Shridula leaned over so that she could get a good look at the Bible on Glory Anna's lap. "*Blessed are the meek,*" she read. "What does 'meek' mean?"

"I do not know," Glory Anna said. "But whatever it is, the Vargheses must be it because they did inherit the earth."

"*Blessed are they which do hunger and thirst after . . . after . . .*"

"After righteousness," Glory Anna said. "It means good-ness. Blessed are those who really want to be good."

Shridula said nothing, but Glory Anna knew exactly what she was thinking and it made her extremely uncomfortable.

"*Blessed are the merciful,*" Glory Anna quickly read. "*Blessed are the pure in heart.*"

Shridula bit her tongue to keep it quiet.

"*Blessed are the peacemakers.* Ha!" Glory Anna snickered. "This family is the troublemakers!"

"*Blessed are they which are persecuted for righteousness' sake,*" Shridula read.

"Well, this family is persecuted," Glory Anna said. "And reviled, too, and all manner of evil is said against them."

"For righteousness' sake?" Shridula asked. "Because of their goodness?"

Glory Anna didn't answer.

"I am a friend of Mahatma Gandhi," Brahmin Rama said to Saji Stephen. "I believe you also to be his friend—in your own way, of course. True, Gandhiji has areas of blindness. But it is in those very areas that he most desperately needs men like me . . . and you. He is, after all, but a Vaisya. If he is to guide India, it is for us, the *Brahmins* and *Kshatriyas*, to guide him."

"Not to guide him," Saji Stephen said. "It is for us to rule over him. And over all of India!"

✦

"Here," Glory Anna said, handing the Bible to Shridula. "You read."

Tracing each word with her finger, Shridula read slowly, "*Ye have heard that it hath been said, An eye for an eye, and a tooth for a tooth: But I say unto you, That ye resist not evil: but whosoever shall smite thee on thy right cheek, turn to him the other also.*"

"There!" Glory Anna announced. "That is not Hindu at all, but it is what the Mahatma teaches." She pulled the Bible off Shridula's lap and ran her own finger down the lines. "And this, too . . .

"*Ye have heard that it hath been said, Thou shalt love thy neighbour and hate thine enemy. But I say unto you, Love your enemies, bless them that curse you, do good to them that hate you, and pray for them which despitefully use you, and persecute you.*"

Shridula shook her head. "I do not care if Jesus said it. I do not care if Mahatma Gandhi does it. It is not right! Love the ones who beat you? And starved your old parents? And called up the evil spirits to fill a snake with poison to kill your mother? No! I will never love such a one!"

✦

"Whenever your son Rajeev speaks, he uses Christian words, laced with Christian thoughts," Brahmin Rama said to Saji Stephen. "Such talk is extremely offensive to Indians."

"The Varghese family is as Indian as you are!" Saji Stephen said. "Everyone in the village knows we are a Christian family with ancient Christian roots."

"True, but the words your Rajeev chooses are abrasive and offensive. Especially when he uses them to argue against a true India."

"You mean a Hindu India?"

A flicker of frustration flashed in the Brahmin's eye. Only for a moment, but long enough for Saji Stephen to see and make note. "What I mean is that your Rajeev pushes the tenets of the Christian religion over Hinduism."

"You mean by agreeing with Mahatma Gandhi and the multitudes that follow him?"

Frustration clouded the Brahmin's face. "Who will you be, Landlord?" he demanded. "Christian or Indian?"

"A Christian Indian," Saji Stephen said. "Just as my family has been for as long as anyone can remember."

"The words 'Christian' and 'Indian' do not fit together as equals," Brahmin Rama insisted. "A *Christian* Indian speaks the way your son speaks. The words of such a one may make Untouchables smile and Englishmen cheer, but they will certainly infuriate the ones who are soon to rule India. An Indian *Christian*, however, can hold to his beliefs while also demonstrating that he truly is an Indian."

Saji Stephen opened his mouth to speak. But because he could think of no clever rebuttal, he closed his lips and said nothing.

"At this moment the entire village is busy getting ready for the *Vishu* festival," Brahmin Rama said. "Do you desire to retain your prestige and power in the area? Then allow me to send a servant to prepare your house for the festival. Let it be known throughout the village that the first thing the Varghese family saw on the morning of the New Year was Lord Krishna reigning over the *Vishukkani*."

"I am not a Hindu."

"Fine. Keep your true religion tucked away in your heart where it belongs," Rama said. "The way to hush up those who would speak against you is to show them you are a true Indian."

✒

As the first light of New Year's dawn streaked the sky, Saji Stephen hurried throughout his house calling, "Come, come! Do not open your eyes until you get to the veranda!"

In other homes in the village, whether rich houses or humble huts, mothers led their young ones, eyes squeezed shut, to their own prepared altars. Everywhere, families opened their eyes to the *Vishukkani*, the first sight of the New Year.

"Really, Father, I never believed you would make yourself so beholden to a Brahmin," Rajeev groused.

"A ridiculous idea!" Nihal Amos muttered as he felt his way along the wall and out to the veranda. "The very idea of kowtowing to that scrawny Rama is absolutely absurd!"

Saji Stephen paid his complaining sons no mind. It was his house and they had no choice but to do as he commanded.

"Will we get a treat?" Rajeev's little son Wafi asked. He danced about excitedly, his eyes shut tight—until he ran into Glory Anna.

"Be careful!" Glory Anna scolded. She grasped more tightly to Shridula's hand.

"Now!" Saji Stephen called. "Open your eyes to a new year of happiness and prosperity!"

What a glorious spectacle lay before them! Golden oil lamps—*nilavilakku*—cast a striking glow over a splendid display of symbols of prosperity: platters of special fruit—coconut halves, mangoes, bananas, and golden cucumbers. All this was set off with a golden spray of *kanikkonna* blossoms. A gilt-edged metal mirror stood in the center. Piled around were new clothes for everyone and special gifts for Wafi and the other children. And over all stood an intricately decorated idol of Lord Krishna, reigning supreme over the dawning new year.

Sheeba Esther gasped out loud. "What have you done?" she demanded of Saji Stephen.

But Wafi squealed with delight, and Saji Stephen busied himself handing around the new clothes.

"Dress quickly," he instructed. "We must hurry to the temple. We must prepare ourselves for the festival to come."

Every member of the Varghese family was to be conspicuously present, dressed in new clothes, for the entire day of festival songs and dancing and feasting and prayer. Saji Stephen demanded it. They paraded to the village marketplace, Saji Stephen on the front seat of his gaily decorated bullock cart and his two sons seated in back of him. The women and children walked behind the cart. They were a sullen group. Glory Anna stayed close to Sheeba Esther, who wrung her hands in continual distress. Only Rajeev's little Wafi bubbled with excitement.

As they approached the marketplace, Amina's constant scolding of her children was interrupted by cheerful calls of "Rajeev! Rajeev Varghese!"

Rajeev looked around in confusion.

"What of the new India, Rajeev?" a villager called out to him.

Only then did the landlord's elder son notice the villagers gathering around the cart and how truly pleased they were to see him. They smiled up and shouted out greetings. Immediately Rajeev's scowl turned into a campaigner's grin.

Brahmin Rama had told Saji Stephen, "The people love Mahatma Gandhi." His words were true. Saji Stephen could see that. But Rama had also warned, "The Mahatma neither likes nor trusts Christians." So Saji Stephen tossed everything Christian from his words and demeanor, and threw himself wholeheartedly into the Hindu festival.

"Ha! Ha!" Brahmin Rama laughed when he saw the landlord. "Change your name, and no one in India will suspect you are a Christian!"

"Oh, but they will," Saji Stephen said. "For I will sit on my veranda and in plain sight of everyone, I will eat an entire platter of roasted mutton smothered in ghee. Only a Christian has the freedom to do that."

✍

Shridula had watched as the Varghese family paraded away, Glory Anna and Sheeba Esther following after the landlord's cart. She had watched as the household servants cleaned up quickly from the morning so that they too could hurry down the road to join the celebration. Only Shridula remained behind.

How strange to be all alone in the landlord's huge house.

"Stay in Glory Anna's room and do not come out!" Udit ordered before he left. He had glared at Shridula as though he expected her to creep around the house and peek about into forbidden places. Of course she would not.

Shridula lay down in her corner of Glory Anna's room and tried to sleep. She couldn't. The pop . . . pop . . . popping of firecrackers drifted from the village. Shridula got up, opened the door a crack, and peeked out. Nothing outside but lonely silence broken by the distant popping. She closed the door and lay back down. How she wished she could sneak down to the settlement to visit her father. But she dare not. She squeezed her eyes closed and forced herself to sleep.

Dancing, dancing in the sunshine, following after the Lord Krishna as the gaily decorated image paraded along the crowded road . . . Laughing, laughing, her mouth sweet with treats . . . Singing, singing, joyous music . . .

Shridula awakened with a start. Jerking upright, she struggled to understand where the festival had gone. No longer did sun stream through the window. Shridula came fully awake to realize she had been asleep for some time.

Out in the great room, something rustled softly. Shridula rubbed her eyes. The servants must be back from the festival. She stood up and listened for their voices.

Nothing.

As Shridula sank back down in her corner, footsteps hurried past. She crept to the door and eased it open just a crack. A single figure—tall and lean and singularly shabby—moved through the gathering darkness of the great room. The figure reached out and grabbed an ivory carving from the tabletop, then snatched up the golden candlestick beside it. Shridula gasped out loud.

The shadowy figure swung around and stared into her face.

"Hari!" Shridula exclaimed.

Jyoti's elder son stared back at her with an even gaze. He didn't even attempt to run.

"What are you doing?" Shridula demanded.

"Helping the landlord share his wealth," Hari said with a laugh.

"No, no! You must not steal from this house!"

Hari's mouth twisted into a vicious sneer. "You would defend this cruel master?" He quickly added, "Oh, I see how it is. You were left here, were you not? Yes, because you are good enough to be Master Landlord's house slave, but too worthless to take part in the festival! Instead of scolding me, you should help me empty out his house!"

"Please!" Shridula begged. "If you take anything away, I will be blamed for it."

"Then do not stay here. Come away with me," Hari said. "Even a girl can fight for the Communists."

"Please, Hari! Please! My father saved your life."

Hari's face hardened. "My life would not have needed saving if the workers had helped the Communists take power from upper caste hands and—"

"The servants will be back any time!"

Hari shot Shridula a look of contempt. He turned and dashed out through the open door, the ivory carving and golden candlestick clutched tight in his hands. What else he may have tucked into his clothes, Shridula couldn't imagine.

As the sun set, as the landlord and his family danced for all to see, as the servants walked the road back to Saji Stephen's house, Shridula sank into her corner and wept.

26

April 1947

𝒮hridula awoke long before dawn. Another day of waiting for the inevitable. Two weeks had passed and no one had yet mentioned the missing ivory carving and golden candlestick. But they would. She knew they would.

That morning, Shridula and Glory Anna occupied themselves in the great room—Glory Anna adding to her growing collection of paintings and Shridula running to and fro in an effort to keep paints and paper before her. Sheeba Esther walked through and stopped directly in front of the shelf where the stolen items had stood. Shridula caught her breath and tried not to watch. For what seemed an incredibly long time, Sheeba Esther gazed at the empty shelf. But then she abruptly turned her attention to Glory Anna's painting of the strutting blue peacock that ruled the landlord's garden.

"Beautiful," Sheeba Esther exclaimed. "You managed to paint the tail feathers in such lifelike detail. And the color you used here . . ."

Shridula stopped listening.

Fetch Glory Anna's supplies so she can paint. Sit by Glory Anna and read with her. Listen to Glory Anna play the sitar.

Every once in a while, squeeze out time to run back to the settlement for a short visit with her father. And all the time, wait, wait, wait for the inevitable.

"Hurry now and move back to your room," Sheeba Esther was saying to Glory Anna. "Amina is coming with her children, and she will be most unhappy to see you here."

✿

Saji Stephen shut his leather-bound book of accounts with an impatient slam. "The British have spoken. It is actually going to happen. I heard all about it on the radio this morning. Before the British leave our country, they will cut it up into portions and give it away piece by piece."

"Do not blame the British for dividing the country," Rajeev said. "All the parties in India agreed to the partition. Nehru and the other nationalist leaders, and Jinnah who speaks so loudly for the Muslim League. Of course, Ambedkar had to whine out his piece on behalf of the Untouchables. Even Master Tara Singh, who represents the Sikhs, had to have his say. Yes, the Sikhs!"

"The lot of them actually *agreed* on something?" Nihal Amos's tone rang of ridicule. "I did not believe that possible."

"India will be partitioned along religious lines," Rajeev said. "The areas mostly Hindu and Sikh will be the new Union of India. Those predominantly Muslim will make up the new Dominion of Pakistan."

"Good," Saji Stephen said. "It is done, then. That was not so bad."

Rajeev shot his father a look of disdain. "Not so bad because you are down here in the south and it will not be your land divided up and given away?"

Saji Stephen tossed his book of accounts onto the carpet beside him and slapped his hand down on it. "It has to be done. And every one of us will share in the cost."

Nihal Amos stared hard at the leather-bound book. "By that, you mean every one of the workers."

Saji Stephen shoved the book under the jasmine vines and out of sight. "By that I mean every single person—except those of you who do nothing but sit and eat and talk!"

"Punjab and Bengal have Muslim majorities, yet they are set to be split," Rajeev said. "I cannot think that arrangement will end in any way that could possibly be called satisfactory."

❧

Aaaaaahh . . . lo! Aaaaaahh . . . lo! A grating shriek echoed through the landlord's house. Aaaaaahh . . . lo!

Shridula awoke with a start and jumped up from her sleeping mat. "What is it?" she cried in alarm. "What is happening?"

Aaaaaahh . . . lo! Aaaaaahh . . . lo! Aaaaaahh . . . lo!

Glory Anna rolled over in the dark and laughed out loud. "The peacock, of course."

"That beautiful bird makes such a terrible racket?"

"Depends on what he wants to say," Glory Anna said. "Sometimes he coos . . . or gobbles. That shriek is his cry of warning."

"Warning about what?" Shridula asked.

"I do not know. Maybe an intruder. But probably just a rival peacock who wants the lady peahen to see him spread out his fancy feathers."

"All that noise just to show off?"

"Birds or humans," Glory Anna said, "that is the way men are!"

Aaaaaahh . . . lo! Aaaaaahh . . . lo!

Rajeev opened his eyes to see his brother already sitting up. "What is it?" he asked.

"Nothing," Nihal Amos said. "No intruder."

"Fool of a bird!" Rajeev groused as he rolled over onto his side.

"The sun is rising," Nihal Amos said. "We should be out at the storehouses early this day, anyway. You get up and I will rouse Father."

"Uhhh," Rajeev grunted. "Fool of a bird!"

"Sheeba Esther says we can go out on the veranda today," Glory Anna announced as Shridula came back to the room with a basin of water for their morning wash. "We can stay all day if we please."

"What about the landlord? He will not want us out there with him."

"He will be away until late afternoon. Rajeev and Nihal Amos, too."

Free! And on such a perfect day! The sun didn't yet burn too hot, and the breeze blew fresh with blossoms and the fragrance of ripening fruit.

"Sit beside me on Saji Stephen's expensive Persian carpet," Glory Anna called as she bounded outside. Shridula hesitated, but Glory Anna insisted. "Come on! No one will see us. The men are gone, and the women will not come around without the men here."

Shridula closed her eyes and breathed in the delicious fragrance of new jasmine blooms.

"We could call for Saji Stephen's servant Udit and tell him to bring us a plate of ripe mangos and guavas," Glory Anna suggested. "Come on, Shridula; sit beside me on this expensive carpet."

Shriudula hesitated. In the end, she settled herself nearby, on a simple woven mat.

"We should sit out here more often," Glory Anna said. "We could watch the road and talk to everyone who comes by."

They did call for Udit to bring a plate of fruit, and they ate every last piece. They also watched the road, though few passed by on it, and those who did ignored the girls. Shridula and Glory Anna talked a bit, but when the fruit was gone, they sat in silence and wondered what to do next.

"Watch this," Glory Anna said. She scrunched her brow, puckered up her mouth, and uttered a loud: *Aaaaaahh . . . lo! Aaaaaahh . . . lo!*

Shridula cried out and slapped her hands over her ears. But to her amazement, an answering call echoed back from the garden: *Aaaaaahh . . . lo! Aaaaaahh . . . lo!*

"How did you do that?" Shridula exclaimed.

"Watch," Glory Anna said. Again she scrunched and puckered: *Aaaaaahh . . . lo! Aaaaaahh . . . lo!*

Aaaaaahh . . . lo! Aaaaaahh . . . lo! This time the answer came from just around the corner.

Again Glory Anna puckered her mouth and called: *Aaaaaahh . . . lo! Aaaaaahh . . . lo!*

No answer this time. Instead, the beautiful peacock paraded from around the corner, its blue feathers glistening iridescent in the sunlight, the feathered crown on its head bobbing in time to its strut. The peacock passed directly in front of the girls, then stopped to fan out its spectacular tail.

"How did you do that?" Shridula gasped.

"Easy," said Glory Anna. "Watch. I will teach you."

✒

When Saji Stephen and his two sons arrived at the laborers' settlement, only a small crowd waited to greet them. On cue, the group cheered, but only in a politely reserved way.

"Perhaps your . . . *Communist* . . . brothers are not as pleased to see you as you expected them to be," Rajeev murmured to Nihal Amos with a smirk.

"Perhaps they are displeased to see me in the company of a stingy landlord and an agent of the British government," Nihal Amos said.

"Agent of the British government? I am no such thing! As a matter of fact, it was I who—"

"Stop it!" Saji Stephen ordered. "Both of you talk and talk and talk about unity. But then you argue and argue and argue to the very brink of exhaustion. I want no part of either of you!"

✒

"Come on, Shridula. Sit with me on Saji Stephen's Persian carpet," Glory Anna insisted.

"No. I must not."

Glory Anna scooted over into the jasmine vines to give her more room. "Come on! You have to obey me because I am your master and I command you. Come and sit on this carpet!"

"Please, no. If someone should see me . . . Because I am an Untouchable, you see, and I . . ."

"Sit beside me! No one will see us except Sheeba Esther, and she likes you."

Slowly—her head bowed low, her face etched with fear—Shridula sank down on the edge of the Persian carpet—but only on its fringes.

"I wish we could come out here more often," Glory Anna said. "Maybe if Sheeba Esther would tell her husband to tell his father that we should have the right to . . . to . . . What is this?"

From the far end of the Persian carpet, tucked back under the jasmine vines, Glory Anna pulled out Saji Stephen's leather-bound book of accounts.

Glory Anna opened the leather cover. "I know what this is," she said. "I never touched it before, though. Or looked inside it." She opened the cover, then turned one page. "Look, Shridula, I will show you how to cipher."

Glory Anna laid the leather-bound book between them, and Shridula leaned in closer.

"These first pages are hard to read," Glory Anna said. "The ink is smudged." She turned another page. "Can you read this writing?"

Shridula bent down close and ran her finger down the page. She started to say no, but then one name caught her eye. "V . . . Vir . . . Vir. . ." Shridula scrunched up her forehead and bent closer over the ink scratches. "Vir . . ."

"Virat!" Glory Anna said. "Can you not see that it says 'Virat'?"

"Virat?" Shridula looked up at Glory Anna. "That was the name of my grandfather."

Shridula took the book and lifted it into her lap. Carefully she traced her finger down the marks. She read: *Virat: Injured son treated at English Mission Medical Clinic. Journeyed to deposit the boy; journeyed to bring him back. Fresh sari, mundu, chaddar for the journey.* ~~20 rupees 40 rupees~~ *80 rupees.* She looked up at Glory Anna. "What does it mean?"

"The twenty rupees was the loan the moneylender gave. My grandfather, I suppose. It is his book," Glory Anna said. "My grandfather doubled the debt because of the journey to the medical clinic. Twenty and twenty more make forty rupees. Adding that together is ciphering. Then he doubled that because of the new clothes. Forty and another forty makes eighty. Do you understand?"

Shridula stared at the marks. Slowly she moved her finger down the page and looked at each of the other marks. So many of them!

"He took away some of the debt because of the work," Glory Anna said. "See? Ten rupees erased down here."

"Yes, but right next to it is thirty rupees added."

"To pay back for food, and for using the hut."

"And then another fifty rupees. What is that for?"

Glory Anna bent low and read the scratched words: "'Interest on the debt.' That means tax for borrowing the money. All the moneylenders charge that."

At one point, young Ashish's earnings also began to count as credit: "5 rupees." But down the page Latha's credits stopped, and finally, so did Virat's. Ninety rupees were added for "body disposal."

"My grandparents died," Shridula said.

Shridula traced further down the page: charges for her parents' marriage, charges for the death of each of their sons, charges for their new child, Shridula, charges for her mother's death. Charges were listed for the used *saris* Sheeba Esther instructed Shridula to wear, the food Shridula ate at the landlord's house, and even for the mat she slept on beside Glory Anna's bed.

Struggling to stop her finger from shaking, Shridula pointed to the last notation: 8,789 rupees. "Is this the last line of the debt of my father?" Shridula asked.

"It is his debt right now," Glory Anna said, "but there is never a last line."

"You knew all this?" Shridula asked.

"Yes. I thought you knew, too."

"As long as I live, I will belong to your family," Shridula said.

"Yes."

Shridula closed the book of accounts and shoved it over toward Glory Anna. She got up from the Persian carpet and walked back to Glory Anna's room.

"I am sorry!" Glory Anna called after her. "I thought you knew!"

⁂

Early in the afternoon, while the bullock cart was still lost in a billow of dust, the girls could hear Rajeev and Nihal Amos shouting at each other.

"Amina is gone from the great room, Glory Anna," Sheeba Esther said quickly. "You can go back in and paint a picture. Or get out the sitar and play for a while, if you wish."

Glory Anna made a face. "I am tired of that. It is all I ever do! I want to see *outside* this house."

Sheeba Esther sighed and glanced about nervously. With a cautious smile, she said, "The day is still pleasant enough. Would you care to accompany me to the market?"

Sheeba Esther intended her invitation for Glory Anna alone. But Glory Anna would not hear of leaving Shridula behind. "She has never seen the market either."

"She is Untouchable," Sheeba Esther explained. "The merchants will not allow her to come around their stands."

Shridula longed to stay behind. For now she knew that every turn of the cart wheel, every bite of a treat, every sip of water would be another notation added to her father's debt. But no one asked her opinion.

All the way to the market, Glory Anna chattered nonstop questions. What would they see? Could she buy a new *sari*? Would people know they were the landlord's family? Would they find sweets to eat?

Sheeba Esther patiently did her best to answer each question, and she never once stopped smiling.

The marketplace bustled with activity. Fruits and squash and cucumbers lay spread out in attractive ways. Behind the displays stood filled baskets. Merchants offered all sorts of wares, including baskets of marigold garlands and coconuts to offer the gods and goddesses. Two fisherfolk sat behind woven baskets of dried fish, and spice merchants displayed a lavish array of sacks filled to the top with exotic spices in many fragrances.

"Look!" Glory Anna cried. "New *saris*, and in so many beautiful colors! Let us find one for me."

Sheeba Esther looked at Shridula. "Not you," she said. Her voice wasn't unkind, but it was firm. "You can wait for us in the cart or you can stand off to the side of the road until we come back for you."

Sheeba glanced further down the road, past the orderly displays of wares. "Wait," she said. "Down there! I almost forgot. Untouchable women sit at the far end of the market with their own wares to sell. You could go down there and look. I will have the driver call for you when we finish."

Shridula almost didn't go down the road to the Untouchable vendors. It would have been much easier to watch from the cart, safely away from prying eyes. But the idea of Untouchables selling at the marketplace was too intriguing to pass up. So she plucked up her courage and walked alongside the road toward the village.

Yes, these women really were Untouchables. Shridula could see the difference—squat, dark, and worn. Definitely her people. Wives of the fishermen sat on the ground behind baskets of hard-dried fish. A girl had a few eggs for sale. The woman beside her, several containers of milk. Another had a few cucumbers, eggplants, and chili peppers spread out on a cloth. Several women sat behind large baskets of wild custard apples. The fruit looked no different from the thick-skinned, seedy custard apples Shridula saw growing high up in the trees beside the road. A woman at the end displayed a stack of mats she had woven from dried river reeds and dyed with vegetable colors.

"Who buys those?" Shridula asked her in amazement. "I mean, they are very nice mats, but does not everyone make their own?"

"Those who have time and no money make their own," the woman said. "Those who have money and little time, buy from me. What about you? Do you have time or money?"

"I have neither," Shridula said.

"Then get away from me," the woman told her. "Make room for those who want to buy."

Shridula stayed at the Untouchable end of the market until the driver of the bullock cart called to her from the road. All the way home, Glory Anna talked of the marketplace, of her new pink and yellow *sari*, of the packet of sweets she clutched in her hand. Shridula pretended to listen, but in her mind she kept seeing the Untouchable women. Imagine them selling at the market! Just imagine!

"Sheeba Esther!" Saji Stephen's voice roared out before the cart had even stopped. "Bring that Untouchable girl to me!"

"What is the matter with him?" Sheeba Esther whispered to the girls. "Did you do something to upset him?"

Glory Anna protested their innocence, but Shridula sat silently in the cart and waited. Even as a wave of terror washed over her, the landlord's words lifted the burden that had weighed on her more heavily every day. The excruciating wait had finally come to an end. What would be, would be.

The landlord's family had already assembled in the great room—Rajeev and Nihal Amos seated side by side on the sofa. Amina perched stiffly on the side of the bed, her little ones around her.

Saji Stephen made a great show of taking his place in a large armchair, conveniently positioned to allow him to glower around at the others. When Glory Anna entered, he motioned her over to the wall. She stood uncomfortably, shifting her weight from one foot to the other.

Next came Sheeba Esther. She looked stricken. Confused. Keeping her eyes on the floor, she led Shridula into the room and told her to stand directly in front of Saji Stephen.

"After all I did for you," Saji Stephen growled at Shridula. "After all I did for your father. You would repay my kindness like this!"

Tears filled the girl's eyes.

"My servant searched Glory Anna's room and found nothing. What did you do with the things you stole from my house? Tell me! I order you to tell me!"

Shridula bit hard on her lip, but she couldn't stop the tears from tumbling down her cheeks. She longed to proclaim her innocence, to tell the landlord about Hari. Maybe Nihal Amos already knew about him. She sneaked a glance at Nihal, but his face was blank. Perhaps Sheeba Esther also knew. Was that possible?

"She passed them along to her father, of course," Rajeev said with a wave of his hand. "You should be searching his hut."

"No!" Shridula cried. "My father knows nothing about it! I was not the one who stole from you, Master Landlord. Please, it was not me!"

27

May 1947

*S*hridula leaned forward and whispered, "A new *sahib* has come from England to send the British away and give India back to Indians, *Appa*. They call him Lord Mountbatten."

"Lord Mountbatten?" Ashish asked. "He is a British god?"

"No, no," Shridula said. "Not like Lord Krishna. A British lord just means a high caste British man."

"A British Brahmin?"

"More like a *Kshatriya*, I think. Like the landlord."

"I see," Ashish said thoughtfully. "Are we to worship this high caste *sahib* who is not quite a god?"

"No, he has work to do," Shridula said. "His job is to give India back to the Indians."

Despite the stifling heat, Shridula and her father talked in hushed tones, crouched together inside their hut with the door pulled closed. Even so, a voice called from outside, "Ask her if the British god will come here, Ashish. Ask her will he set us free."

"I do not know," Shridula said to the voice. "No one at the landlord's house ever speaks about Untouchables."

❦

"Still more violence in the Punjab!" Rajeev stormed. "The Muslims will not stop until they carve the crown off the head of India and keep it for themselves!"

Saji Stephen's eyes narrowed. "Let them have it if that will quiet them. Or throw out every last Muslim and keep the country for the Hindus. Why should I care? The Punjab is far away from here."

Rajeev heaved an irritated sigh. "Really, Father, is it impossible for you to think any further than the end of your own fields?"

"It would do well for you to think a bit more about our own fields! Our storehouses are all but empty. The workers demand more food, even though they know I have no more to give them. When I fail to do the impossible, they punish me with their laziness."

"Those are but small troubles compared to—"

"Now I am told my winter fields are stunted, too, and that they overflow with weeds. I pray for a good harvest, but I know I will not get one. Soon the entire village will be hungry, and who will they blame for their aching stomachs? The Muslims in the Punjab? No. They will blame me!"

Scowling and muttering about the state of the nation, Rajeev made a great show of pulling himself to his feet.

Saji Stephen ignored him.

Rajeev stalked back into the house, slamming the door behind him. "Udit!" he called. "Udit!" The Sudra servant hurried over and Rajeev ordered, "Prepare the cart for me! Not the slow bullock cart. The fast cart pulled by the horse!"

❦

By pushing the horse to make all haste, and forcing those on the road to scurry for their lives, Rajeev arrived at the English Mission Medical Clinic in record time. He strode confidently up to the door, balled his hand into a fist and banged on it.

"You again," Dr. Cooper sighed when he saw Rajeev. "I really am quite busy. What do you want this time?"

"I be coming to see the lady called as Miss Abigail Davidson," Rajeev said. He held his head high and assumed the most condescending tone he could manage.

Dr. Cooper looked the Indian up and down, from his dusty sandals to the nicely woven fabric of his *mundu* to the *kurta* shirt that covered him above the waist.

"Isaiah!" Dr. Cooper called, his eyes still on Rajeev.

When no one responded, the doctor called again, but more loudly: "Isaiah!" Still no response. Finally, with undisguised irritation, the doctor shouted, "Krishna!" Immediately the scarred man with the twisted face appeared.

"Take this . . . *Indian* . . . to Miss Abigail," Dr. Cooper stepped back into the clinic and slammed the door shut.

⟡

The first thing Shridula noticed amiss was the grain scattered around the earthenware pots in her father's hut. And although her *appa's* skin was baked dark and tough as leather, she was certain that bruises showed through the dirt on his chin and around his eye. She leaned close and whispered, "I did not steal anything."

"I know," Ashish said.

"But I know who did."

Ashish said nothing, nor did the expression on his face change.

Leaning in closer still, she breathed, "It was Hari."

"The scavenger, then," Ashish said. "The one whose life I already saved."

"He thinks he is doing the right thing by making the land-lord share his wealth with the people."

"The people?" Ashish asked. "Have you seen any of that wealth? I have not seen any of it. Only Hari has seen the wealth. What you and I see is the punishment he left for us to endure."

"What should I do, *Appa?*"

"I have no answers for you, Daughter. I do not know."

"Of course I shall not return to England!" Miss Abigail Davidson insisted to Rajeev. (Miss Abigail didn't even try to converse in Malayalam any more. It was up to Rajeev to do his best in English.)

She handed him the porcelain cup decorated with forget-me-nots and filled it with tea. Passing him the pitcher of cream, she said, "In the forty years I have been in India, I have gone back to England but once, and then only with great reluctance. My mother had arranged a marriage for me, you see, and I was duty bound to at least make the acquaintance of the unfortunate young man."

"But . . . your husband, then?" Rajeev asked. "He is not to be coming to India beside you?"

"Alfred was not a pleasant man," Miss Abigail said. "Not a pleasant man at all. Shallow and doughy: those were my impressions when I first saw him. On further association, I found him to also be whiny, somewhat like a spoiled child. When I expressed my dismay to my mother, she responded that I should be thankful to have a young man with any breeding at all. She said he was the best husband one such as I could hope to secure. Can you imagine? The following day I left London, still a single woman. I went straight to the docks and eagerly awaited the next ship to Madras."

Rajeev stared at her.

"You do think me foolish, do you not?" Miss Abigail asked.

Rajeev lifted his cup to his lips and noisily sipped his tea. Foolish was exactly what he thought her, though he knew better than to say so. This white-haired woman with skin like wadded-up paper. With blue eyes so pale and filmy, she must surely be too blind to tell an Englishman from an Indian. A foolish English woman who ran away from the husband her father's family found for her so that she could sit out her life on a rooftop in India, dressed up in a *sari*, and sip tea all alone. Oh, yes, Rajeev thought her foolish indeed!

"The doctor and his wife. They are to be leaving India?" Rajeev asked Miss Abigail.

"Most assuredly. Already they have begun to pack."

"The English Mission Medical Clinic. It is to be belonging to you, then?"

"No, no, not to me. Most certainly not to me. Whatever happens, the clinic will still belong to the Medical Mission— although I do intend to stay here, and, as much as possible, to be of help to those who need me."

With some difficulty, Rajeev replaced the fine porcelain cup on its fine porcelain saucer. Without looking up at Miss Abigail, he said most delicately, "It is being to your benefit to be having a member of the government of the new India at your personal disposal, no?"

For some time, Miss Abigail sipped at her tea in silence. Finally she cleared her throat and said, "My dear sir. Do you have some specific proposal you wish to present to me?"

"India is to be changing," Rajeev said. "English peoples are to be needing friends. Indians also are to be needing friends.

I am coming here today to be offering you my friendship, and also my protection in the days that are to be coming."

"More tea?" Miss Abigail asked.

"I am to be offering more protection right now, in these present uncertainties, do you see, but also in the greater uncertainties after the British peoples are to be going away. In return, I am to be asking for your friendship and your support when the British are to be making India ready for a new government."

"More tea?" Miss Abigail said again.

Rajeev sighed in exasperation. He leaned forward and his voice took on a tone of urgency. "I cannot be knowing what you might be needing," he said. "I cannot be knowing what I might be needing. But if matters are not well for you—or for me—we might be agreeing to be protecting . . . mutually, that is . . . to be protecting—"

"Are you asking me to shelter you from the British soldiers?" Miss Abigail demanded. "Why, yes, I do believe you are. You want me to hide you here in the clinic! Why, my good sir, what a thing to ask of me!"

Miss Abigail, who had risen from her bed as soon as the first rays of sun peeked through her window, longed to sink back into her bed with the setting sun. Certainly she did not fancy an evening with the long-winded Dr. Cooper and his tiresome wife. Nor, she was quite certain, did they fancy an evening with her. What the good doctor would want to discover was why the Indian man had been so interested in conferring with her. Not only was it none of his business, but she wasn't at all certain herself. As she thought back on the afternoon, she found it all most confusing.

Still, the Coopers were leaving India soon, and they had requested her presence through a politely written note of invitation. Were Miss Abigail to beg off, they would consider her extremely rude. Really, what choice did she have? She would go, but she wouldn't stay long. Perhaps she would plead a headache. Yes, that's exactly what she would do—plead a dreadful headache!

Krishna walked her to the clinic, but the doctor met them at the door and bid him a curt farewell. To Miss Abigail he said, "Ah, my dear Miss Davidson, so good of you to come." He ushered her to the straight-backed chair she so disliked.

"There, now, are you quite comfortable?" Susanna Cooper asked in a tone Miss Abigail found terribly condescending. "We cannot have you sitting in a draft, can we, Miss Davidson?"

Miss Abigail insisted she was perfectly comfortable.

"I must say, I did not realize you were in the habit of sharing your wisdom with Indians," Dr. Cooper said in an attempt at levity.

Miss Abigail raised her eyebrows and shot him a stiff, noncommittal smile.

"That Indian . . . Raja, or some such name, I do believe. He has been here before. Is he in need of something from us?"

"What sort of something might you have in mind, Doctor?" Miss Abigail asked.

Wicked of her to so thoroughly confound him, perhaps, but she did enjoy the game.

"Well, yes . . ." Dr. Cooper did his best to hide his growing agitation. He coughed, then cleared his throat.

Miss Abigail fixed him in an impassive stare.

"Rather," Dr. Cooper continued. "Well. I am pleased, then, that there is nothing about which I must need concern myself."

Miss Abigail held her gaze steady.

"Dash it all, Miss Davidson, those people are not to be trusted! I should think you would understand that after so many years out here among them!"

Indignation lit Miss Abigail's aged face. "'Those people,' Doctor? I suppose Indians might say the very same thing of the British. And with far more justification, all things considered."

Foolish man, that Dr. Cooper! Silly woman, his wife, Susanna. Miss Abigail could not imagine living in India as they had, rigidly resisting everything Indian. Both husband and wife refused to learn the first words of Malayalam. Both refused to taste a bite of Indian food. And although it had caused the cook who had been at the clinic since Miss Abigail first came to leave in disgust, Dr. Cooper insisted they be served cooked meat every day of the week.

"Isaiah informed me that—"

Isaiah! Right there was another thing! Imagine changing the name of a grown man—such an insult! Krishna refused to answer to this new name, yet the stubborn doctor would not call him by his Hindu name.

"Isaiah?" Miss Abigail asked with feigned ignorance. "I do not believe I have had the pleasure of meeting . . . Oh! Could Krishna be the one of whom you speak?"

"Excuse me, Miss Davidson," Dr. Cooper said. "I have no desire to enter into a dispute with you tonight. But I think I have made myself clear on this particular matter. I will not have that heathen name spoken in my house."

"I see. Krishna means 'defender of justice.' Your given name is William, is it not? What does that name mean?"

"I am sure I have not the faintest idea," Dr. Cooper huffed. "Nor do I care. William is a strong English Christian name."

"Old German, to be accurate," Miss Abigail said. "And, therefore, perhaps not Christian at all."

Dr. Cooper grunted in frustration. "The point is, Miss Davidson—"

"The point is, Dr. Cooper, we are in India, not England. Have you had the pleasure of learning about the Indian Christian holy man, Sadhu Sundar Singh?"

Dr. Cooper sighed loudly and lifted his eyes toward heaven.

"No," Abigail said. "I see you have not. How unfortunate for you. Sundar Singh once told the story of a high caste traveler who grew faint under the relentless Indian sun. Barely conscious, the traveler slumped onto a bench at a train station. A passerby thought to do a good deed and brought him a cup of water. But the traveler waved it away without tasting it. 'He will not drink that,' the train man said. 'He is high caste and an Untouchable may have used that cup.' Fortunately, the train man spied the traveler's own cup lying on the bench beside him. He grabbed it up and ran to fill it with water. The traveler readily drank the water and, fortunately, was revived and able to continue his journey. The thing is, the high caste man would rather die than risk drinking from the cup of an Untouchable."

"Ridiculous. Utterly ridiculous!"

"I tell you that story, good doctor, because of Sadhu Sundar Singh's concluding words. He said, 'Indians will not receive Christianity from an English cup. If they are to receive the Gospel, it must come to them in an Indian cup.'"

At the landlord's labor settlement, Shridula told her father, "Everyone at the landlord's house talks of independence. They talk and they talk, but I do not think anyone really knows what will happen."

"No," Ashish agreed. "I am sure they do not."

"Nihal Amos says the Communists will take over. But Rajeev says no, that Indian men will be elected to run the country, and he will be one of them even if he is a Christian and he has a Muslim wife."

Ashish shook his head. "They cannot both be right."

"No," Shridula agreed. "I wish neither of them was right."

Ashish took his daughter's hands in his and held them tightly. "The scavenger Jyoti and her son no longer live in this settlement," he said. "I went to bed one night and they were next to my hut. I awoke the next morning and they were gone."

Shridula opened her mouth, but the question died on her lips.

"I heard nothing," Ashish said. "No sound of struggle."

Several minutes passed before Shridula spoke again. Remembering all the ears pressed against her father's door, she whispered, "Glory Anna reads with me from her Holy Bible. I can read almost every word now, though I do not know what they all mean."

"I miss reading with you, Daughter," Ashish breathed.

"I found a special verse I want to read to you," Shridula whispered.

Ashish took his leather-bound Bible from its hiding place, and with nimble fingers Shridula flipped halfway through to the book of Jeremiah, to chapter 31 and down to verse 16. "Listen, *Appa: Thus saith the* LORD: *Refrain thy voice from weeping, and thine eyes from tears: for thy work shall be rewarded, saith the* LORD; *and they shall come again from the land of the enemy. And there is hope in thine end, saith the* LORD, *that thy children shall come again to their own border.*"

She stopped reading and looked up at her father. "Do you think there will be independence for us too, *Appa?*"

"I do not think so," Ashish said.

"But the Holy Book says refrain from weeping, and work shall be rewarded, and come back—"

"Those words are not for such as us, little one," Ashish said. "They are for the children of God. We are nothing but Untouchables."

28

August 1947

Shridula awoke with a start. Could that be rain she heard? Rain, in the searing month of August? When the sun scorched the earth and every grain of rice that the harvesters missed roasted in the fields? Shridula eased herself from her sleeping mat and moved quietly across the room on tiptoes. Carefully she pulled the door open. Glory Anna snuffled in her sleep and rolled over, but she didn't awaken.

Unexpected rain in the middle of hot weather—how wonderful! Healing to both the body and the soul. That's what Shridula's mother used to say.

Shridula slipped out the door and tiptoed to the veranda. In the last twinkling of the last stars before dawn, she lifted her face upward and waited expectantly. But, alas, no drops of rain touched her. Something else was crackling through the sky. Something unfamiliar. Something disquieting and strange.

"Fireworks," Saji Stephen said in a weary voice. "The fires of independence hang heavy in the air."

Shridula gave a start. "Master Landlord! I am sorry! I did not see . . . I did not know . . ." As she stammered her attempt at an apology, she moved back toward the door and the safety of Glory Anna's room.

"Come, come. No need to run away," Saji Stephen said in a strangely gentle voice. "Everything is different this day. On the English calendar, it is the fifteenth day of the month of August in the year nineteen hundred and forty-seven, A.D. Remember that date, girl. Last night at midnight, the British Indian Empire disappeared from this country. The morning dawns on the new Union of India. This is the day of Independence."

"What does that mean, master?" Shridula whispered.

"It does not mean justice," Saji Stephen said. "That scavenger boy who robbed my house is independent, yet you who protected him are not. That is the way independence works. Some benefit even though they do not deserve it. Others never benefit though they do deserve it."

Shridula, her eyes wide, stared at the landowner.

"You think the whispers do not reach my ears? You think I do not know?" Saji Stephen said. "I am no fool. Of course I know."

The flames of revolt that brought independence to India left no family untouched. Not of any caste. When the sun was fully up, Rajeev hoisted the old tricolor Swaraj flag Mohandas Gandhi had designed, and flew it high above the house so that everyone in the village could see it.

Nihal Amos squinted up at the saffron, white, and India green flag of the Indian National Congress. "Is that not a bit out of date?" he asked.

"Good enough," Rajeev said. "The new flag will be these same three colors. The only real change is that spinning wheel in the middle. It will be replaced with an *Ashoka Chaka*."

As the Sudra servant brought platters of *idli* cakes and bowls of *sambar* for their breakfast, Rajeev turned on the radio, which crackled and sputtered to life. "Patriotic speeches," he said. "We need to hear them."

"Yes," Saji Stephen agreed. "Someone should explain to us what all this means."

"Not much. That is what I say," said Nihal Amos. "Nationalism is just another word for dominance by the Brahmin caste."

"The Untouchables would never allow that," Saji Stephen said. "I have 692 of them in my labor settlement. How long do you think they will be willing to continue to bow under the Brahmins' Hindu social order? How long will they stay crushed at the bottom of the heap? When they decide to rise up and fight, Brahmin Rama will not be the one hurt. I will."

"So what do you think of your favorite, Mr. Gandhi, now?" Nihal Amos asked. "He called those Untouchables *harijans*, Children of God. Yet the thought of them quitting Hinduism terrified him. And well it should. Hinduism would be nothing without the Untouchables."

"Utter nonsense!" Rajeev exclaimed. "Once the government is put into place, every Indian will have a say in it. From highest of the Brahmins to lowest of the Untouchables. Yes, even the scavenger!"

"I do not know." Saji Stephen shook his head doubtfully. "I just do not know. Perhaps I should call a fortune-teller to advise us where to cast our lots."

"Father!" Rajeev scolded. "You sound like an ignorant old woman. What could a fortune-teller possibly have to say to you? Use your intelligence. We have only to watch which way the government inclines, then cast our lots alongside it."

"Oh, yes, Father, by all means!" Nihal Amos said in his most mocking tone. "Why not listen to the words of Brahmin Rama, too? Throw away every vestige of your Christian principles. Forget what is right and do anything that looks to be in your best interest."

In honor of the day, Glory Anna instructed Shridula to dress her in Grandmother Parmar Ruth's vibrant green and yellow silk *sari*. "Everything about today is terribly exciting!" she exclaimed. "I must look exciting, too."

"Yes," Shridula said. "Of course."

"Do not sulk!" Glory Anna ordered. "You are fortunate to be here with me. Whatever happens, we will be safe in this house."

"But my father is in the labor settlement," Shridula said.

"Even so, you cannot go down there. I forbid it! Stay here with me."

Shridula said nothing. She helped Glory Anna into the yellow blouse and fastened it, and then into the yellow *pavada*—petticoat. She wrapped the length of green silk around her, taking care to make perfectly spaced tucks across the front the way Sheeba Esther taught her.

"You can choose any one of my *saris* to wear today," Glory Anna offered. "Except my new one, of course. But any other one you can wear."

"Thank you," Shridula said. She already knew what she would wear this day—her own worn hand-me-down *sari*: the clothes of an Untouchable fortunate enough to be a servant in a fine house.

"The British Parliament passed the Indian Independence act a month ago," Rajeev said. "Today independence is official. Yet still I have heard nothing about my own position with the government."

"You expect too much," Saji Stephen told his son.

"Not at all! It is not as if the country must start a whole new government from the beginning. Or this partition arrangement, either. For both the new India and the new Pakistan, it is simply a matter of adapting the legal framework from the India Act 1935."

"Surely you are not the only person vying for a government position," Nihal Amos said.

"No. But unfortunately I made the mistake of counting on a united India," Rajeev said with a sigh. "Me, a Christian; Amina, a Muslim; our offspring, true children of India. But now, with the country splitting, no one cares about a united Indian family."

"You did your part by dropping your Christian name," Nihal Amos said. "What do you propose to do now? Change the name of your wife as well?"

"Why not? A Muslim wife is no longer an asset to me."

Slowly and carefully, Miss Abigail Davidson climbed the steps to the roof of her cottage. The sun was fast rising in the sky, yet Lelee had not yet brought her morning tea. It wasn't like the child to be late. But never mind. Miss Abigail had no pressing engagements. She never did anymore. She could afford to wait. Still, she did like her morning tea on time.

Immediately, the suffocating heat closed in around her. Miss Abigail raised her hand to her chest and gasped a deep breath. She sank into a chair and closed her eyes. Where was that girl with the morning tea?

"*Mem*, you should not be sitting outside on this day."

Miss Abigail jerked her head up to see Krishna standing over her. She blinked at him in confusion. How could he have gotten up the stairs so silently? Could she possibly have fallen asleep?

"Please, *mem*, stay inside this day."

"I dare say, this morning is no hotter than yesterday morning," Miss Abigail said. "Once I have had my tea, I shall consider my plans for the remainder of the day, but not until then."

"*Mem*, are you to be forgetting what day it is?"

Miss Abigail stared back blankly.

"Today is to be the first day of the new independent India," Krishna said.

Independence! Of course. How could she have forgotten?

"But where is Lelee with my morning tea?"

"Lelee is no longer here," Krishna said. "Please, I am to be bringing your tea to you in your room."

"What do you mean the child is no longer here? Wherever would she go?"

"Before the doctor and the *memsahib* left, they send everyone away. Are you not remembering? No one is here anymore, *mem*, but only you and only me."

With a sense of growing dread, Miss Abigail pulled the handkerchief from the waist of her *pavada* and blotted at her eyes and forehead. Dr. Cooper and Susanna had left? Had anyone told her? She had been dreadfully forgetful of late, but surely she could not have forgotten that.

Miss Abigail sat up straight and gathered together the pieces of her shattered dignity. "Would you be good enough to help me down the stairs?" she asked. "Perhaps it would be the best idea if I were to lie down for a bit."

"Yes, *mem*. Yes, that is being the best idea."

Miss Abigail grasped Krishna's arm and moved forward with unsure steps. *Perhaps there will be riots*, she thought. *I should go down to the clinic and make certain everything is ready to care for the injured when they come.* She leaned heavily against Krishna. *But not just yet.*

"You will bring me the tea, then, Krishna?" she asked. "I do like my morning tea."

"I will not, I will not!" Amina's angry voice echoed through the house, from the back room she shared with Rajeev and their children clear to the veranda where Saji Stephen and Nihal Amos sat in silence, taking in her every word. "You are my husband, but you cannot force me to change who I am!"

What Rajeev said in response, they could not make out. But Amina's answer was perfectly clear.

"My father never would have agreed to the marriage had he known you would make such a demand of me! He will be most angry. Furious!"

Again, the mumble of Rajeev's unintelligible response.

"You may go against your God, Husband. Your entire family may go against your God. But I will not go against Allah!"

Sheeba Esther stepped softly onto the veranda. "A treat to refresh you," she said to her husband and her father-in-law. "Nothing cools the temper and eases the heart like a sweet dish of *payasam*." Mmmm. . . . Rice boiled with milk and sugar, and flavored with cardamom, raisins, saffron, and pistachio nuts. With a demure smile, she handed the first bowl to Saji Stephen. He thanked her with a broad smile.

After Sheeba Esther went back inside, while Saji Stephen and his son enjoyed their rice pudding, Rajeev's angry voice once again echoed through to the veranda. "If you will not help me, Wife, neither will you stand in my way. That I promise you!"

Nihal Amos swallowed a bite of the *payasam*. "I wonder," he said to his father, "does Rajeev have any idea what kind of government he struggles so hard to join?"

"He thinks he does," Saji Stephen answered.

"Mr. Nehru wants a modern India, but Mr. Gandhi wants a modified and purified caste system. Mr. Ambedkar demands more power for the Untouchables. Put them all together and India will be an independent republic stewing with confusion and contradiction. No one will be happy."

After several moments of silence, a small child's wail echoed from the back of the house. Nothing more.

⁊

"Why did you come?" Ashish exclaimed when he saw Shridula hurrying down the path. "It is not safe for you to be out!"

But he was not the first one to see his daughter. The young man with an old man's face had been gathering thorn brush to patch holes in the fences around the fields of ripening rice when he caught sight of her. "Shridula has come!" he called as he ran back to the settlement. "Shridula is here!"

Jinraj picked up his cry: "Shridula! She brings news!"

"Shridula has come!" Dinkar called. "Now we will hear the truth."

As word spread of Shridula's arrival, people dropped whatever they were doing and hurried to gather at Ashish's hut.

The woman with three teeth lifted her scrawny arms and cried, "Do not go inside your father's hut so we cannot hear your news, Shridula. If you do, we will push the door down and listen anyway!"

Shridula didn't even try to go inside. The gathering crowd listened with rapt attention as she told them everything she knew about Independent India. She told about Mr. Nehru and Mr. Gandhi, of course, but also about Mr. Ambedkar who was fighting so hard to make certain that Untouchables also had rights.

"Are we also free?" an old man called out.

"I do not think so," Shridula answered. "Not yet. But no one seems to know for certain."

"We will fight!" the young man with an old man's face yelled. "We want independence for everyone! That means for us, too!"

"Especially for us!" someone called out from the back of the crowd.

So much anger and excitement! So very many questions! One after another after another, many shouted out at the same time. Shridula did her best to answer each one, but there was much she simply did not know. Finally Ashish stood up and said to the crowd, "I know you still have concerns. I have concerns, too. But Shridula is running out of answers, and I am running out of time with my daughter. Please, let us have some time together."

No one wanted to leave. Several ignored Ashish and shouted out more questions. But Dinkar stepped forward and ordered, "Go home! Shridula has done us a great kindness. Listen to what Ashish says and be on your way."

In the simmering heat, Shridula and Ashish could not bear to sit inside the stifling hut. They might as well have sat in the cooking fire. So even though it meant giving up their hope of privacy, they huddled close together under the shading branches of the *neem* tree and whispered to each other.

"Jyoti and Falak are gone?" Shridula asked.

"Yes. But two different watchmen whisper that they caught sight of Hari stealing rice from the fields. We think he is hiding out in the marsh. Perhaps his mother and brother are there, too."

"How could that be?"

"No one actually saw the landlord's men come for Jyoti. Maybe it was Hari who came for her and Falak. Or it could be that the two of them ran away and met up with Hari."

Shridula looked doubtful.

"It could be," Ashish said.

Shridula nodded. "It could be."

For several minutes the two fell silent. Finally Shridula said, "I really do not know anything for certain, *Appa*. I hear things, but I do not know what will happen. All I can do is hope."

"No one knows what will happen," Ashish said. "As the saying goes: *Ruling India is like clanging on the head of a cobra.*"

Shridula leaned close and whispered, "Do you still read the Holy Book?"

"More than ever, Daughter."

"I copied this for you from the part called Romans. Chapter 8, verses 24 and 25." Shridula handed her father a crumpled slip of paper. "Can you read the way I wrote it?"

Slowly, pointing to each word as he pronounced it, Ashish read, *We . . . are saved . . . by hope: but hope that is seen is not hope . . . for what a man seeth, why doth he yet hope for? But if we hope for that we see not . . . then do we with patience wait for it.*

"We can still hope, *Appa*," Shridula said. "Even if everyone else is clanging on the head of a cobra, we can still hope."

"Even when we cannot see it," Ashish said.

"Especially when we cannot see it. That is what makes it hope, is it not? Not being able to see it but continuing to wait anyway?"

"Yes, Daughter," Ashish said. "Continuing to wait with patience."

29

August 1947

"Durga," Rajeev informed his wife. "No longer is your name Amina. From this day forward, you will be called Durga. And a proud name it is, too. Durga, the invincible Mother Goddess."

"Never will I answer to such a name!" Amina shouted. "Nor will I call my sons by the names of Hindu gods. Or my daughter . . . I will not call my daughter by any Hindu name at all. No, I will not!"

Anger rose in Rajeev's dark eyes. His voice turned hard and cold. "You forget yourself, woman. You are my wife. The decision is not yours to make. I alone will decide what you will and will not do."

"I will not be called by the name of a Hindu goddess! You could not make a Christian of me, and you cannot make a Hindu of me either."

"Soon I shall be a man of great importance. Surely, even you would not be such a fool as to risk all the advantages of being my wife on something as unimportant as a name. You were born a Muslim, but you need not remain so."

Amina looked him straight in the eye. "I *am* Muslim," she insisted. "Nothing in the past changed that, and nothing will change it in the future."

Such insulting insolence! And in his father's own house, where his entire family could hear every word of the disgraceful exchange. Rajeev fumed. He burned with rage. "You stubborn woman! If you will be a Muslim, gather up your belongings and take yourself away to the new Muslim country of Pakistan. Carry your daughter along with you, too. But do not think you will take my sons from me. They will remain with me always. And from this day forward, they will be Hindus!"

Amina turned away and said no more.

Rajeev, extremely pleased with his show of strength, strode out to the veranda where his father and brother sat in silence enjoying a respite after the exhausting heat of the day. He strutted about, waiting for one or the other of them to offer him praise for the way he had handled his hardheaded wife. When neither one did, Rajeev harrumphed loudly in an effort to catch their attention.

"Cup of tea?" Saji Stephen asked Nihal Amos.

Rajeev sucked in noisy breaths of evening air. "Ahhhhh," he sighed loudly. "Wonderfully welcome after so decisive a day."

Saji Stephen poured a cup of tea and handed it to Nihal Amos, then he poured another for himself.

His irritation growing, Rajeev made a great show of preparing himself to sit. When neither his father nor his brother paid him any mind, Rajeev grunted his annoyance and settled himself on the far side of the veranda.

"A Muslim can never go to hell no matter how black his sins might be," Rajeev stated. "A strange belief, that. Would you not agree?"

"In good time, we shall see for ourselves whether or not that is true," Nihal Amos said.

Rajeev ignored the mocking tone of his brother's voice. "The Muslims say a dispensation exists for every kind of sin. Still, no one who fails to believe in Mohammad as the prophet can ever go to heaven under any circumstances, according to their belief. They say heaven is a place reserved for the believers of Islam alone."

"In that case, how surprised they will be," Saji Stephen said.

"Of course, I shall not be quick to give up on my wife," Rajeev said. "My Durga. She is not the kind of woman who can be fooled forever. By tomorrow morning she will come to her senses."

Glory Anna could make out mounds on the veranda, each one snoring loudly in the pale gray before sunrise. It would be the men of the family, of course. Perhaps Rajeev's children, too. She eased past the doorway and through the great room to the back of the house where Rajeev's and Nihal's wives slept. Glory Anna hardly ever went back there. The very thought of her days under Amina's angry rule sent shivers down her back.

"Sheeba Esther!" Glory Anna called quietly. "Sheeba Esther!"

All was quiet. No children's voices, no morning preparations, no smoke from a cooking fire. Overhead, the last stars faded from the sky.

Glory Anna tapped on Nihal Amos's door. "Sheeba Esther!" she called again.

"What is it?" Sheeba Esther answered, her voice muffled through the panels and thick with sleep. She stumbled to the door and opened it a crack. Sheeba was still in her sleeping garment, her hair hanging long and undone down her back. But as soon as she saw Glory Anna, she shook herself awake. "What is it?" she asked. "Is something wrong?"

"It is Shridula. She has been crying all night."

"Is she ill?"

"She is afraid. She wants to go back to her father's house."

Despite the heat, Rajeev walked down the road to the marketplace. He paused at one vendor's stall after another to take in the village gossip. Everyone was out, in a rush to accomplish as much as possible in the cooler hours of the morning. To Rajeev's great pleasure, everyone's chatter revolved around the same topic: independent India. What would befall their village? Even more, what would independence mean to them personally?

Rajeev smoothed down the high caste folds in the front of his crisp white *mundu* and cleared his throat. "I am quite aware that no person, not even Jawaharlal Nehru, could rightly call himself an expert on the affairs of the new India," Rajeev stated in a loud voice. "So much has come to pass so quickly that everything is far too new for everyone."

Conversations quieted, and eyes turned toward the landlord's son.

"Yet it is with all humility that I confess to having more knowledge about it than do most men. If I may say so, more knowledge by far."

"Is that so?" challenged an eager young man. Despite his age, he sported a most impressive beard and moustache, which gave him an air of authority beyond his years.

Rajeev looked the young man up and down. "Most certainly it is so. I am also a humble servant to my countrymen, I might add." A look of mild disgust flashed in Rajeev's eyes, and the corners of his mouth twisted upward, though not in a pleasant way. "Even to you, Mani Rao. Even to a spice merchant. Even to one far more lowly than myself."

"You are acquainted with the partition of India, then?" Mani said. "You know of the new border lines that sever Pakistan from the mother country? That cleave Sikh regions in half?"

"Yes, yes. Of course I know," Rajeev said, but not without a noticeable degree of hesitation.

"You know that villages are split in two, right down the middle of the road? You know that the line chops through fields and severs houses, leaving one room in India and the other in Pakistan?" Before Rajeev could gather his wits and stammer an answer, Mani added, "You know, too, I suppose, that blood flows in the streets and soaks the roads?"

"A line had to be drawn," Rajeev said. "Of course some conflict is inevitable. Unfortunate, to be sure, but unavoidable."

"Since you are so well informed, surely you also know that the family of your wife decided to cast their lots with the new Muslim country," Mani said. "Surely you know that they boarded a train to Delhi this morning."

"The family of my . . . wife?" Rajeev stammered. "But they . . . Surely they will—"

"Your wife and all your children went with them," Mani said. "But of course you know that, do you not? That they are right now on their way to Pakistan? Since you are more knowledgeable than most men by far, this cannot be news to you."

✐❧

With trembling hands, Shridula struggled to braid her hair. "Let me help you," Sheeba Esther said gently. First she combed her fingers through the uneven lumps, then she picked up Glory Anna's brush and pulled it through Shridula's thick locks. "You should look nice for your father," she told Shridula.

The girl gasped and lifted guilty eyes to Glory Anna.

"I do not mind if she uses my brush in your hair," Glory Anna said. She did, however, cast a disapproving eye at Shridula's worn garment. "But you should not wear that dingy old thing. Take one of my bright *saris* for today. Even my new pink one, if you promise to treat it carefully."

Shridula lowered her eyes and said nothing. Self-consciously she pressed at the unpleated front of her own shabby garment.

"Never mind," Sheeba Esther said brightly. She picked up one of Glory Anna's ribbons and tied Shridula's braid fast. "You could not look more lovely, Shridula."

"Everyone will want me to tell them everything," Shridula said to Sheeba Esther. "They will ask me questions and questions and more questions. But I know nothing. What answers can I give them?"

Sheeba Esther clasped Shridula's hands in hers. "Tell them the truth," she said. "Right now two new countries hang in the throes of frightening birth pangs. What the end will be, no one knows. We would all be wise to turn away from anyone arrogant enough to claim to have more answers than that."

Sneering, Rajeev kicked at a bag of dried peppercorns propped up at the end of the spice stall. "You dare to instruct *me*, Mani Rao? Such a brazen young man you are!" The bag tipped over. Hard, black peppercorns spilled out and rolled across the ground. Rajeev strode through the river of pepper. With each step, he ground the corns into the hard dirt.

"A spice merchant, are you not? Grandson of a spice merchant? Son of Irfan Rao, a *Vaisya*?"

Rajeev sucked in a deep breath and made a great show of taking in the pungent pepper fragrance that filled the air. He turned back to Mani. "You know nothing of my family, Mister Spice Merchant, so I would suggest you hold your tongue."

Mani pulled himself up to his full height. "A spice merchant, yes, but one whose father, Irfan Rao, is right now with his army regiment in Malabar. I went to meet him when he arrived by train, fresh from the bloody road to Pakistan. I heard the horrible truth from soldiers who witnessed it with their own eyes. It was there that I saw your family boarding the train for Delhi."

The smirking smile left Rajeev's face.

"I am a spice merchant who knows you determined that power was more important than your family. Your own wife told me as much. And I fear, Landlord's Son, that the road to Pakistan will turn redder still with their blood."

Rajeev, trembling uncontrollably, turned his back on Mani Rao. Stumbling over bulging sacks, he hurried away from the spice stall.

"You turned your wife and children away!" Mani shouted after him. "You turned them away because they were an embarrassment to you!"

Shridula waited until the sun was halfway to its zenith, a time when she thought the laborers would all be busy in the fields. As she hurried along the sun-baked path, her eye caught sight of a small patch of weeds not yet roasted dry and dead. She bent down to touch them. So limp. So thirsty. An overwhelming sadness swept over Shridula. Why must everything die? Why must every person die?

The girl pulled herself up and tried to run, but she could not. The heat sucked every bit of strength from her body. She felt as limp as the poor weeds. But she must not stop.

"She is coming!" a young voice shrieked as she rounded the last bend in the path. "Shridula is coming!"

By the time Shridula arrived at her father's hut, a crowd had gathered, eager questions already poised on anxious lips.

Shridula tried hard to say the right things. But after a few minutes, she cried in frustration, "Stop! You must not ask me so many questions, because I do not know the answers! All I know is that India is now an independent country and so is Pakistan. Muslims have to move to Pakistan and everyone else has to come to India, whether they want to or not. Everyone is terribly angry with everyone else, but the British army went home, and now too many people are dying. That is all I know. Nothing else."

"What will happen to us?" someone called out.

"What of the harvest?" Dinkar demanded.

Shridula covered her ears and burst into tears.

"Go away, all of you!" Ashish ordered. "Let my daughter be! Go to your homes and leave us alone."

Words, words, words! Rajeev had come to the marketplace with one purpose in mind: to show off his knowledge and political strength before as many people as possible. How would it look if he were to let the words of a humble spice merchant drive him away? Pulling himself up tall, he removed the anxiety from his face and replaced it with a confident smile. He turned back toward the spice trader's stall and called out, "Thank you! Thank you to everyone for your attention!"

Actually, it quite amazed him to see the size of the crowd that had assembled behind him. And every person was watching him.

Rajeev raised his arms high and called out, "You ask what independent India means to you? Even now, a constitution is being written that will determine the answer to that question. I wish to see your rights included in it. Since I have had the singular foresight to forge valuable alliances with each of the personalities and factions charged with establishing the new government, I see myself, more than any other individual in this village—indeed, more than any other person in this entire area—in the position to assume a leadership role in the new Union of India!"

He paused, waiting to graciously receive the villagers' praise and shouts of encouragement.

"What is your position on the Radcliffe Line, Master Landlord's Son?" Mani Rao called out.

Rajeev's smile froze and his eyes narrowed.

"What of the millions of poor souls forced from their homes and ordered to seek refuge on the other side of that line?" Mani demanded.

"Not millions!" Rajeev shouted back.

"Yes, Master Landlord's Son, millions! My father saw the endless line with his own eyes. Men and women and children. Babies and old people. In bullock carts and piled onto lorries and stuffed into buses. But most of all, on foot, carrying their pitiful sacks of belongings on their heads, and their old grandmothers on their backs."

"Go back and sweep up your spilled pepper!" Rajeev called. He tried to laugh, but his face dripped sweat and his throat choked.

"What have you to say to the thousands who lie starving beside the road?" Mani challenged. "Or to the living who scratch in the dried earth to bury their dead?"

The silent crowd stared at Rajeev.

"What of the rivers of blood from the uncounted masses slaughtered along the roadside?"

Not a sound from the crowd as they waited for Rajeev's answer.

Rajeev's eyes darted from one person to another to another, then back to Mani. "The British assured us of a smooth transition," he offered lamely. "Of course there will be unfortunate circumstances. That cannot be avoided. But for the most part . . . with the British army and the Indian army working together to keep order—"

"The Boundary Force?" Mani said. "Is that what you mean by working together to keep order?"

"Yes," Rajeev answered. He took a deep breath and relaxed a bit. "Yes, the Boundary Force. Exactly. They will keep the peace."

"Then they would have to do it with fewer than one soldier for every murderous roadway mile," Mani shot back. "And since they are not even able to protect the cities along the route, what can they hope to do for the endless caravans of refugees that clog the roadways?"

Rajeev opened his mouth, but for once in his life, he could think of absolutely nothing to say.

"Refugees that, by now, may well include your family," Mani added.

"Now see here! You—"

"Especially your half-and-half children. For they are like the houses divided between two countries. The Radcliffe Line divides the very spirits of your children in two!"

Suddenly, the heat of the day was more than Rajeev could bear. Trembling and perspiring, he turned his back on Mani Rao and the rest of the crowd. He wanted to run, but he was far too unsteady on his feet. Curious eyes bored into his back. He knew it was so, even though he couldn't see them. Determined to do no further damage to himself, he raised his head high, took a deep breath, and fixed his eyes on the road for home.

"Servant!" Rajeev called as he approached his father's house. "Udit! Make the cart ready for me immediately. With the horse!"

Udit hurried out, his face lined with confusion. "But, master, the sun is still high. Surely you do not mean now. Not in the heat of the day!"

"Immediately!" Rajeev ordered. "Without one moment's further delay!"

30

September 1947

*W*ith Rajeev lashing wildly at its flanks, the horse jerked the cart away at a fast trot. Choking dust billowed up behind it and hung heavy in the simmering heat.

"Have you no respect for the beast?" Brahmin Rama scolded from the shade of his mango tree. "The sun is too hot for so fast a ride in an open cart."

Rajeev knew that. Of course he knew it. He grabbed hold of the *chaddar* that flapped about his shoulders and swiped at his burning face. Then he slapped the switch across the horse's back harder than ever.

When he arrived at the English Mission Medical Clinic, Rajeev led the exhausted horse to a scraggly stand of trees. He climbed down from the cart and, ignoring the main clinic, headed directly for Miss Abigail's cottage.

Krishna stepped out to see who was approaching, but Rajeev didn't slow his pace. "Get water for my horse!" he ordered in the Malayalam language. "Now!"

Had circumstances been different, or his intentions less urgent, Rajeev would have behaved in a more civilized manner. But this day, with only one thing on his mind, he strode quickly toward Miss Abigail's door, bellowing all the way, "*Mem* Davidson! We be needing to talk together. *Mem* Davidson!"

Rajeev shifted impatiently from one foot to the other as he waited outside the closed door. After what seemed an inordinately long wait, he slammed his open hand hard against the door frame. The door swung open a crack, and Miss Abigail's anxious face peeked out.

"*Mem* Davidson, please, I must be talking with you. Now!"

Miss Abigail squinted at him with her filmy blue eyes. She waved her hands about her head, as if swatting at flies, although it was much too hot for insects of any kind.

"Immediately, *Mem* Davidson. Please. Please!"

Miss Abigail opened the door a bit wider. "I am afraid you have missed Dr. Cooper," she said. "He no longer resides here."

"In that case, you more certainly are to be needing protection," Rajeev said. As he talked, he pushed his way through the doorway. "Yes, *mem*, more certainly you are!"

Miss Abigail frowned, but she stepped aside.

"It is being most fortunate for both you and me, my coming here today," Rajeev said as he moved past Miss Abigail and settled himself in the nearest of the two chairs. "I am to be needing your help now. The British government, you see, officials who are to be staying in India. They can be helping me when I am arriving in Delhi, do you see, and that is the reason why—"

Miss Abigail, who had been glancing nervously at the closed door, interrupted him in an urgent whisper, "Oh, sir, the most terrible things have happened! Horrible things, really. A massacre, sir! An absolute massacre!"

Miss Abigail hustled over to the table, which was strewn with newspaper clippings. She rifled through the pile with shaking hands, then pulled out a photograph and held it out to him. "Refugees in a long train of oxcarts," she said. "Children. Even babies! God in heaven knows what will happen to them." Tears filled her cloudy eyes. "Look here. A poor, poor old man! He must carry his wife on his back! How far can he go bearing such a burden?"

Rajeev stared at the pictures. Every woman's face looked to him like Amina's face. And in the faces of every child, he saw his own little ones.

With tears streaming down her wrinkled cheeks, Miss Abigail grabbed up yet another photograph from the pile and thrust it to him. "Look! Burial mounds alongside the road. Distressing! Most distressing!"

Rajeev's face had gone white. He pushed the clippings away from him.

Miss Abigail sat down in the second chair. "I have not always agreed with the British way of doing things, but they are a people of laws. One must appreciate that fact. We English do cling to decorum. Ours is a country of order."

"A country of order? It is being a country in a maddening rush to get India's independence over before the chop, chop, chopping begins! For three hundred years, your people are to be taking India's wealth away from us. Now you are having to go away so quickly that you are to be muddling everything up for us. You are to be confusing everyone!"

Miss Abigail stared at the Indian man in confusion. "What?" She shook her head and squeezed her eyes shut.

"You are to be tearing away Muslim wives and leaving them to be burying their sons beside the road!" Rajeev swatted at the stack of clippings. "Look at the order your great country is to be leaving behind for the new India to sort out!"

"I do not understand, sir," Miss Abigail said. "Did you Indians not want independence?"

"It could be that those are being my own baby sons in the line of oxcarts!" Rajeev exclaimed. "It could be my family that is to be lying in those burial mounds on the side of the road. No, *mem*, this is not what we are to be wanting. None of us. We are not to be wanting this!"

The troubled look ebbed from Miss Abigail's face. Brightening, she turned her eyes to a picture pinned up on her wall. It was a faded photograph of her as an energetic young woman with blonde hair, and freckles sprinkled across her nose, sitting on the back of an elephant. "Do look at that silly elephant and me," she said with a laugh. "We are both smiling, do you see? What a lovely day that was."

Rajeev's eyes darted up to the wall, then back to the scattered newspaper clippings.

"I well remember that day," Miss Abigail continued dreamily. "I had just come back from England determined to spend the rest of my life in India. How Dr. Moore scolded me for permitting that picture to be made! He called me an unprofessional child. Yes, that was his exact word—'child'!"

"Yes. Well . . ." Rajeev began. "Were we not discussing the importance of us to be working together? Perhaps you might be good enough to be writing for me a letter of reference. Do you see? As we are to be helping each other? I am being certain you will be protected always, and you can be helping me to be making the acquaintance of important people in Delhi who can also—"

"Oh, yes, the times are hard." Miss Abigail shook her head sadly. "Most surely and definitely. Horrible things are happening. A massacre—"

"Yes, yes," Rajeev interrupted. "As you are still to be having connections to the British government, I am holding to the hope that you might also to be having—"

"I have lived a long time," Miss Abigail said in a hushed, conspiratorial tone. "I remember when the world was a very different place."

Confusion clouded Rajeev's face. "I am also remembering, *mem*. But what I am to be requesting from you at this moment is—"

"I remember when we feared cobras and tigers more than we feared each other. Do you remember such a time, young man?"

Rajeev sighed in exasperation and ran his hand across his face. "The British government, *mem*," he began. But Abigail wasn't listening. She had dropped off to sleep.

Naturally, the summer sun had long since baked the marshes and streams until they lay hard and cracked. Certainly the withering heat had scorched the rice paddies dry. Of course parched rice stalks withered brown, and drying rice heads hung heavy. All this was to be expected. It happened every year as the end-of-summer harvest approached.

None of this disturbed Saji Stephen. In fact, when he climbed into the bullock cart and settled himself beside Udit, his spirits were high and his only intention was to survey his fields. Death and mayhem might plague the north of India, uncertain winds of charge might whip through the new government, his sons might dash to and fro in search of a new world order, but this one constant remained: harvest. The promise of storehouses refilled and coffers replenished. Soon, grateful villagers would envelop him with adoration and praise. And after the deprivations of a long summer, more of them would come to him begging for loans. Whatever happened elsewhere in the world, in Saji Stephen's village, life would go on just the same as it always had.

Saji Stephen gazed overhead. Nothing but hot, blue sky. He turned and stared back toward the mountains. Not so much as a tiny wisp of cloud. Good. Nothing to disrupt his harvest.

"What is this?" Saji Stephen exclaimed to Udit. To his left lay an empty field. Not empty as in harvested, but empty as in never planted.

"It is the farthest field from the labor settlement, master," his servant said. "The least fertile and most unproductive of all your lands."

This answer did not satisfy Saji Stephen. He was still voicing his dismay when the bullock pulled the cart toward the next field. It had been planted and rice was growing, but the ground was so dry that the paddy had opened up in large cracks. And the rice—nothing but sparse, stunted stalks growing in a sea of weeds.

"This is . . . this rice paddy . . . it is . . ." Words piled together in a helpless jumble on Saji Stephen's shocked tongue.

Slowly the lumbering bullock pulled the cart past the weed-choked edge of the second field and on to the main paddies beyond. Although this ground had received better care, it, too, had been baked dry. Stunted rice stalks barely topped the weeds. Saji Stephen's dismay turned to blinding fury.

"I do not see even one of my laborers at work in the paddy!" he bellowed. "Where are my workers? Where are my overseers?"

His servant didn't even attempt an answer.

"Take me to Dinkar! Find that lazy Ashish! I will have the skin whipped from both their worthless backs!"

As the bullock lumbered down the path, the cart behind it bounced and lurched over deep gullies left over from the rainy season, now baked hard as rock.

"No one even bothered to smooth out the pathways!" Saji Stephen cried. "Enough! Turn the cart around and take me home!"

With a tug on the rope and a click of his tongue, Udit stopped the bullock. The beast flicked its tail and flattened its ears, then it pulled the cart around and headed back up the path.

"I will not forgive any of them!" Saji Stephen vowed through clenched teeth. "Not Dinkar and not Ashish, and certainly not a single one of the workers. Every one of them will pay! And I will not forgive my worthless sons who live in my house like lazy princes, either!"

A bullock is a steady beast, but it is also slow. The rutted road back allowed Saji Stephen plenty of time to storm and yell. But once his outbursts were spent, he sank back in silence and let his rage simmer.

✍

". . . if the doctor and his wife even managed to get out of India, and I cannot be absolutely sure that they did, Mrs. Cooper would have nothing but to go north to Agra, you understand. To see the Taj Mahal with all its marble treasures, she said, which are all quite wonderful I am told, though I have never seen them with my own eyes. I told her it was nothing but an enormous tomb—magnificent, yes, but a tomb all the same. Of course, the gardens surrounding it can be most splendid and well worth the effort it takes to get there, but with the world in such a state of flux, it did not seem the time to undertake such a journey, although I quite understand Mrs. Cooper's point about taking advantage of being so close—relatively speaking, of course. One should see the sights while one is already in the country. She was most insistent on this point. But when I read the newspaper accounts, and when I see the photographs . . . well, you do understand my concern, do you not?" Miss Abigail Davidson paused to grab a breath and await her guest's reply.

Lulled by the endless prattle of the old woman's voice, Rajeev had turned his attention to the open window. Only now did he notice a spindly tree—some species he didn't recognize—growing just outside in the courtyard. Its shadow stretched out alarmingly long.

"Sir? You do understand my concern, do you not?" Miss Abigail repeated.

"What? Oh . . . Yes. Yes, I do indeed," Rajeev said quickly. "But I must to be excusing myself. The afternoon, it is becoming late, and I must to be going on my way."

"Oh, dear. I'm afraid I have bored you with my endless blather. It's just that everything has happened so quickly, and no one is here to help me set it to rights in my mind." Miss Abigail's face suddenly brightened. "You wouldn't happen to have made the acquaintance of Lord Mountbatten, would you?"

Rajeev glanced again at the scattered pile of newspaper clippings. Immediately Miss Abigail's smile melted into wrinkled distress.

"Dear me, dear me, where is my brain? I have not yet offered you tea." Miss Abigail turned in her chair toward the door and called out, "Lelee! Lelee, dear! Do bring a pot of tea, and two of my porcelain cups. Biscuits, too, if you please. There's a good child!" She turned back to Rajeev and beamed. "Perhaps the good doctor and his wife will join us."

Rajeev's eyes darted to the empty doorway. "Perhaps another time," he said quickly. "The hour is being late. I must to be going."

"Oh, I am so very sorry," Miss Abigail said. "Please, you must come again. I did so enjoy our visit."

"Yes," Rajeev said as he backed toward the door.

"You will not mind if I remain seated, will you? Excitement does go to my head and I find it difficult to move about. Why, when I was younger, I would—"

"I am not to be minding at all," Rajeev said as he moved toward the door. "Please, *mem*, not at all."

"I will be sure to give your regards to the doctor and his wife," Miss Abigail called after him. "And do greet Lord Mountbatten for me when next you see him, won't you?"

Rajeev closed the door behind him and ran all the way to his horse cart. The sun had begun its descent, yet the air remained hot and perfectly still. Hauntingly silent, too, he couldn't help but notice. Not a whisper, not a footfall, not the rustling of a leaf. Rajeev whipped up the horse, and he never looked back.

Before he even clambered down from the cart, Rajeev could hear his father's rants echoing out from the veranda. He considered going around the back of the house to his own room, but he quickly discarded that possibility. Like it or not, he needed to stay on the good side of his father. Nothing else seemed to be working in his favor. Besides, family influence just might help in his quest for a position with the new government, even though that was up north in Delhi and his family was in the south. Of course, his father's wealth wouldn't hurt any. So Rajeev sucked in his pride, pasted a smile on his exasperated face, and strode as casually as he could to join his father and brother.

"I may as well have no sons at all, for all the good you two do me!" Saji Stephen shouted. Nihal Amos sat beside him, sucking the last of the juices from a lamb bone. When Rajeev entered, Nihal looked up with relief.

"It should be much quieter in the house now," Nihal Amos commented. "What with fewer people living here, and no screaming children about."

"It does not sound any more quiet to me," Rajeev said, looking directly at his father. "Besides, you should not get used to it. My family will be back after Amina has a chance to bid her family farewell."

"Do you not mean Durga?" Nihal Amos grinned broadly.

A blush tinged Rajeev's face.

"Never mind!" Saji Stephen snapped. "While we sat on the veranda discussing the state of India, and arguing about communists and Gandhi and all the others who would bind us up with laws, our fields have turned into a wasteland!"

"You are the landlord," Nihal Amos reminded him.

"I am also the father of two sons who sleep under my roof and eat my food and give orders to my servants, yet who do not one thing to assist me!"

Rajeev lifted his hands to his throbbing head. Humiliated in the village by a lowly spice vendor. Worried over his willful wife who might at this very moment be on the road to Muslim Pakistan with his children. Enduring the entire village's gossip. Watching the safe haven he took such great pains to procure dissolve into a nest for a madwoman and her disfigured servant. It was too much for such a suffocating day. Absolutely too much. Rajeev's face burned bright red as he turned blazing eyes on his father.

"Sleep all alone under your roof, Father. Lick every last morsel of food off your platter until you choke." Rajeev didn't roar or bellow, but his even voice seethed with red-hot fury.

"Do with your servants as you will. What does it matter to any of us? Will not Glory Anna's husband take possession of everything of value in the end?"

"Stop!" Saji Stephen ordered. "You will not talk to me this way!"

"Tend to your fields or not, whichever pleases you. I no longer care. The world has changed, but you have not."

"Now see here—"

"Winston Churchill once claimed India as Britain's brightest jewel. As England's daily bread," Rajeev said. "But now India is *our* jewel. As for our daily bread, I have no desire to grow the grain for it. If I wish to be a part of the government, I must be where the government is. Tomorrow I shall pack my belongings and board the train to Delhi."

31

September 1947

*S*omething disturbed the peacock. A prowling animal, per-haps, or maybe just the shimmering light of the moon as it rose on a night that refused to give up the day's heat. At twi-light the bright blue bird flapped his way up into the trees to roost with its lady hen as was his wont, but once the moon rose it started to cry.

Aaaaaahh . . . lo! Aaaaaahh . . . lo! Aaaaaahh . . . lo!

Nihal Amos, sleeping alone on the veranda, stirred and sighed. When the ruckus continued unabated, he growled and clasped his hands over his ears.

Aaaaaahh . . . lo! Aaaaaahh . . . lo! Aaaaaahh . . . lo!

For a while, the peacock would settle down, lulled by the cooing of the peahen or intimidated by Nihal Amos's threats of boiled peacock, but as soon as Nihal started to snore, the bird started up again. As the first light of dawn touched the sky, Nihal Amos was wide-awake, most weary, and in a foul mood. He splashed water on his face, kicked his sleeping mat into the corner, and stomped around toward the garden.

The peacock flapped down from its roost and strutted directly in front of Nihal Amos, trailing its magnificent tail behind it. "You may impress your lady, but you do not impress me!" Nihal Amos growled. "Lucky for you, you are too old and stringy for the cook pot!"

Pots clattered at the back of the house. Soon the entire household would be stirring. Nihal Amos stepped into his sandals and hurried toward the road.

✏

Saji Stephen, washed and oiled and dressed in new linen clothes, sat impatiently on his carpet under the jasmine vines. He had almost finished his breakfast of spiced rice and curry with coconut, yet still Nihal Amos did not come. Udit returned bearing a plate of bananas, mangoes, and guavas, which he set down before the landlord.

"Where is Nihal Amos?" Saji Stephen demanded. He made no attempt to hide his irritation. "The harvest begins tomorrow. Where is my lazy son?"

"I do not know, master," the servant answered. "When I came out to see that the veranda was in order, he had already gone."

Saji Stephen jumped to his feet. "Find him! I will not go to the worker settlement alone. Find my son!"

Udit bowed low and backed away as quickly as he could.

Saji Stephen kicked at the plate of fruit. The banana bunch fell off to one side and the mangoes to the other. The guavas rolled every which way across the veranda. Saji Stephen glared at the spilled fruit, and rage overtook him. Roaring, he stomped on the mangoes, squishing them into the ground. Then he chased down the guavas and trampled them, one by one, until nothing remained but a mess of fruit pulp.

"Find him!" Saji Stephen yelled. "Find Nihal Amos!"

"Nihal Varghese!"

Nihal Amos started at the sound of his name. "Hari?" he asked, glancing quickly from side to side. "Is that you?"

Instead, Mani Rao stepped out from the shadows.

"Where is Hari?" Nihal Amos asked. "I demanded to see him, not you."

"I speak of your brother, Rajeev," Mani said. "While he searches for a place of power with the new government, will he also search among the Muslims for his own family?"

Nihal Amos's eyes narrowed. "That is neither your worry nor mine. Our concern is Communists who steal. Was it just the house of my father, robbed by one angry boy, or is this now an accepted way of bringing down the rich?"

"Your brother will not find what he wants in Delhi," Mani said.

"First you have my house robbed, then you make threats against my brother!"

"I tell you the truth. Men do not establish themselves in the new government and gain power simply by going to Delhi. Delhi is the gathering place of Muslims—*lakhs* of them from all over the country."

"*Lakhs* of Muslims? Hundreds of thousands?"

"They fill Purana Quila and Nizamuddin. No room remains even in the open space around the Red Fort. Soldiers push the refugees out of Delhi as fast as they can and onto trains headed for Pakistan."

Stunned, Nihal Amos stared at Mani.

"If your brother is fool enough to impose himself uninvited on the government in Delhi, would he not also be fool enough to trek among the refugee camps?"

"It is a vicious business," Nihal Amos said shaking his head.

"Especially for your brother. Angry Muslims target Hindu moneylenders."

"My brother is not a Hindu! He is a Christian, descended from a long line of Christians."

"Still today? When it no longer suits his purposes?" Mani shook his head. "Your brother boasts of the wealth of his landholding family. And he bears the name of a Hindu moneylender . . . should he live long enough to identify himself."

Nihal Amos hesitated. "Do you threaten my family, Mani Rao? Is that the way of the Party now? Robbery and . . . and—"

"Perhaps you do not know as much about us as you think you do," Mani said. "Could it be that you are nothing but a Varghese landowner after all?"

Then Mani was gone. Slipped down to the road already filled with villagers eager to get their work under way before the heat of the day. Nihal Amos turned back to his father's house. He never knew that the entire time, Hari hunkered in the shadows, listening to every word he said.

"The man who will be my husband came to see Saji Stephen," Glory Anna bubbled to Shridula. "I was not allowed to see him, of course, but Sheeba Esther did. She said he is very handsome."

Shridula pulled the brush through Glory Anna's hair. "Do you suppose he stomps his feet when someone displeases him?"

"Certainly not! He is a fine man, patient and kind and extremely generous."

"Is that what Sheeba Esther told you, or is that what you hope?" Shridula gave the brush a bit of a yank.

"Ow! Be careful!" Glory Anna scolded. "Sheeba Esther did not have to say so because I already knew it to be true. My grandmother would not have approved a man to be my husband unless he was like that."

"Maybe she only knew him as a boy, before he grew into a man."

Glory Anna pulled away from Shridula's rough brush strokes. "What is wrong with you today? You pull my hair, you criticize my handsome almost-husband, and now you try to stir up an argument with me."

Shridula slammed the brush down on the table. She grabbed up her sleeping mat and tossed it into the corner.

"I have been thinking about asking Saji Stephen to give you to me as a wedding gift," Glory Anna stated. "Then you will have to come to my new house and be my servant forever. And if you act like this to me, I will punish you, and then I will . . . I will . . ."

Shridula turned away. She refused to let Glory Anna see the tears that welled up in her eyes. She jerked the door of the wardrobe open and sifted through the carefully folded stacks of beautiful silk *saris*.

". . . and then I will never let you see your father again!"

Tears spilled down Shridula's cheeks. She swiped at them with the back of her hand before she turned around to face Glory Anna. "Would you really do that?" she asked softly. "Really?"

Glory Anna shook her head. "No," she said. "When I marry, you can go back to your father."

"Back to my father and the fields and the rice paddies," Shridula said. "Why does the whole country go free, but not us? Why not Untouchables?"

"I do not know," Glory Anna said. "It is not fair. It is not right. But that is our way."

⁂

"Because I know nothing about growing rice and even less about keeping a book of accounts," Nihal Amos said to Saji Stephen. "Because I care nothing about the harvest and I do not approve of owning other people. Because, despite India's independence, I am still a Communist in my heart. That is why I will never work alongside you, Father."

"We are landlords," Saji Stephen insisted. "We are money-lenders. That is what our family has been for countless generations. It is what we are."

"Not Rajeev. He is a politician. And not me. I am a fighter for freedom."

"Rajeev is gone," Saji Stephen said. "His sons are gone. One day this land will belong to you. But I confess, my son, until that day comes, I do not know how to be a good land-lord. I need your help."

Nihal Amos shook his head in frustration.

"Come, sit beside me on my fine Persian carpet. I will teach you all about my book of accounts. *Our* book of accounts." Saji Stephen's voice had drifted off into a pleading whine. "Come with me to see the harvest. Come and see all the good you can do for our own laborers. You can talk to the overseers."

"Overseers. Right there is a major problem. How can two men be in charge at the same time? When the laborers fail to do their job, which overseer should be punished? When the labor-ers succeed, which one of the two should receive a reward?"

"Yes! Of course you are right!" Saji Stephen exclaimed. "See how naturally the responsibility of landowner comes to you?"

But Nihal Amos was just getting started. "Even now, as the laborers go out to the harvest fields, we could be speaking to them of the rewards that await them when they finish. The feast should be especially lavish this year, a celebration of India's independence. Bonuses of extra rice and wheat and spices for all, of course, but additional gifts as well. New clothing, perhaps?"

"Wait, wait!" Saji Stephen protested. "I have seen the paddies. The rice is stunted and sparse. This harvest will not be a plentiful one. Why should I hand out such generous rewards?"

"To buy the allegiance of the workers, of course," Nihal Amos said. "An extra measure of rice and a set of cheap clothes is a small price to pay for loyalty among your bonded laborers. Anyway, what good are profits this year? If you do not spend the money on the workers, it will go to pay for Glory Anna's wedding."

Saji Stephen's face broke into a grin. "Yes, I see, I see! Ha, ha!"

"Glory Anna's wedding would be especially lavish, but what good would that do you? You still might well have little cooperation from the workers."

"Yes!" Saji Stephen said. "We shall do this together, Nijal Amos. Two landlords today, then when I lie in my grave, the land will all be yours."

Nihal Amos stared out toward the road. "I do believe a rain cloud has begun to form over the mountains, Father. The hard season is almost behind us."

"Did you hear them talking?" Shridula whispered to Glory Anna. "One overseer will have to go. Dinkar hates my father because he thinks my father is trying to push him out, but my father never wanted to be overseer in the first place. Dinkar will fight to keep his job, but my father will not fight back."

"Saji Stephen likes your father," Glory Anna said.

"No, he does not! He only likes to torment him. If my father was gone, Dinkar could be the overseer again the way he was before, and everyone could be satisfied."

"Gone where?" Glory Anna asked.

"Away! With me. Do you not see? India is free from England. You will soon be married, and then you will be free from this place. But what about my father and me? Should we not be free too?"

"I do not know," Glory Anna said doubtfully. "Where would you go? Maybe you would starve to death."

"Maybe I would not," Shridula said. "Other Untouchables live free. I saw them when we went to the market."

"Do you really think you could?" Glory Anna asked. She paused only a moment, then she grabbed Shridula's hands. "If you truly think so . . . Well, maybe then I could help you."

*

The next evening, after the last meal of the day, Glory Anna spread out a long silk scarf and stacked five *chapatis* on it. She tucked a bag of rice up close to them. "Do you want to take my hair brush with you?" she asked.

Shridula laughed. "It is silver. Untouchables cannot have metal."

Glory Anna opened the wardrobe and pulled out her dowry box. "Ten rupees and twenty annas," she said. "That is all the money I have. You take it."

"No," Shridula said. "I could not."

"It is my gift to you. For all you did for me." Glory Anna laid the coins beside the food and wrapped everything together in the scarf.

Many times, Shridula had gone to the settlement to see her father. She could easily go again and no one would ask questions. But if she did go to the settlement, word would quickly spread from worker to worker that she was there and she wouldn't be left alone for a single moment. With so many eyes on her, how could she and her father hope to sneak away? Better to wait until everyone in the landlord's house was asleep. She could go get her father, and they could be away from the settlement well before dawn.

After the sun had set, Saji Stephen and Nihal Amos settled themselves on the veranda to enjoy the cool of the evening. Glory Anna opened the door of her room, and the girls peeked out at the men. Shridula would have to cross the veranda in order to get to the path that led to the settlement.

"Those two might sit there all night!" Glory Anna whispered.

But Shridula knew they would not. She just had to wait. Just wait.

". . . no sleep last night," Nihal Amos was saying. ". . . fool of a loudmouth bird!"

Shridula could only catch snatches of their conversation.

". . . early tomorrow morning . . ." Saji Stephen replied. ". . . most important day of all . . ."

Glory Anna caught her breath. "I think he is almost ready to go to bed," she whispered.

Nihal Amos said something that made Saji Stephen laugh. Saji stood up and stretched. ". . . right after dawn. Or perhaps even before . . ." He made his way toward the house. Quickly the girls scampered inside and shut the door.

After a few minutes, Glory Anna eased the door open. Out on the veranda, Nihal Amos busied himself spreading his sleeping mat. He stretched out across it, and within minutes his soft snores reverberated back to the house.

"Now!" Glory Anna whispered.

Shridula grabbed up the silk scarf.

Glory Anna threw her arms around Shridula and hugged her tight. "I will pray for you," she promised. "Every day, I will pray for you."

With a sudden rush, Shridula's mind flooded with all the things she wished to say. *Thank you for letting me sleep in your room. Thank you for reading with me. Thank you for allowing my Untouchable hands to hold your silver brush. Thank you for daring to be my friend.* But in the end, all she could manage was to choke out, "Thank you. Thank you!"

Shridula eased out the door and wove her way along the side of the veranda. Hugging the shadows and hardly daring to breathe, she crept around Nihal Amos. Never before had she seen him so close. His lips were full and loose. With each breath, he sucked them in with a snort, then puffed them out with a resounding snore. With a sudden gasp, Nihal Amos swatted at something on his face. Shridula froze. She was close enough to reach out and touch him. But then he rolled over, and the floppy-lip snoring started up all over again.

If only the moon were not so bright! Shridula thought. *If only the night were not so clear!*

Shridula's pounding heart made her head throb. Yet she dared not slow her pace. Finally she managed to duck around the corner of the veranda. Once her feet touched the safety of the garden edge, she lunged forward . . . only to plunge headlong into a handcart filled with rocks. The cart tipped over with a crash, and the rocks clattered out onto the ground.

"Who is there?" Nihal Amos called.

Shridula crouched down low. She was stuck out in the open, halfway between the wall and the road. Her eyes darted back and forth. She could see no place to hide.

"Who is it?" Nihal Amos demanded. "Who is in the garden?"

Shridula could picture Nihal Amos sitting up on his sleeping mat and craning his neck to get a better look toward the garden. Terrified, she froze. Soon he would make his way toward her. Perhaps he had already picked up a stick. Or a knife.

Then an idea came to Shridula. She stretched out her neck and, in the voice of the peacock, she called *Aaaaaahh . . . lo! Aaaaaahh . . . lo!*

Aaaaaahh . . . lo! the peacock answered from its roost in the tree. *Aaaaaahh . . . lo!*

"Fool of a loudmouth bird!" Nihal Amos said. He lay back down, clamped his hands over his ears, and went back to sleep.

Shridula slipped away in the moonlight under the watchful eye of the confused peacock.

32

September 1947

"Leave the settlement?" Ashish exclaimed. "Sneak away in the dark of the night?" He stared at Shridula with uncomprehending eyes. "But where would we go?"

"To freedom!" Shridula said.

"I have never been out of the settlement. Our kind . . . Untouchables like us . . . we have no place in the village."

"I have been out there, *Appa*, and I saw our kind," Shridula insisted. "Untouchables live out there, and they are not owned by anyone."

"What would we do? How would we eat?"

"We can make a way." Shridula grabbed her father's arm and shook him. "But we have to go now, *Appa*. Tonight! Do you not see? The landowner will not allow two overseers in his harvest fields. He is coming tomorrow. When he gets here, you must be gone!"

"I do not want to be overseer," Ashish said. "I will say that to Dinkar. I will say it to the landlord. I do not want to fight with anyone."

"Of course not!" Shridula could barely hide her exasperation. "Please, *Appa*, we must go now. While it is still dark and everyone sleeps. In the morning, when the harvest begins, it will be too late."

Shridula scooped up the earthenware container of spices and the bag of rice and tossed them into her silk scarf. "We will only take the food and the water jar. Maybe one pot for cooking. Leave everything else."

Ashish didn't move. "They will come after us," he said.

"Not with the harvest starting. They will be too busy. Come, *Appa*. Please, come now!"

"The Holy Book," Ashish said. "I should get that from its hiding place and take it along. Unless we will be coming back. Will we be coming back?"

"Take it," Shridula said. "We will not be back."

Shridula grabbed up the loaded scarf and hung it over her shoulder. She grabbed her father by the arm and pulled him toward the door. "Be very quiet. We must not let anyone hear us. Come, come! Quickly now."

Outside the door, Ashish stopped to stare at the giant *neem* tree. "I planted this tree myself. Twenty-nine years ago, for your mother. It was only a little sprout then, but I knew it would grow. It keeps our hut cool in the hot sun."

"Yes," Shridula whispered gently. "But look at the branches, *Appa*. They wave a farewell to us. Do come now. We must step quickly!"

ℒ❧

How grateful Shridula was for the same bright moon that had so upset her when she sneaked across the veranda. Now it cast a welcome glow that lent a bit of light to the rough path. Only occasionally did they stumble on the dried crevices or trip on rocks.

"If anyone sees us, we will act as though we are simply enjoying a cool respite together," Shridula told her father.

"With a bulging silk scarf hanging over your shoulder?" Ashish asked. But his voice was easier, and he laughed when he said it.

Once they were safely out on the thornbush-lined path and away from the settlement, Shridula picked up the pace. "Hurry," she urged. "Before the workers awaken and someone sees that you are gone."

"Do you know where you are taking us?"

"Yes. Well, sort of . . . Away from the landlord." Shridula laughed. "You do like an adventure, do you not?"

"No, I do not," her father answered. "But if your mother was here, she would love it."

"I wish she was here," Shridula said. "She would be so happy to finally be free."

Ashish touched his daughter's hand. "You are very much like her, you know."

Together Shridula and Ashish hurried along the narrow path that ran between the two largest of the landowner's fields. They could almost make out the most productive of the rice paddies off to the right. In a few hours, it would be filled with workers.

"This harvest will not be a good one," Ashish told his daughter. "I am happy to be gone."

For a long while, the two walked in silence. The farther they moved from the settlement, the narrower the path became. With fewer feet treading this way, the ground grew increasingly uneven and bumpy.

"Slow down," Ashish warned. But Shridula would not.

As the moon set and the shadows thickened, it became more and more difficult to see the path. Several times Shridula stumbled, but she quickly righted herself. Still she refused to slow her pace.

"I do not think it will be very much— Oooof!"

Shridula's foot hit against a jutting tree root, and she landed flat on the ground. The silk scarf slipped from her shoulder and struck the baked ground with a clatter.

"We are away from the settlement," Ashish said as he helped Shridula to her feet. "Slow your pace." She started to argue, but he stopped her. "Listen to me, Daughter. Do you hear the river? The road to the village is up ahead. Slow your pace."

✐

When Saji Stephen stepped out onto the veranda, all ready for a new day, he found his son pacing impatiently.

"You said sunup," Nihal Amos said.

Saji Stephen looked up at the last splashes of orange fading from the already hot sky. "Better to see the laborers in the field." He moved to his place under the jasmine vines. "Come. Sit beside me. We will go to the paddies with our stomachs full."

Nihal Amos sighed with frustration. "Better to see the harvest started well," he said. "You can fill your belly when our work is done."

"Now see here—"

"If we are to work together, I shall have my share of the say," Nihal Amos said. "And I say we get ourselves out to the paddy immediately."

"It will take time for the servant to ready the horse cart," Saji Stephen said. "I will give the word, and Udit can bring *idli* cakes and curry for us to eat while we wait."

"I have already given word," Nihal Amos said. "The cart is ready and waiting."

"But smell the curry," Saji pleaded. "Surely it would do no harm to wait for a bit of rice!"

"Even now we waste time!" Nihal Amos exclaimed. "I am going. Come with me or stay here and eat."

Nihal Amos strode toward the waiting cart. Saji Stephen frowned and scolded after him. Nihal Amos, ignoring his father's protests, climbed up into the cart. Saji Stephen started to stamp his foot, but already Nihal Amos was giving orders to the servant.

"Wait!" Saji Stephen called as he ran for the cart. "Now I am ready!"

As the rising sun shimmered pink and orange, Shridula and Ashish stood together at the end of the landlord's pathway, at the place where it joined the village road. Alongside the juncture, the river flowed brown and lazy, cutting the village road in two. Ashish stood still and stared at the rickety bridge that connected one side of the road with the other. "There it is," he said in wonder. "That is the place that haunts me in my dreams."

"You have been here before?" Shridula asked.

"No . . . Or . . . maybe. I almost remember, but not quite. I do know that it is a bad place. A place of evil and great pain. We must leave at once."

On the other side of the road, in a rice paddy ripe for harvest, a sprinkling of men stood up from their work and stared across at the two.

"The Untouchable women I saw at the market," Shridula said uncertainly. "They were on this side of the river. I know they were, because I did not cross over. But I did cross it when . . . when I was with Glory Anna."

"This is a bad place," Ashish murmured. He started to tremble. "Maybe we should go back. Maybe we would be better off working for the landlord."

"No!" Shridula said. "We can find those other Untouchable women who sell at the market. We can ask them—"

"This is Sudra land!" a worker called from across the road. "Untouchables belong on the other side of the river!"

"Come, *Appa!*" Shridula said. She grabbed Ashish by the hand and pulled.

"No, no," he protested. "We must not!" But Shridula ran on toward the bridge. Ashish had no choice but to follow.

⊘

"Not one worker will be in the fields," Saji Stephen said.

"The harvest begins today," Nihal Amos insisted. "Everyone who can stand will go to the fields."

"Those lazy laborers know how to get out of work. One will say to Ashish, 'We cannot cut the rice because Dinkar told us to clean the storage sheds.' Another will say to Dinkar, 'We cannot clean the storage sheds because Ashish told us to cut the rice.' Then they will lie down together in the shade while the rice goes uncut and the shed stays dirty."

"One overseer," Nihal Amos stated. "He will have our backing, and we will punish all who go against him."

"But what if it is the other overseer who goes against him?"

"There will be no other overseer. One overseer only, and he will have our backing."

"But if Dinkar says one thing and Ashish says another—"

"One overseer!" Nihal Amos insisted. "Only one, and everyone will do as he says."

As the horse cart passed the empty field, Saji Stephen snorted in frustration. The horse continued on, picking its footing along the path to the second field. "Weeds!" Saji Stephen exclaimed. "Nothing but weeds!" When the main field came into view, Saji Stephen caught his breath.

Already, a long line of men had started their way through the paddy, swinging their scythes high and chopping the rice stalks low and close. As one, they stepped forward and chopped again. Another step and another chop. Behind them, women readied themselves to gather up the stalks and bind them into sheaves.

Saji Stephen leapt up, trying his best to stand in the moving cart. "Look! Just look!" he cried, beside himself with joy.

"Separate the weeds!" Dinkar called out to one group of women. "Work faster, Arun!" he shouted to a man in the line. "Keep up with the others!"

"You did it!" Saji Stephen sighed as he sank down beside Nihal Amos. "One overseer, just as you said! And everyone at work. Just as you said, my son!"

"But, Father, I . . . I . . ." Perplexed, Nihal Amos looked about him, searching for Ashish.

"You what?"

"Never mind," said Nihal Amos. "One overseer, just as I said."

$\mathcal{L}\!\blacktriangledown$

On the Untouchable side of the river, on the far side of the pond—although the pond was now nothing but a large pool of slimy mud—the roadside had been chopped bare of brush and trees. A woman passed by them with a basket of custard apples balanced on her head.

"See, *Appa?*" Shridula said eagerly. "That women must be taking those custard apples to the market on the other side of the river. We could do that. Custard apples grow on the trees between the landlord's fields."

"Those trees belong to the landlord!" Ashish said. "We could not take fruit from them."

"Other trees, then. We can go far down this road and find other trees. And the reeds along the river. You can gather them, and I can weave them into mats. I saw another woman selling reed mats at the market."

"My father was a *chamar*," Ashish said thoughtfully. "He gathered up the animals that died and made fine leather from their skins. But I do not know that skill."

A boy passed by leading two goats along the road.

"Maybe we can get a goat," Shridula said. "We could sell milk."

"We are not of the milking caste," Ashish said. "Anyway, goats cost money. And they need food and a roof over their heads."

Up ahead stood the first shelters in a settlement of thatched roof huts. Ashish stopped and stared at them.

"What is it?" Shridula asked.

"When I was very small, we used to live in a hut, but it was made of mud. My mother told me about it."

"Here? Is this where you lived?"

"I do not know," Ashish said. "I cannot remember."

As they walked beside the settlement, three girls who hurried along together passed by them. All three carried water pots on their heads. In front of one hut after the other, women hunkered down over kitchen fires, thin lines of smoke rising up into the air. A tiny child chased after a chicken that flapped its wings wildly and squawked in protest. A boy kicked a rock over toward the road. He started to run after it, but when he saw Shridula and Ashish, he stopped and stared at them until they passed on out of sight.

"Go past the last of the huts, then on a bit farther still," Ashish told Shridula. "We must not upset the people of this settlement with our presence. We will make a place for ourselves apart from them."

In the gathering twilight, Saji Stephen looked up from his place on the veranda and surveyed the smattering of clouds that had begun to gather over the mountains. "It will be a good harvest," he said to Nihal Amos. "Dinkar will see to that. You made the right choice for overseer."

"Tomorrow, we shall go to the settlement at dawn," Nihal Amos said. "Before the workers go to the paddy, we will tell them of the great feast we have planned, and the gifts with which we will reward them after the harvest."

Saji Stephen hesitated, but only for a moment. "Yes, yes," he agreed. "We will go at dawn. Before dawn, if you like!"

For a long time, the two sat together watching the sun set and the stars come out.

"Nihal Amos," Saji Stephen finally said. "About Ashish . . ."

Nihal cleared his throat.

"You did the right thing," Saji Stephen said. "He was not a good overseer. I trusted him, but he only made trouble for me. You did the right thing."

Beyond the last of the huts, past the place where the village scavengers made their home, Ashish and Shridula moved off the road and pushed their way back into the bushes. As Ashish gathered sticks and palm fronds, Shridula collected stones for a cooking pit. By the time Ashish finished erecting a simple lean-to shelter, Shridula handed him a bowl of boiled rice flavored with dried chili peppers.

"I used almost all our water," Shridula said to her father. "Tomorrow morning I will have to walk to the river to get more."

"No!"

Shridula stared at Ashish.

"I do not want you to go to the river alone, Daughter. You and I will go together."

"Getting water is the work of women," Shridula protested.

But Ashish was adamant. "Tomorrow we will go to the river together."

They had no sleeping mats, so Ashish took the *chaddar* off his head and spread it on the ground for Shridula to lie on. By the light of the moon, she watched her father walk toward the road and back again, around the lean-to and back to where she lay. She watched him sit, then get up, then sit again.

"Do you fear evil spirits, *Appa?*" Shridula asked.

"Hush," Ashish said. "Sleep now."

"Because of the dreams that haunt you?"

Ashish said nothing.

"I do not believe in the evil spirits," Shridula said. "Remember the song you sang to me . . . *Jesus loves me, this I know . . .*"

"That was a long time ago."

"We are free, *Appa*. No one owns us anymore."

"It took us only one day to walk here and find this place," Ashish said. "The landlord, in his bullock cart, could be here much faster."

"The Holy Book says: *When a man's ways please the* LORD*, he maketh even his enemies to be at peace with him,*" Shridula said.

"Perhaps it will please the Christian Lord to let us live our lives in peace."

"I do not know." Ashish slumped down and clutched his head in his hands. "I am too old to understand. But maybe you can, my daughter. Maybe you can understand."

33

October 1947

*S*hridula turned over on her father's *chaddar*. At night it was her bed, in the morning he wrapped it around his head. Rain had fallen during the night—gentle rain, but enough to leave Shridula feeling clammy and uncomfortable. Her father's *chaddar* stuck to her back and clung to her arms. The uneven ground—and every clump of dirt, every little stone—dug into her aching body. Still, she refused to think back kindly on her sleeping mat spread out on Glory Anna's floor. She was a slave then. Now, though her body may ache, she was free.

Stretching her legs and arms, Shridula blinked into the fading darkness. The ground next to her was empty. Where was her father?

The lean-to rattled, stopped, then shook hard. Shridula jerked upright. "*Appa?*" she breathed.

"I am out here," her father answered. "Patching palms over holes left by the wind." Shridula knew her father too well to be fooled by the lightness of his voice. She could hear his worry. A small rain last night, and today everything inside the shelter dripped. What would happen once the monsoons began to pour down? Their little lean-to would quickly wash away. What would they do then?

Shridula stepped out of the shelter. "I will go to the river to fetch water," she said.

"No!"

Shridula was taken back by her father's harshness.

Ashish took a deep breath and, in his artificially light voice said, "I will go with you, Daughter. I want to gather custard apples."

"Custard apple trees grow farther down the road, not up toward the river."

"In that case, I will gather firewood. I will walk along with you and gather something."

Shridula sighed.

Ashish went along with her to collect water. He followed when she searched for firewood. At the market, he stayed close beside her, and if she did more than exchange the most basic pleasantries with anyone, he intervened and cut the conversation short.

"I know this does not please you, Daughter," Ashish said gently. "But you are young, and I am old. I understand much more than you do. You and I, we do not know the rules of the village, and so we must be ever so careful. Because we do not know whose eyes are on us, we must constantly be wary."

"What good is freedom if I must live my life in a new kind of cage?" Shridula demanded.

"For our kind, someone will always be watching," Ashish said. "A cage will always await us."

"Tea leaves, of course," Miss Abigail Davidson said to Krishna. "And kidney pie, I should think. Perhaps with a nice Yorkshire pudding."

Krishna waited patiently. The expression on his scarred face never changed.

"Would you fancy that?" Miss Abigail asked. "Would you fancy a kidney pie and Yorkshire pudding for supper this evening?"

"Yes, *mem*," Krishna said. "Certainly, *mem*."

"Be off with you, then," Miss Abigail said. "I do believe I shall take advantage of the quiet to catch up on my reading."

Of course, she would not. Krishna knew she would be asleep before he left, and however long he was away, she would still be snoring softly in her chair when he returned. Good. That would be for the best.

"And strawberries, dear boy," Miss Abigail called after him. "Wouldn't that be lovely? Perhaps you would be good enough to choose especially ripe berries. And do remember the cream. Oh, to have a bowl of strawberries and cream just now!"

"Yes, Miss Abigail," Krishna said. He had no more idea what a strawberry was than Yorkshire pudding or kidney pie. He would purchase what he always purchased—a bag of rice, a wrapper of tea leaves, and a measure of curry. Whatever Miss Abigail called the meal, he always prepared the same thing: boiled rice, with chili peppers from the garden and a hefty pinch of curry thrown in. He knew how to cook nothing else. Every morning and every afternoon he brewed a pot of tea and served it to Miss Abigail, and every morning and every afternoon she drank her tea and thanked him for the biscuits.

"Never mind!" Miss Abigail suddenly exclaimed. "You will botch the entire project. I shall have to go to the marketplace with you and select the strawberries myself."

It would be a long, dirty ride, Krishna explained. Clouds were gathering in the sky and it looked like rain. And what of the reading she had planned for the afternoon?

But Miss Abigail would not hear his excuses. She did not mind dirt one bit, she insisted. As for rain, she could think of nothing more refreshing than a cleansing downpour. And her reading would easily wait for another day. "I'll just change into fresh clothes," she said. "I shan't be but a moment."

Krishna waited, pacing back and forth, and growing more and more impatient with each turn. It was not his place to hurry Miss Abigail, but she often fell these days. And she became so easily confused. What if something had happened to her? Krishna was ready to call out when the door to Miss Abigail's bedchamber opened.

All Krishna could do was stare. For many years, since he was a boy, he had seen Miss Abigail in nothing but Indian *saris*. But now she stood before him in a long blue skirt with matching top, its sleeves full at the top, and all trimmed in fading eyelet. Around her gray hair she had tied a navy blue straw hat, now brittle and broken with age.

"Well?" Miss Abigail said. "Do you plan to spend the day gawking or may we be off?"

With the harvest consuming all their energy and attention, neither Saji Stephen nor Nihal Amos realized Shridula was gone from the house. Glory Anna stayed in her room, out of their way. That was enough. But Sheeba Esther knew at once that something was amiss.

"She went to visit her father," Glory Anna explained.

"During the harvest?" Sheeba Esther asked. "When everyone works from the break of dawn until dusk? When the laborers are too weary to do anything at night but fall onto their sleeping mats?"

"She loves her father," Glory Anna answered with a shrug.

"Yes," Sheeba Esther said. "Of course she does. I know for a certainty that she loves him very much."

When Sheeba Esther asked Nihal Amos about the overseer difficulty, he said, "I worked it out. Dinkar is the only overseer now. Ashish crept away into the shadows and is hardly visible in the fields."

"How very clever of you," Sheeba Esther said to her husband. But she knew.

When the harvest ended, everyone in the landlord's household turned all their efforts toward the great feast, and after that, to Glory Anna's wedding.

One morning, when the house was finally quiet again, Glory Anna said to Sheeba Esther, "I shall miss the sitar."

"Take it with you," Sheeba Esther said. "If you ask Saji Stephen, he will say no. But if we load it on the cart among your other belongings, he will never miss it."

Glory Anna laughed. "Sometimes to be forgettable is not a bad thing."

"No," Sheeba Esther answered. "Not a bad thing at all."

⁊❧

The only animal left at the mission was a worn-out donkey. Krishna fastened it to the cart and urged it up the road toward the village.

"The day is to be pleasant," Krishna said. "Please, you are to be waiting in the wagon until I return. I will not be away for long."

"Find some good haddock for tonight's supper," Miss Abigail called after him. "And root vegetables, too. That would be quite nice, I should think."

Krishna hurried over toward the Sudra rice seller's stall. He didn't see the silk scarf spread out on the ground with its small pile of custard apples and unevenly woven mats. But Shridula saw him. "Look, *Appa*," she gasped. "Do you see that man?"

The twisted face. The mouth scarred into a perpetual O. Ashish caught his breath and stared. Something stirred in the back of his mind. Something about the river . . . About the bridge . . .

"I think he must be a leper," Shridula said.

"Then we must not allow him to approach us," Ashish warned. "Leprosy is a terrible curse."

But already the man was gone, folded into the crowd of villagers. Shridula turned back to her wares. Ashish, however, could not take his eyes from the crowd.

"Strawberries? Strawberries?" Miss Abigail tapped her walking stick on the ground in front of Shridula. "I say, young lady, have you any strawberries today?"

Shridula was too taken aback to say anything. It didn't matter, though, for Ashish had already caught sight of the pale English lady in the old-fashioned blue dress. He shook his head slowly, as if attempting to rouse himself from a dream. His mouth dropped open, but no sound came out.

"Miss Abigail!" Krishna cried as he ran up behind her. "You were to be waiting in the cart!"

Ashish's eyes turned to the scarred face. "Krishna," he whispered. Then he turned back to stare again at the woman in blue.

"Listen," Glory Anna said to Sheeba Esther. "The rain has started." A light patter, patter sounded on the roof. Glory Anna wrung her hands anxiously. "It is falling softly now, but soon it will pour down in torrents."

"Shelter can be found in many places," Sheeba Esther said gently. "Even for Untouchables."

Glory Anna started. "I only meant . . . maybe the harvest . . . because if . . . if . . ."

"They will be all right," Sheeba Esther said gently. She sat down beside the girl and clasped hold of her hands. "No one will go after them."

Glory Anna stared at Sheeba Esther. "How can you be certain?"

"I asked Nihal Amos to pass along to Saji Stephen your gratitude for his wedding gift of two servants."

"Shridula and her father?"

"Yes. I told him they were already on their way to the house where you will live with the family of your new husband. I told him they must prepare for your arrival next month."

"He did not argue with you?"

"Not when I said you would require no other gifts from him. That is true, is it not? You will not require any other gifts from him?"

"No!" Glory Anna said. She laughed out loud. "No, no, no!"

"*Mem* is like my mother to me," Krishna said to Ashish as the two men sat together on the floor in Miss Abigail's cottage. "But I am worried for her. I cannot do for her all she needs."

Ashish looked over at Miss Abigail. Shridula had cut a custard apple open for her. The old woman lifted it to her mouth and noisily sucked at the fruit. She spat out a mouthful of seeds and asked, "Strawberries, my dear?"

Shridula smiled. "Yes. Strawberries."

"Delicious!" Miss Abigail sighed. She sucked out another bite.

"Her mind is not well," Krishna told Ashish. "I do not know what to do. I am afraid for her."

"Who are you, dear?" Miss Abigail asked Shridula.

"Shridula. I am the daughter of Ashish."

"Oh!" Miss Abigail exclaimed. "I know a boy named Ashish! Would you happen to know him? He is smaller than you, I fear. I will tell you a secret. That sweet boy has my dear father's Bible."

✑

Miss Abigail sat in one of the two chairs in her sitting room. "But of course you shall live with me, Ashish!" she said, slipping back into her fluent Malayalam. "Why would you live elsewhere? This is your home."

Ashish shook his head hard, but he could not make sense of it all. The pale English lady on a horse . . . Krishna writing letters in the dirt with a stick . . . the frightening clinic at night. So many memories.

"Your blue dress, Miss Abigail," Ashish whispered. "I remember that."

"I was wearing it when I took you home in the cart," Miss Abigail said. "That's when I gave you my Bible. Did you ever read it?"

"Yes," Ashish said. "Eleven times."

"I read it, too," Shridula added. "In our hut. *Appa* taught me the words."

Miss Abigail chuckled. "Dr. Moore said I was a fool to give my Bible away. I knew he was wrong. *Cast thy bread upon the waters: for thou shalt find it after many days.*"

Shridula looked up at her father, but he seemed as confused as she.

Miss Abigail turned to Shridula. "My dear, do you know how to make kidney pie?"

"No," Shridula mumbled. "I . . . I . . ."

"I will show her, *mem*," Krishna said.

"There's my boy," Miss Abigail cooed. "My Krishna and my Ashish, my two boys, home from school. I never should have sent you away. Never!"

Krishna cooked rice with chili peppers and a large pinch of curry. Shridula cut open more of her seedy custard apples, their creamy flesh sweet and fragrant. "My favorite," Miss Abigail said. "What I wanted more than anything for my supper. Strawberries and cream!"

Ashish and Krishna sat together and talked through the evening while Miss Abigail dozed in her chair. From time to time, the old lady roused herself enough to make a comment— sometimes confusing and sometimes profound, sometimes in English and sometimes in Malayalam. As for Shridula, mostly she just listened.

"We are clean. We work hard. We do right," Ashish said. "Why must we still be Untouchable?"

"Because that is how we were born," Krishna said.

"Perhaps things will change now, I do not know," Ashish said with a sigh.

"If God commands it, then things get better. The crops will grow and everyone will prosper," Krishna said. "Perhaps hearts will grow softer, too, and more generous."

"I do not believe in the Hindu gods and goddesses any-more," Ashish told Krishna. "I am not sure I can even believe in the Christian God."

"Did you really read the Bible eleven times?"

"Yes," Ashish said. For a moment he was silent. "On a clear night, I look at the sky and see the stars twinkle. But in the time of the monsoon, I see nothing but clouds. I am not like Shridula. She sees stars ahead, but I cannot see a good future. Only clouds. All I can see for us is clouds."

"How can you say that, *Appa?*" Shridula asked. "Here we sit in a dry house with people who do not want to hurt us or make us slaves. The landlord would never dare come and get us away from here. We are free!"

"We are still Untouchables," Ashish said.

Miss Abigail sat up and gazed around her with bright eyes. "Brahmins dislike Christians," she said. "Because if one removes the inequities and injustices, and the belief in karma, where is Hinduism's foundation? Crumbling away, that's where."

"Without us, who would be slaves for the upper castes?" Ashish asked.

The boisterous call of a pitta bird echoed through the open window: *wheeet-tieu, wheeet-tieu.*

"So loud a voice for one so small," Shridula said.

"Like too many people I know," Krishna added with a laugh.

Miss Abigail's blue eyes cleared. "When the pitta bird has something worth saying, he throws his head back, points his bill to the sky, and says it with all his might. He says it tonight, and tomorrow he will come back and say the same thing all over again."

"I want to be like that," Shridula whispered.

Miss Abigail laid her head back and let her eyes drift closed. "Matthew chapter 10, verse 31. *Fear ye not therefore, ye are of more value than many pitta birds.*"

"The Holy Book says that?" Shridula asked with a gasp. "It says *pitta birds?*"

Krishna laughed out loud. "Fear not, young one. God's hand is on you and your father. You are especially blessed."

"But does the Holy Book really say *pitta birds?*" Shridula insisted. "Does it, Miss Abigail?"

Miss Abigail didn't answer. She was already snoring softly.

Glossary of Terms

Ahimsa: A Buddhist and Hindu doctrine promoting non-violence toward all living beings.

Amma: Malayalam for mother

Anna: An old Indian coin, worth one-sixteenth of a rupee

Appa: Malayalam for father

Ashoka Chakra: Depiction of the Buddhist Dharmachakra represented with 24 spokes. It is so called because it appears on a number of edicts of Ashoka, the most prominent of which is the Lion Capital of Sarnath, adopted as the National Emblem of the Republic of India. The most visible use of the Ashoka Chakra today is in the center of the national flag of the Republic of India.

Benares: Located in Varanasi, in the present state of Uttar Pradesh, India, this revered and spiritual city located on the sacred Ganges River is considered holy, the city of "Lord Shiva."

Brahma: Creator god of the Hindu "trinity." The other two gods are Vishnu, the preserver, and Shiva, the destroyer. (Not to be confused with *Brahmin*. See below.)

Brahmin: The highest and most honored of the *varnas*, or castes, in Indian society. Brahmins are the Hindu priests and spiritual leaders. They put great and minute emphasis on ritual purity, and are forbidden from doing any manual labor. They make up approximately five percent of India's population. (Not to be confused with the god *Brahma*. See above.)

Caste: Traditional Hindu society is divided into four main *varnas*, or hierarchical groups known as castes: Brahmins (5 percent), Kshatriyas (5 percent), Vaishyas (5 percent), and Sudras (50 percent). Below this four-fold caste structure are the "outcastes"—now called Dalits—an oppressed people forced in all ways to occupy the lowest positions of this social order (25 percent). Also outside the caste system are the "tribals," the indigenous Indian peoples. Technically, Christians and Muslims are also outside the system, since caste is really part of the Hindu religious philosophy, though in actuality most outcaste Christians and Muslims remain mired in its oppression. These and people of other nationalities and religions make up the other 10 percent of the population. Each caste has its own group of occupations associated with it.

Chai: Indian spiced milk tea. It starts with a black tea, then various spices are added. The spices vary from place to place, but often include cloves, cardamom, cinnamon, and ginger.

Chaddar: A long strip of cloth, half the size of a mundu, worn by men as a shawl or turban.

Chamar: One of the many Untouchable occupational sub-castes, this one being that of leather tanners.

Chapati: Round, flat baked bread, similar to unsweetened pancakes or tortillas.

Chital: A reddish-brown deer with white spots, native to South Asia. Its antlers, which it sheds each year, are three-pronged and curve in a lyre shape. They may extend to 2.5 feet.

Cows, sacred: In India, "Mother Cow" is respected and looked after. It is considered sacred, and to harm a cow is a great sin. It is likened to harming one's own mother. The cow is also associated with mythological stories that surround several Hindu deities, including Krishna, said to have been raised by the son of a milkman.

Dharma: A moral law, or righteousness. This can vary, person to person, caste to caste.

Dowry: Money and/or property required of the family of the bride by the family of the groom in order to secure a marriage. The amount varies, depending on the "value" of the bride, but it is crippling for many families of girls. Dowry is a major cause of the abandonment and even killing of female children.

Ganges River: "Mother Ganges," sacred river of the Hindus, runs for 1,560 miles, from the Himalayas to the Bay of Bengal. It is revered as the source of life and purity, and is itself considered a goddess. Though the river is horribly polluted, people flock to it to bathe, to perform ceremonies, to float their dead, and even to drink from it. For the belief is that anyone who touches these purifying waters will be cleansed of all sins.

Ghee: Butter, boiled and clarified. It is greatly prized, both as a food, and as a part of ritual worship and the preparation of food for gods and goddesses.

Harijan: Children of God. The name Mohandas Gandhi used for Untouchables.

Jati: Each caste, or *varna*, is further divided into sub-classes, each representing a stratum in the strict hierarchy of Indian society. While there are only four castes, those are broken into thousands of *jatis*, as is the outcaste stratum.

Kanikkonna: A fast-growing, medium-sized tree with deeply fragrant yellow flowers that hang down in lovely profusion. The official flower of Kerala, it is used to arrange *kani* during the Festival of Vishu.

Karma: the sum total of a person's actions that is believed to lead to his or her present fate. This major tenet of Hinduism easily brings about an atmosphere of fatalism which can lead to hopelessness.

Kshatriyas: The second of the varnas, or castes, in Indian society. Formerly the kings and soldier-warriors, they, like the Brahmins, are respected and privileged. Also like the Brahmins, they may be "twice-born." Many are in the military, and many others are successful business owners and landlords. Kashatriyas make up about five percent of the Indian population.

Kurta: A collarless Indian shirt.

Lakh: A unit of Indian numbering that is equal to 100,000.

Lord Krishna: The most popular of the Indian gods. Krishna is believed to be an incarnation of Vishnu, the Preserver.

Mahatma: Great Soul. The title was often applied to Mohandas Gandhi.

Malayalam: The language spoken on the Malabar coast of South India, in the state of Kerala.

Mantra: Sacred words and sounds used for rhythmic chanting.

Manusmriti: The writings of Manu (though said to be authored by the god Brahma) that codified the caste system and sanctified it as religious institution.

Mem: Short for *memsahib* (see below).

Memsahib: Respectful address for an Indian to use toward a white woman.

Monsoon: The July to September season of torrential rain and wind. While the rains bring relief from the suffocating heat, it can be a time of treacherous downpours and flooding.

Mundu: A piece of thin cotton, linen, or silk cloth, fifty inches wide and five yards long, worn by men as a lower garment. It can be an ankle-length "skirt" or tied up to more closely resemble shorts.

Naga: Snake. In India, snakes are so revered that even temples are erected in their honor. The Naga culture was fairly widespread in India before the Aryan invasion, and continues to be an important segment of worship in certain areas. After the invasion, the Indo-Aryans incorporated the worship of snakes into Hinduism.

Naga Panchami: One of the most ancient celebrations in India, Naga Panchami, or the Festival of the Snakes, occurs on the fifth day of the bright half of the Shravan month (July/August). In Hindu culture, snakes hold a prominent place. Hindu mythologies are filled with stories and fables about snakes.

Neem: A common and appreciated tree in India. Every part of this wonderful tree is used for medicinal purposes—bark, roots, leaves, branches, flowers, fruit.

Nilavilakku: A flickering lamp integral to all celebrations and festivals in the Indian state of Kerala.

Outcastes: Now called Dalits, these are the people who fall outside and below India's caste system. They are forced to occupy the lowest position in the Indian social order. For many centuries they accepted their miserable lot as their justly deserved karma, a result of their own sins in a former life. More recently they have attempted to assert the rights afforded them when India gained independence from Britain. These attempts are often met with strong resistance from the upper castes, and the results can be horrendous: torture, rape, massacres, and other atrocities. The dominant castes have deliberately prevented the outcastes from rising to the level of equality by imposing on them impossible limits in every area of life, from occupation to dress to the very right to eat and drink. The social order has been constructed to keep them helpless and subservient. A conservative estimate of the number of "outcastes" is 25 percent of the Indian population.

Paddy: This can refer to a food, in which case it means rice with the husk still on. Or it can refer to the rice field—the paddy field.

Pallu: The loose end of a sari. In fine saris, the pallu is beautifully decorated.

Panch-kos: Sacred road that forms a boundary around the sacred city of Benares.

Purification: A ritual washing to remove sin and/or pollution.

Rupee: The most commonly used Indian currency.

Sadhu: An Indian holy man. Often, sadhus dress in saffron-colored robes that set them apart as dedicated to sacred matters.

Sahib: An Englishman. Often times, one who is very important.

Sari: A thin garment, fifty inches wide and five to six yards long, worn by Indian women, wrapped around the body to form a dress.

Sacred thread: A thin rope of cotton threads worn over the left shoulder by all initiated males of the Brahmin caste—and, though less frequently, by those in the second and third castes, too.

Sanskrit: The ancient language of India, and the language of the Vedas. Now it is used almost exclusively by the Brahmin caste for religious purposes.

Sharvan: The name of a month in the Hindu calendar, roughly falling July to August.

Shiva: Hindu god of creation and destruction. (See "Brahma.")

Sudras: The fourth of the *varnas*, or castes, in Indian society, supposedly created from the feet of the creator god, Brahma. Although they are still people of caste, they are of much lower status and privilege. They cannot be "twice-born." They are relegated to such jobs as laborers and farmers and servants. In fact, they are believed to have been created for the purpose of serving the higher castes. Sudras are not allowed to read, study, recite, or even to listen to the Vedas. The stated penalty for doing so is horrific maiming or death.

Thag: An Indian word that is the source of the English word "thug." The meaning is the same.

Untouchable: An outcaste, as determined by the laws of Manu. Depending on stratum, and on the area of the country in which one lives, this could also mean a person is unseeable (meaning laying eyes on them is polluting). Not long ago, polluting a member of an upper caste, even with a shadow, a footprint, or a drop of spittle that may result from speaking or sneezing, was crime enough to result in drastic punishments.

Vaisyas: Members of the third *varna*, or caste, in Indian society. Businessmen and traders, they are also high caste and may be "twice-born," although their status is much less than the two higher varnas. Vaisyas make up approximately five percent of the Indian population.

Vedas: Ancient Hindu scriptures, written in archaic Sanskrit in the form of a collection of mantras and hymns of praise to various gods. *Vedas* means sacred, revealed knowledge. The four Vedas are: the Rig Veda, the Sama Veda, the Atharva

Veda, and the Yajur Veda. The Yajur Veda is considered to be the oldest and most important. The foundation of the philosophy of Hinduism, the Vedas set forth the theological basis for the caste system.

Veranda: An external covered platform that sits at ground level of an Indian house. Most of a family's living took place on the veranda.

Vishnu: Hindu preserver god. (See "Brahma.")

Vishukkani: New Year festival celebrated in the Indian state of Kerala.

Discussion Questions

1. It is always difficult to move ourselves into another time and culture, then to attempt to understand it. Yet isn't that precisely the point of reading outside our own experience? What elements in this book's setting, either physical or cultural, surprised you? Confused you? Enlightened you? If you read the first book of the Blessings in India trilogy, *The Faith of Ashish*, did you expect more change in the almost half a century since that saga ended? One element of the Indian social system that seems especially difficult for Westerners to grasp is the powerlessness of outcastes. How did you see that evidenced in Shridula? Ashish? Jyoti?

2. A common response to criticism over caste issues is that the Indian social order is not really so very different from class divisions in other societies. To what degree do you think this argument is valid? In what ways do you see the Indian caste system as different? How is the plight of Indian outcastes similar to that of Africans enslaved in the U.S. a century earlier? How does it differ?

3. The landlord Varghese family takes great pride in their long and distinguished Christian heritage, which they claim goes all the way back to the Apostle Thomas. What does "Christian" mean to them? What separates them from the Hindu majority? What compromises were various family members willing to make in order to secure social or material gains? Why do you think Brahmin Rama encouraged Landlord Saji Stephen Varghese to so thoroughly embrace and participate in the Hindu festival?

4. Despite his Christian background, what do you think persuaded Nihal Amos Varghese to join the Communist Party? He claims to be both a Christian

and a Communist. Could this have been possible? Why or why not? What compromises would it require? In his insistence that he could be both at once, do you see any parallels to some professing Christians today? If so, in what ways?

5. In the bleak social order in which this story is set, hope is a difficult commodity to come by. When did you first recognize signs of hope in Shridula? Where does that hope come from? How does it mature? Do you see elements of hope in any other characters? Who, and in what way?

6. "Rice Christians" is a derisive term for people who declare themselves Christians purely for the material benefits it brings them. Is this situation a danger for Ashish? For Shridula? Why or why not? Do you see any ways in which Abigail Davidson might have unwittingly encouraged this? Do you think this is a concern for outcastes—now called Dalits—in India today?

7. Mohandas Gandhi is widely recognized as the leader of India's independence. Although this book is in no way intended as a comprehensive expose on his life, and although the book's scope ends before India's constitution was passed in January 1950, do you see any ways in which Gandhi failed to champion the cause of Untouchables? Why or why not? In what ways was he influenced by Christianity? How did his actions influence subsequent movements in other countries (e.g., U.S. civil rights; apartheid in South Africa)?

8. After all Ashish went through, after all he learned about the landlord's deceptive ways, why do you suppose it was so difficult for him to leave the labor settlement? What enabled Shridula to take the initiative in their escape? Do you think the two of them could have made it without the help they received from Glory Anna and Sheeba Esther?

9. Miss Abigail repeats a story attributed to the revered Indian Christian holy man Sadhu Sundar Singh about a man of high caste birth who, even to save his life, refuses to drink from a cup that might possibly have touched the lips of an Untouchable outcaste. The Sadhu's conclusion: "Indians will not receive Christianity from an English cup. If they are to receive the Gospel, it must come to them in an Indian cup." What was Miss Abigail's purpose in telling this story? Is it a valid point? Why or why not? How might this principle apply to Christians today?

10. In what ways does Shridula cast a face of hope over a social landscape many might consider hopeless? Do you see in this book a development of the budding faith that began with the child Ashish in book 1? If so, in what way? What is the vehicle for any such development? What might be required for the full blossoming of that faith? What might be required for the fulfillment of the hope of Shridula?

The Blessings in India saga concludes with *The Love of Divena*, which will be published in Fall 2012. Here's a sample of the final book of this enthralling series.

❧

1

March 1985

A breeze wafted along the marketplace and stirred up the fragrance of spring. Cooler air rustling through the palm fronds refreshed Shridula as she sat with her basket of chili peppers before her and four small cucumbers laid out to one side. A near-perfect market day.

Shridula pushed back an unruly lock of gray hair and dared to dream of selling enough vegetables to earn a whole *rupee*. More than a *rupee*, perhaps. Maybe enough to buy a small bag of rice. Even a coconut. What a treat that would be.

A steady stream of women in brightly colored *saris* passed by. Married women, whose husbands had *not* deserted them. Women with sons who could look after them as they grew old. But only a few paused to look over Shridula's fine peppers. Mostly they fixed their eyes on other vendors' piles of green mangoes, the first of the season, and on their fresh leafy greens, and coconuts, and packages of peppercorns. Women even stopped to pick through old Arpana's pile of woven mats, despite the fact that everyone already had woven mats, and if they needed new ones, they could make them themselves.

"Beautiful hot peppers!" Shridula called out. "Plucked from the garden this morning!"

But each shopper hurried past without pausing to look.

Shridula held out the finest of her peppers and called all the louder, "Beautiful peppers! And cucumbers, too!" She thrust the cucumbers out toward the women shoppers. Still no one stopped.

Hours later, when the sun reached its zenith—the cooling breeze long gone—Shridula still had not earned even one *paise*. Not one penny.

"Lovely peppers, spicy hot," Shridula sighed.

No, no! She must not allow that note of desperation to creep into her voice. When she was young and her voice still rang with hope, shoppers had flocked to buy from her. She brushed a calloused hand across her weathered face.

"Cucumbers! Cucumbers, fresh from the garden!"

She didn't dare call the cucumbers "lovely." Not when she had picked them so early in the season that faded blossoms still clung to the ends. The cucumbers were too small and immature to bring a good price. Shridula knew that. Yet if someone should have a particular hunger for cucumbers, and if hers were the only ones at the market . . .

A woman with two whiney little ones tugging at her green *sari* stopped to pinch Shridula's peppers.

"Fresh and firm," Shridula offered.

"We shall see about that," the woman sniffed. She dug through the basket and pulled out an especially nice pepper. She laid it aside and chose another, and another, and another until she had piled up the best from Shridula's basket. The woman scowled at her squealing children. "I suppose these will do," she said with a sigh. She scooped the peppers into her bag and handed Shridula a ten *paise* coin. Ten cents.

"No, no! Fifty *paise!*" Shridula insisted. Even that was less than she had hoped for.

"Hah!" laughed the woman in the green *sari*. "Do you think you are the only woman selling peppers at the market today? You most certainly are not!"

Shridula tried to barter, but the woman's loud shouting frightened her children and they began to cry. Other women stopped their shopping to gawk at the seller who had obviously done something to provoke such an outrage. In the end, Shridula accepted the coin simply to get rid of the woman. The woman in the green sari pushed her little ones ahead of her and hurried away, a triumphant smile on her lips and her bag filled with Shridula's finest peppers.

❧

By mid-afternoon, Shridula gazed with despair at her wilted chili peppers and shrunken cucumbers. The early stream of shoppers had melted down to an impatient trickle. A great weariness settled over Shridula. With a sigh of resignation, she put the cucumbers back in the basket and balanced it on her head. Clutching the single thin coin, she set her feet on the road toward home.

Over the years, the dirt road between the marketplace and Shridula's small hut had grown so familiar to her feet that she no longer paid it any mind. It used to be that she prayed to the God of the Holy Bible as she walked the road. But that was before her husband had left. When her sons still lived.

"My soul is weary," Shridula's father, Ashish, used to say. Back then, she couldn't understand what he meant. She did now.

Far down the road, the old woman's weary feet turned off onto the narrow path that led to the far edge of the untouchable end of the village. Except that people were not supposed to use the word "Untouchable" for outcastes anymore. Now the acceptable term was *Dalits*. Broken people.

As she approached her wooden hut, Shridula slowed and stared ahead in confusion. A few more careful steps, then she stopped still and squinted hard into the gathering shadows. Someone sat crumpled against her door. A filthy, muddy someone with wild hair and ragged clothes. A beggar! Yes, a beggar dared take up residence in her doorway!

"Get away!" Shridula ordered. "This is my house."

The beggar unfolded herself. She was only a skinny child of no more than ten years. A boney wisp of a girl who stared up at her with red-rimmed eyes.

"*Ammama?*" the girl whispered.

Shridula's legs went limp and the basket slipped from her head. Cucumbers and red peppers tumbled to the ground. The girl stared hungrily at the vegetables as they rolled through the dirt.

"Why do you call me Grandmother?" Shridula demanded. She had not intended her tone to be so sharp. "Who are you?"

The girl buried her face in her hands and sobbed.

"What is your mother's name?" Shridula pressed. For the girl had called her *Ammama*—"mother of my mother," not *Achama*—"mother of my father."

The girl wiped her hand across her dirt-streaked face. "Ritu," she said, tears catching in her voice. "My *amma's* name was Ritu. But I do not have an *amma* anymore."

"Where is she?" Shridula asked, her own voice shaking.

"One day she did not wake up and *Appa* said we must leave her on the sidewalk where she lay. We said goodbye to her and walked and walked. For many days we walked . . ."

The girl could say no more, for tears overtook her once again.

Shridula sank to her knees. Her daughter. Her sweet Ritu, who had married so young. Whose husband had taken her from the village. How many years ago? Shridula had no idea.

"Why did you come here?" Shridula demanded of the girl.

"I did not come. My *appa* brought me. But when we got near the village he said he was tired of taking care of himself so he found a new wife. He left my sister at an orphanage and he brought me here." When Shridula said nothing, the girl insisted, "I did not want to come! My *appa* brought me here and left me!"

Shridula opened her hand and looked at the single thin coin. Ten paise. In the earthenware container on the shelf in the house was, at the most, two handfuls of rice. Enough to last the two of them three days. Maybe four, if they ate only one small meal each day. She would take her peppers back to the market tomorrow, of course, but she couldn't make women buy them.

"What is your name?" Shridula asked as she walked toward the girl. She forced her voice to be more gentle and kind.

"Anjan," the girl said.

"Anjan! Why would my daughter name her child 'fear'? What kind of name is that to give a little one?"

The girl looked at the ground and said nothing. But Shridula had seen her face, and she recognized the look in the waif's eyes. It was fear. The poor child was doomed to live down to her name.

"Come," Shridula said. "You must be hungry. I will cook us some rice with spicy peppers. We will have cucumbers, too. They are not quite ripe, but they will still be good."

For the first time, the hint of a smile touched the edges of the girl's mouth.

As Shridula pulled dried sticks from her small pile of firewood and started a fire in the cook pit, she positioned herself in such a way that she could see the girl in the doorway. She poured water into the cooking pot and set it over the fire. The girl watched her.

From the almost-empty rice container, Shridula got half a handful of rice to stir into the pot. No more than that.

"We shall eat slowly," Shridula told the girl, a false smile on her face. "That way we won't need as much rice in our bowls."

The girl said nothing.

Shridula dropped a handful of peppers into the pot, too. And because it was a special occasion, she added a pinch of precious spices.

"Two cucumbers," Shridula said to the girl. "Do you like cucumbers?"

The girl wrinkled her brow in puzzlement. "I do not know," she answered. "I never ate one."

"Good!" said Shridula. "Then you will not know whether these are ripe or not."

*

When Shridula handed a bowl of rice and peppers to the girl, the young one grabbed it and lapped it up like a starving animal. Then she started on her cucumber. She ate the entire thing. Even the wilted blossom on the end.

"I am not particularly hungry," Shridula said as casually as she could manage. "Would you be able to finish my rice as well?" She reached out her bowl.

The girl's eyes narrowed suspiciously.

"Please take it. I have had enough."

The girl looked straight up into Shridula's eyes, but only for a quick moment. She grabbed for the bowl and scooped the rice into her mouth.

"Tomorrow I will take the water pots and fill them at the pond," Shridula said. "Then you can wash the mud from your face."

"No," the girl said. "Getting water is my job. I will take the water pots to the pond."

The dirt-floor hut, small and cramped and almost always too hot, was not a pleasant place to sleep. Like most everyone else, Shridula pulled her sleeping mat outside at night and slept under the stars except during the rainy season.

"I only have the one sleeping mat," she said to the girl as she spread it out. "Come, lie down beside me."

Gingerly, the girl crept to the side of the hut, but she would come no farther.

"You must be very tired," Shridula said. "Come and lie down."

The girl didn't move, so Shridula settled herself on one side of the mat. For a long time she lay still. Out of the corner of her eye, she watched the shadow of the girl.

"My *appa* was called Ashish. Blessing," Shridula said softly. "From the day he was born, his parents knew he would be a blessing to them."

The girl said nothing.

"My *appa* and *amma* named me Shridula. I was their blessing, even though I was only a girl."

Still the girl said nothing.

Shridula watched the stars in silence. The girl didn't move.

"You did not want to be left in my doorway. And I did not want you left here, because I have no money to buy food for you," Shridula said to the small shadow pressed against the side of the hut. "But here you are, so we will live together. We will find a way."

Do you have questions or comments?
Would you like to learn more about author
Kay Marshall Strom?

Visit her at her website www.kaystrom.com
and on www.GraceInAfrica.com

You are also welcome to join in the discussions on her blog:
http://kaystrom.wordpress.com

Abingdon Press has many great fiction books and authors
you are sure to enjoy.

Sign up for their fiction newsletter at
www.AbingdonPress.com
You will see what's new on the horizon, and much more—
interviews with authors, tips for starting a reading group,
ways to connect with other fiction readers . . .
even the opportunity to comment on this book!

Abingdon Press fiction
a novel approach to faith

Plan your escape.

BKM122220002 PACP01110786-01

What They're Saying About...

The Glory of Green, by Judy Christie
"Once again, Christie draws her readers into the town, the life, the humor and the drama in Green. *The Glory of Green* is a wonderful narrative of small-town America, pulling together in tragedy. A great read!"
—Ane Mulligan, editor of *Novel Journey*

Always the Baker, Never the Bride, by Sandra Bricker
"[It] had just the right touch of humor, and I loved the characters. Emma Rae is a character who will stay with me. Highly recommended!"
—Colleen Coble, author of *The Lightkeeper's Daughter* and the *Rock Harbor* series

Diagnosis Death, by Richard Mabry
"Realistic medical flavor graces a story rich with characters I loved and with enough twists and turns to keep the sleuth in me off-center. Keep 'em coming!"—**Dr. Harry Krauss, author of *Salty Like Blood* and *The Six-Liter Club***

Sweet Baklava, by Debby Mayne
"A sweet romance, a feel-good ending, and a surprise cache of yummy Greek recipes at the book's end? I'm sold!"—**Trish Perry, author of *Unforgettable* and *Tea for Two***

The Dead Saint, by Marilyn Brown Oden
"An intriguing story of international espionage with just the right amount of inspirational seasoning."—***Fresh Fiction***

Shrouded in Silence, by Robert L. Wise
"It's a story fraught with death, danger, and deception—of never knowing whom to trust, and with a twist of an ending I didn't see coming. Great read!"—Sharon Sala, author of *The Searcher's Trilogy: Blood Stains, Blood Ties,* and *Blood Trails.*

Delivered with Love, by Sherry Kyle
"Sherry Kyle has created an engaging story of forgiveness, sweet romance, and faith reawakened—and I looked forward to every page. A fun and charming debut!"—Julie Carobini, author of *A Shore Thing* and *Fade to Blue.*

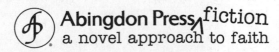

Abingdon Press fiction
a novel approach to faith

AbingdonPress.com | 800.251.3320

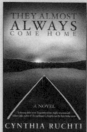